PENGUIN CANADA

SWITCH

GRANT MCKENZIE is a Scottish-born writer
living in British Columbia. He began his
writing career at the *Calgary Sun* cover-
ing the 'Dead Body Beat,' and his short
stories have appeared in *Out of the
Gutter* and *Spinetingler* magazines. His
debut novel, *Switch,* was published in
Germany and the U.K. in 2009.

SWITCH

Grant McKenzie

PENGUIN
CANADA

PENGUIN CANADA

Published by the Penguin Group

Penguin Group (Canada), 90 Eglinton Avenue East, Suite 700,
Toronto, Ontario, Canada M4P 2Y3 (a division of Pearson Canada Inc.)

Penguin Group (USA) Inc., 375 Hudson Street, New York,
New York 10014, U.S.A.
Penguin Books Ltd, 80 Strand, London WC2R 0RL, England
Penguin Ireland, 25 St Stephen's Green, Dublin 2, Ireland
(a division of Penguin Books Ltd)
Penguin Group (Australia), 250 Camberwell Road, Camberwell,
Victoria 3124, Australia (a division of Pearson Australia Group Pty Ltd)
Penguin Books India Pvt Ltd, 11 Community Centre, Panchsheel Park,
New Delhi – 110 017, India
Penguin Group (NZ), 67 Apollo Drive, Rosedale, North Shore 0745,
Auckland, New Zealand (a division of Pearson New Zealand Ltd)
Penguin Books (South Africa) (Pty) Ltd, 24 Sturdee Avenue, Rosebank,
Johannesburg 2196, South Africa

Penguin Books Ltd, Registered Offices: 80 Strand, London WC2R 0RL, England

Published in Penguin Canada paperback by Penguin Group (Canada),
a division of Pearson Canada Inc., 2010.
First published in Great Britain by Bantam Books, an imprint of
Transworld Publishers, a Random House Group Ltd. company, in 2008.

1 2 3 4 5 6 7 8 9 10   (WEB)

Copyright © Grant McKenzie, 2008

*Publisher's note: This book is a work of fiction. Names, characters, places
and incidents either are the product of the author's imagination or are used
fictitiously, and any resemblance to actual persons living or dead, events,
or locales is entirely coincidental.*

Manufactured in Canada.

LIBRARY AND ARCHIVES CANADA CATALOGUING IN PUBLICATION

McKenzie, Grant
Switch / Grant McKenzie.

ISBN 978-0-14-317335-9

I. Title.

PS8575.K397S95 2010   C813'.6   C2010-900582-1

British Library Cataloguing in Publication data available

Visit the Penguin Group (Canada) website at **www.penguin.ca**

Special and corporate bulk purchase rates available; please see
www.penguin.ca/corporatesales or call 1-800-810-3104, ext. 2477 or 2474

To Kailey — Who will always know that dreams
can come truc.
To Karen — Who already knew.

Prologue

Rick Ironwood staggered back from the blow, his trick knee giving out with a pop as his feet twisted sideways in a puddle of grimy engine oil.

Twin jolts of pain took his breath away, the shock turning his scream into a pathetic squeak. His feet failed to find traction and slid out beneath him. For a moment he was airborne, his body twisting unnaturally until all 260 pounds came crashing down. He landed hard, sending a dozen flimsy oilcans clattering across the floor. The back of his skull struck the garage's concrete pad with a loud crack.

Rick groaned as every pain sensor in his body flashed red. His face was a mask of blood, his left cheek and upper lip gashed open, his twice-broken nose snapped once more from the unexpected assault.

He held up his hands.

'Take anything you want! Fuck! The car! Anything! Jesus! There's nothing here!'

The tall black man with the gun stared at him, his eyes so wide and pupils so small the whites were like soft-boiled eggs. He held his mouth half open as though struck dumb at how easily the larger man had gone down.

Lying on his back with torn skin and pulled muscles, Rick knew the years hadn't been kind: hard muscle of youth turned to blubber from years of sitting on his ass and guzzling too many beers; skin a sickly white from a lazy diet of high-fat convenience foods and a liver disease only recently diagnosed. Even his shaved head, spotted with two days of growth, was a poor attempt to hide a hairline that had begun to recede before he was even out of his twenties.

Despite those flaws, he hadn't been prepared to be knocked flat by a skinny-assed spook in a business suit who looked too weak to part his own hair. Sure, the attack was a complete fucking surprise, but still, it wasn't so long ago that he'd had a reputation for kicking serious ass.

Gagging on blood, the broken nose making it difficult to breathe, Rick couldn't fathom why *anyone* would break into his garage. The only thing of value was his black-and-Bondo '79 Trans Am Firebird with the silver screaming eagle logo on the hood. But since it was sitting on cement blocks, it wasn't worth more than a couple hundred. He had been meaning to restore it, like that *Pimp My Ride* show on MTV, but money didn't grow on trees, at least not in his neighbourhood.

His attacker, a lanky, smoke-steel silhouette, pointed a tiny, blood-flecked pistol at Rick's face. The Detonics Pocket Nine still looked comical, its three-inch barrel no larger than the man's coal-black fingers. Rick had almost laughed when the well-dressed stranger pulled it out of his pocket, but that was before the barrel had gashed open his face and sent him sprawling.

The man finally spoke, his voice low.

'I had almost forgotten you.'

'For . . . gotten?' Rick's broken mouth was having trouble forming words as bubbles of crimson foam popped on his lips. 'I don't know . . . who the fuck . . . you are!'

'Yes,' the man said quietly. 'Yes, you do,' he paused before adding, 'Ironman.'

Rick's eyes narrowed in puzzlement, the nickname sparking cherished – *hell, sacred* – memories.

'And for what it's worth,' the man continued, 'I am sorry.'

'Wha—'

Rick's face imploded as the ball-bearing-sized bullet punched through his nose to become an explosive pinball. Ricocheting off bone, the bullet ripped tissue and muscle with abandon before finding the soft palate for a destructive exit.

Remarkably, even with the lower half of his face unhinged and his brain on fire from the shock, Rick stayed alive. He tried to speak, to reason with the man, but his tongue was no longer whole. He felt cold concrete against his cheek and found he could no longer lift his head.

Rick struggled to find a reason for his attack. His gaze came to rest on a wooden bench containing an unfinished birdhouse and an old metal tool-case that had once belonged to his father.

The tool-case, rusted and worn like everything else in his life, had been his favourite hiding spot at a time when he still had a wife to hide things from. The case held a half-dozen dog-eared *Hustler* magazines, a small metal pipe a buddy who joined the army had made from brass bullet casings, and a glass vial containing two tiny rocks of yellowed crystal meth. The grand worth of his secret stash was about ten bucks and change.

The gunman stepped closer. His polished black shoes acted as twin mirrors to reflect the horror of Rick's face. Rick whimpered then, his mind finally unravelling as he felt the hot gun barrel touch his temple with a brief sizzle.

Rick's eyes flicked skyward and suddenly, with the man's dark, unsmiling face filling his vision, he remembered him.

It was the last thought he ever had.

1

The thin man felt as fragile as glass.

With shaking hands, he dropped the warm gun into the pocket of his suit jacket and removed a folded triangle of white cotton. After wiping the sweat from his face, he noticed the handkerchief had become spotted with blood – Ironwood's blood.

Christ, he thought. *What have I become?*

His cellphone chirped and the unexpected sound was almost enough to make him drop to his knees and stick the damn gun in his own mouth. But he hadn't come this far to fall apart now.

He answered the phone.

'It's done.'

'I know,' said a voice scrambled by cheap electronics to flatten its pitch and cadence.

'You're watching?'

'You made quite the mess, Dr Parker.'

Zack Parker scanned the rafters of the garage for the camera. It didn't surprise him that he couldn't see one. When today's engineers made cameras so small they could swim in your bloodstream and identify plaque in the vessels of a beating heart, any object in any room could hide a thousand of them.

The scrambled voice laughed.

'Would you like me to send you a copy of the footage?'

Zack closed his eyes, struggling to hold back the madness that would send him so far into the abyss, return would never be an option.

'I've done everything you asked.'

'Perhaps,' said the voice.

Zack waited, not noticing he was holding his breath until his lungs began to burn.

'They're waiting,' said the voice. 'Here's what I need you to do.'

2

Inside the house, mother and child began their nightly ritual.

It was like watching a soap opera on a rabbit-eared TV set. When they crossed a window, he could see their features as clearly as if he were in the same room, but then they would fade out of sight behind a wall and he would need to use his imagination to fill in the gaps. But that was OK, he had developed a good imagination, and he could hear their voices.

The familial sounds emanating from the speakers floated around him, surprisingly static-free considering the cheap wireless microphones he had planted inside the house. He had considered planting cameras, too, but the idea of spying so intimately on the child had bothered him.

Better simply to listen.

'Are you wearing your retainer, MaryAnn?'

'Uh-huh.'

'Are you sure?'

'Uh-huh.'

'If I come up there—'

'OK, Mom. Geez. I'll get it.'

'MaryAnn! Do you know how much money your father and I have spent on your teeth?'

'OK, you don't have to yell. I was gonna do it.'

'And floss, too.'

'Yes, Mom.'

In the darkness of his lair, the watcher played with a disposable lighter. Its dyed plastic skin gradated from red to orange to yellow, the colours any amateur artist would use to depict flame. It took a true *auteur* to see the full spectrum of a fire: the blood reds and puss yellows, crisp blacks and molten ginger, and the deep, deep violet that told you it was a living thing.

Fire lulled you into the belief that it could be tamed, controlled, like a performing white tiger in a Vegas magic act. But all it took was a flick of thumb to release its true nature, and if you listened closely enough, to release its true voice: not unlike a human scream.

'No more Facebook, MaryAnn. It's time to sleep.'

'But, Mom—'

'No buts, it's late. Switch off your computer and get to bed.'

'Yes, Mom.'

Once the child had retreated under the bedcovers, the house grew silent.

Switch

The watcher leaned forward, closing his eyes and listening intently to the gentle padding of feet as the woman poured herself a glass of chilled Chardonnay (she preferred the vineyards of Southern Australia) and settled in her favourite armchair.

The bookshelves in the cozy den that over-looked a well-tended garden were lined with paperback thrillers. There was also a short shelf of plays and bound TV scripts with small speaking roles highlighted in yellow. But all those books belonged to her husband.

In these quiet hours, the watcher knew that Hannah would dig deep into the side pocket of her recliner and pull out one of the Victorian romances that she bought by the sackful from a used bookstore in Burnside. She liked her bodice-rippers full of old-fashioned romance and British accents, plus teary middles, tender-hearted rogues and, most of all, happy endings.

The faint crinkle of thin foil signalled that she had also dug out her other favourite indulgence, a Terry's Chocolate Orange in dark rather than milk chocolate. The watcher admired her discipline. She ate only two or three segments a night, which made the treat last a whole week.

Satisfied that both woman and child were settled for the evening, the watcher lifted a tiny remote control with two buttons: one blue and one red. The remote was unremarkable in design

15

or function and, like the lighter, it was inexpensive and easily disposable.

He pressed the blue button.

From his vantage point inside an olive-green van parked a short distance away, nothing seemed to happen. But inside the house, in a dark corner of the neglected basement, a perfect hole was punched in the natural gas line that led into the furnace.

Within forty minutes, enough deadly gas would escape to pack the furnace cavities and begin creeping upstairs to the main floors. By the time the rotten-egg odour became noticeable, both woman and child would be in a deep slumber.

Within seventy minutes, the slightest spark would be enough to turn the quaint two-storey, lemon yellow and white trim home into a blazing pyre. For each additional minute, the gas would build until the entire block was in danger of being reduced to an impressive crater.

The watcher looked once again at the plastic lighter in his hand. The continual motion of his thumb had worn away a patch of orange paint. Like all the others he had handled in his time, the colour underneath was a pale, almost translucent white.

With a sad smile, the watcher eased back into his chair, rolled the metal thumbwheel against the flint and watched as a tiny flame leapt from its plastic womb. In the silent darkness, he could hear the creature begin to scream.

3

Dr Zack Parker pulled his silver, four-door Mercedes E320 sedan to the kerb, his heart pumping so hard he could hear the blood rushing through his veins.

He wiped the back of his hands across his dripping forehead, and glanced out of the window at the cheerful yellow house across the street.

As he blinked away more nervous sweat, he saw a brief flicker of life from the upstairs bedroom. It could have been the shadow of a lace curtain fluttering in the night breeze, but Zack was sure he had seen the soft, dark skin of his daughter framing the prettiest little mouth he had ever kissed.

The lips were turned up in a smile.

As Zack threw open the car door, his cellphone rang.

No. Please, no, he whispered to himself.

The phone continued to ring as he stood frozen in

the middle of the road, eyes locked on the bed-room window and the unmoving darkness beyond.

With building dread, he flipped open the phone and lifted it to his ear.

'Change of plans,' said the distorted voice.

'Nooooooo!'

Zack's protest became an agonized wail as he began to run, leather soles slapping tarmac, hands outstretched. The names of the two people he loved most in the world erupted from his throat.

His eyes were blurred with tears when the force of the blast hit him like a locomotive.

Zack was lifted off his feet and tossed back the way he had come. His limbs flailed and his lungs screamed from sudden decompression. He felt his feet skim the top of his sedan before his body arced down, feet lifting higher, his head and shoulders dipping towards the ground.

His solid German-made car rocked against the blast, but its heavy chassis kept its wheels firmly on the ground. The calm pocket of dead air behind the Mercedes lacked the force to hold Zack aloft and he crumpled onto a green lawn, as all around him car alarms began to howl.

Where the yellow house had stood, a column of flame licked the sky.

Lying on his back, winded, bloody and bruised, Zack watched as a giant cloud of fiery debris began to fall like hell's own rain.

Switch

Let it come, Zack thought as his mind retreated into a silent darkness so deep that he prayed to stay there. *Let it come.*

4

Crunch!

Sam White bit down on a tuna and potato-chip sandwich and admired the sixty-inch, high-definition, widescreen plasma television in the window of the Sony store. The television wasn't switched on as the store was closed and the mall long emptied of its customers.

Even switched off, the screen was impressive: thin, sleek and with a sticker price greater than anything Sam could take home in a month. Hell, two months with no overtime.

Sam finished his sandwich and licked his fingers before topping up his plastic mug with coffee from a new red thermos emblazoned with the winking mascot of the Portland Beavers. With a smile, he dug back into his brown paper lunch bag and produced a large, misshaped oatmeal cookie. Baked by his daughter, the cookie was overloaded with chunks of chopped Mars Bar. It was a recipe he had taught her when she first started taking an interest in the kitchen.

Sam dunked the cookie in his coffee and sucked the melting mess into his mouth just as his two-way radio squawked to life.

'Come in, Sam. You there? Over.'

Sam rolled his eyes at the sound of Kenneth Baker's tremulous voice. The twenty-two-year-old was studying to be a criminal psychologist at the local university, but Sam had serious doubts he would ever make it to graduation.

Sam unclipped the radio from his belt, held it to the side of his mouth while he finished chewing, then pressed the transmit button.

'What's up, Ken?'

'Uh, nothing much. What you doing? Over.'

Sam chuckled.

'Just having a bite to eat and admiring this TV I'll never afford.'

'Cool. Hey, I saw your commercial this afternoon on the sports channel. You were great. Over.'

Sam groaned.

'I transform into a giant rodent, Ken. Not exactly Oscar-winning material.'

'Uh, no, but . . . uh, I thought you were very convincing. Over.'

'Thanks, Ken, I appreciate it. Gotta keep my hand in, you know?'

'Sure, sure. Lots of actors get discovered doing commercials, don't they? Over.'

'Yeah,' Sam said. 'Me and Jodie Foster, kid.'

'Jodie Foster did commercials? Over.'

'When she was two she starred in a spot for Coppertone. Eleven years later she was nominated for an Oscar.'

'Oh, wow. Uh, I didn't know that. Over.'

'Yep.' Sam laughed. 'But then, she's Jodie Foster and I'm playing the freakin' Portland Beaver.'

'Uh, but you did it well, Sam. You had me laughing, anyway. Oh, and I burned it on disc for you. I'll give it to you later, OK. Might be good for your résumé. Show you in action, you know? Over.'

Sam paused, touched by the support of his co-worker and embarrassed by his own ingratitude.

'That's really thoughtful, Ken. I don't think my daughter has seen it yet. That'll be nice to show her.'

'No problem. I just thought it was so cool seeing you on TV. I showed my mom, too, and she was thrilled. I heard her bragging to the neighbours that I was working with a famous actor. Over.'

Sam laughed again. 'Why don't you do your rounds, Ken? Check all the doors. We'll meet up later for coffee.'

'Yeah, OK, sure. Over.'

Sam swallowed the last mouthful of coffee and screwed the plastic cup on top of his thermos. As he walked to the trashcan to dump his empty sandwich bags, he caught himself reflected in the dark store windows.

The security guard's uniform – crisp black

trousers, light blue shirt with darker blue accents on the pocket flaps and shoulder epaulettes, rugged black belt and holster with gun, flashlight, aerosol mace and expandable baton – was designed to mirror the Portland City police. That illusion was intended to instil fear in shoplifters and respect in the regular shoppers.

In theory, anyway.

Over the last few years, the daytime security guards' role had changed from a babysitting service for the stores' merchandise to the more pro-active chore of making sure the customers felt safe. That meant working in tandem with local authorities to crack down on drug dealers, pimps out to recruit naive schoolgirls, hopped-up muggers in need of a quick fix, plus patrolling the parking lot for opportunistic car thieves.

The overnight shift, however, was still just glorified babysitting. And that's exactly the way Sam liked it. As a mall sitter, he didn't have to think too much, and more importantly, he didn't have to care.

As he walked the long, lonely halls, checking doors and sipping coffee, he could allow his mind to ponder the screenplay he was going to write one day. He often imagined himself pulling a Stallone and telling the major studios they could only produce the movie if he got to star.

Unlike *Rocky*, however, Sam still hadn't come up with a sure-fire plot that would make money-lenders salivate.

His two-way radio crackled again.

'Uh, Sam, you there? Over.'

'Yeah, Ken. What's up?'

'I heard something. Over.'

Sam sighed. The kid was so nervous, he would jump a mile at the sound of a mouse fart. And everyone knew vermin in the Pacific North-west were never that rude. This wasn't L.A., after all.

'What did you hear?'

'Err, voices, I think, and a muffled bang on the side door behind the jeweller's. Over.'

'Did you check it out?'

'Yeah, the door wasn't locked. I must have missed it on my first pass. I think someone's inside. Over.'

Sam dropped his trash in the circular bin and brushed the cookie and potato-chip crumbs off his shirt.

'Stay where you are, Ken. I'll be right there.'

He walked at a steady pace across the mall, past the food court and down the frozen steel teeth of the sleeping escalator. On the ground floor, he headed up the hallway towards the public washrooms and through the *Authorized Personnel Only* doors to the labyrinth of corridors and storage bays beyond.

He found Ken biting his nails beside a set of double doors that led out to the rear parking lot. Even in his blue-and-black uniform, Ken looked exactly like what he was: a geeky, knob-kneed kid who had just enough upper-body strength to

24

wrestle an eight-year-old girl to the ground. If she happened to be on Ritalin, so much the better.

Ken had also been cursed with a bout of late-blooming acne that, despite a vigorous cleansing routine, turned his cheeks, forehead and chin into a lunar landscape of shiny pink pits. When you combined this with his general geekiness, Sam was amazed at how the kid still managed such a positive outlook on life.

He knew the credit must belong with Ken's loving mother who always put sweet little notes (which Ken was never embarrassed about reading aloud) in his bagged lunches. She was so thoughtful it wasn't unusual for her to send along extra treats for Sam.

As he approached his partner, Sam was relieved to see that Ken hadn't unclipped his company-issued revolver from its holster on his hip.

'I stayed where I was, Sam.'

'Just like we practised.'

Ken's smile grew wider. 'That's right.'

'So what's next?' Sam encouraged. He knew that if Ken could concentrate on all the things they had taught him, he was less likely to collapse to the floor and curl into a foetal position.

'We confirm there's an intruder, secure the area, and then call the police.'

'Excellent. Now, where did you hear the voices?'

Ken pointed down the short, dimly lit corridor that turned sharply behind the jewellery store.

25

'I'll take point,' said Sam. 'Stay close behind, and keep your weapon holstered. Do you understand?'

Ken nodded and gulped.

Sam moved quickly and quietly down the corridor, stopping at the corner to regulate his breathing before darting his head out to take a quick peek beyond. The next corridor was empty, too, but Sam caught a ripple of sound that didn't belong.

'There's someone here,' Sam whispered. 'But we need to make sure it's not one of the store owners. Someone might have forgotten to tell us they planned a late-night stock-take.'

Ken reached for his weapon.

'Leave it,' Sam said sharply. 'I don't care what kind of training the company gave you, this isn't the shooting range. We don't use our weapons, OK?'

'But the manual says—'

'Fuck the manual, Ken. We're not paid nearly enough to put our lives on the line for some over-priced junk. If the intruder has a weapon, we back away and let the cops handle it. OK?'

Ken nodded, but still looked unsure.

Sam grabbed him by the shoulders.

'You have to be with me on this one. More security guards lose their lives from friendly fire than anything else. That's because we don't have the practical training to really know what the fuck we're doing. We get paid shit wages because our job is to eat sandwiches, drink coffee and stop the bums from sneaking in and using the storage closets as personal drug dens and toilets. So keep it holstered or go home right now.'

Ken sighed his agreement.

'Good. Now wait here while I check the situation.'

Leaving Ken at the corner, Sam moved cautiously down the hallway, past the undisturbed rear entrance to the jewellery store, and stopped outside the sliding door that led to *The Candy Factory*. The latch on the door was broken.

Sam pressed his ear to the door and heard soft grunting noises beyond. Nervous sweat began to bead on his forehead as he unsnapped his baton and slid open the door.

In the darkness, the store's gaily coloured tubes of bulk candy – jawbreakers, boiled sweets, Licorice Allsorts, gummy soothers and jelly beans in 1,001 flavours – looked sadly plain. The grinning plastic clowns and cuddly bear masks that protruded from the ceiling and walls had a creepy, haunted-house quality.

Sam moved slowly and carefully to the cash register and looked around. The register hadn't been disturbed. He stood listening, his right hand gripping the metal baton by his side.

A rustle of plastic wrap whispered from beyond a large metal rack filled with brightly coloured gumballs.

Sam crept to the far side of the rack. The

rustling had turned to wet slurping and Sam suddenly wondered if, instead of a burglar, he was about to catch some creepy store manager giving a naive new employee the unauthorized after-hours tour.

Click!

Sam froze at the unmistakable sound of a gun being cocked.

Then the candy rack exploded – packets of gumballs, Pez dispensers and gummy spiders flew around him like sugared shrapnel.

Startled, Sam stumbled backwards, stepped on a runaway cluster of jawbreakers and lost his balance. As he crashed into the overstocked candy shelves, two teenagers launched themselves through the cloud of confusion, their pockets and cheeks stuffed with sweets. Grinning, teeth coated a raspberry red, one of the boys turned, his hands clutching a highly sophisticated gun.

Sam recognized the weapon's silhouette as a variant of the Heckler & Koch MP5 submachine-gun. With a retractable stock and its barrel threaded for a silencer, it was the type of gun favoured by the US Navy and anyone else who needed to fire 800 lethal rounds per minute. To enhance its accuracy, the teen had attached a sophisticated laser sight.

Sam saw the sight's red laser cut through the darkness and candied flotsam. Then the boy found his target and squeezed the trigger.

Sam grunted as he was punched twice in the

belly, the impacts buckling his knees and sending him sliding on to his ass.

Gasping for breath on the floor, his heart thundering in his chest, Sam reached for the wound in his belly and felt a warm, sticky mess oozing over his shirt. When he lifted his hand, his fingers were covered in bright Day-Glo yellow paint.

Shit, he thought as he tried to calm himself, *a bloody paint gun.*

Then a second, more alarming thought: *Ken!*

He scrambled to his feet and rushed out of the store, screaming at the top of his lungs to warn his partner the intruders were only kids. His warnings were lost in metallic thunder as something meaty slammed into the exterior exit doors.

When Sam breathlessly reached Ken, the guard was standing rock still, his hands raised in surrender, five bright-yellow splotches of paint decorating his uniform from crotch to chin. His face was streaked with tears.

'I–I thought I was a goner, Sam,' he said shakily. 'I didn't know what to do.'

Sam smiled, relieved he wasn't the only useless member of mall security working tonight. He patted the young man's shoulder.

'You did exactly the right thing, Ken. You didn't panic, and more importantly, you didn't put a bullet into two stupid kids. Hell, you're practically a hero.'

Ken smiled weakly. 'Really?'

'Why not? If you had pulled your gun, we both would have lost our jobs and those kids' parents would have sued our asses off. And I, personally, have precious little ass left to sue.'

Ken pondered this information for a moment before adding, 'I think I peed myself.'

Sam snorted with laughter and slapped him on the shoulder again. 'You know something, I think I did, too.'

5

At the end of his shift, Sam unloaded and secured his gun inside its locked case, which he kept inside his locker, and hung up his heavy holster and belt.

He slipped out of thick-soled work shoes and changed his uniform for street clothes: comfortable, over-washed GWG jeans, plain black T-shirt that he bought in packs of three at Wal-Mart, a pair of black Reebok sneakers and an insulated, sleeveless Eddie Bauer vest to keep off the pre-summer chill.

Once dressed, he bundled his soiled uniform in a plastic shopping bag for the dry cleaner's.

Before leaving the converted broom closet, shared by the six full-time and two part-time guards, Sam looked at himself in the full-length mirror and sucked in his stomach.

The face reflected back at him was still handsome. Not soap-star pretty, granted: more Clive Owen with a fuller face, slightly sharper nose,

Paul Newman eyes and thick black, close-cropped hair that could stand up to a tornado and barely move.

His mother once told him the hair, and his bone stubbornness, came from his great grandmother, the first black Mrs White. That mixing of the gene pools had also miraculously kept away the inevitable grey from his temples, at least for the moment. The same couldn't be said of his beard, which he now preferred to keep clean-shaven.

At forty-two, he was too damn young to display grey hair.

Sam had moved his family to Portland from L.A. nearly ten months earlier on the promise of a steady acting gig on a new weekly TV series. As it turned out, the show, like so many others, didn't get picked up beyond its pilot. When the series went under, his wife of fifteen years gave him an ultimatum: get a real job or leave your family behind.

Sam surprised himself by how quickly he agreed not to return to the lights of L.A., and instead settle down in his original home town. His wife had been good about it, too. She didn't complain about the lousy wage his lack of useful skills earned, and she still encouraged him to audition for the occasional commercial, voice-over or small-budget movie that came to town.

His last gig had been just three weeks earlier: a thirty-second TV spot to kick-start excitement for the Beavers' new season of Triple-A ball. The two-day shoot, in which he played a face-painting fan magically transformed into the team's furry mascot, gave him a newfound appreciation for the Sci-fi actors who had to wear elaborate masks every working day. It had taken him almost a week to remove all traces of the beaver make-up, rubber, clay and glue from his ears, nostrils and other crevices.

Sam couldn't say he was happy with his new life, his failure to realize his acting dream still made him feel less than whole. But by removing himself from the constant rejection of L.A., he had to admit he felt closer to its embrace.

He exhaled and watched his stomach roll out into the formative stages of a middle-age paunch. He needed to get back to the gym. After all, he told himself, one of these days, Hollywood might finally come callin'.

The door to the cramped locker room opened and Ken walked in. He had already changed out of his uniform. The kid was too shy to change in front of other people, and often disappeared at the end of the shift to some other closet somewhere. Sam never questioned him about it. He had his own quirks.

'You left this upstairs.' Ken handed Sam his red thermos.

'Thanks. I must have put it on the bench when you called about those intruders.'

Ken opened his locker and grabbed an ugly

orange and black-striped leather jacket off the hook. He dug in the inside pocket. His hand re-appeared with a DVD, complete with a custom-made label that showed Sam as the wink-ing mascot. He handed it over.

Sam accepted it graciously, making sure he took a moment to look at the label.

'Nice work. You do that?'

Ken beamed. 'Yeah, on the computer. I like teaching myself new things, you know?'

There was a knock on the door and a gruff voice called out: 'Are you night turds done in there? We gotta get changed.'

Sam slipped the disc and thermos into the plastic bag beside his uniform before opening the door. Two day-shift guards stood in the hallway, arms folded to pretend fat was muscle, with shit-eating grins creasing their ugly mugs.

'We're just leaving, ladies, keep your knickers on.'

Sam glanced over his shoulder. He didn't like leaving Ken alone with the day-shifters. Too many people joined security as a way to flex their muscles without the restrictions of the police force. And no matter how much he may be part of the mall squad, Ken would always be easy prey for the bullies in their midst.

'You ready?'

Ken snatched up his motorcycle helmet and followed Sam out.

6

In the mall parking lot, Sam climbed into the black vinyl and duct-taped driver's seat of his navy blue '81 Jeep CJ5 and started the engine. The lack of doors and flimsy soft-top made him glad for his insulated vest. Cold air blasted over his legs as the engine coughed into life and the Jeep began to purr.

Sam switched off the heater fan and reached into the pocket of his vest to dig out a tin pack of small Dominican Republic cigars. From the same pocket, he produced a gunmetal Zippo lighter adorned with The Who's red, white and blue Mod target logo. After licking the chocolate-brown outer leaf to slow its burn, Sam stuck the cigar in the corner of his mouth and touched it to flame.

As he exhaled the sweet, pungent smoke, he turned the fan back on low. Mild warmth began to fill the open interior of the rugged two-seater. If he restored it to its prime, Sam knew it could easily fetch several thousand dollars on the collectors' market. The catch, of course, being that he would first need several thousand dollars to fix it up.

As he put the Jeep in gear, Ken buzzed by on his orange and black Vespa scooter with matching bee-shaped helmet.

Chuckling, Sam took off across the deserted parking lot to wind his way home. The one benefit he found in his job – hell, the only benefit – was how quiet and peaceful the streets were at 6 a.m.

7

Zack Parker stared at the Willamette River, the neck of a whiskey bottle gripped so tight it should have turned blue.

His tailored silk suit hung from his bony frame, its shark-grey sheen streaked with ash and a confetti rash of ember burns. The knees of his trousers were smudged with grass stains, the once perfectly creased fabric stretched out of shape. The manicured lawn that had broken his fall had been smooth and soft and free of rocks, but that had been before Zack and the shattered remains of a pretty yellow house fell from the sky.

Less than a week ago, Zack would have been mortified by his appearance. He was a man for whom clothes advertised not only wealth and status, but also confidence and attention to detail. And although he didn't like to admit it, dressing for success was necessary in a town where he had to bring an extra edge to his game if the porcelain blondes and sun-kissed brunettes were to trust a black man with their skin.

Now, however, his appearance seemed so inconsequential as to make him wonder why it ever mattered at all.

Apart from two homeless men, the river path had remained deserted in the dark, silent hours leading up to dawn. The men had stumbled past on their way to find late-night shelter amid the dank concrete crannies and wide iron rafters under Burnside Bridge.

Their faltering footsteps as they caught sight of the bottle had gone unnoticed by Zack. As did a low growl from the throat of one, which made the other shake his head.

The Mercedes' powerful engine had grown cold while Zack sat on the hood, his back against the windshield, oblivious to the icy fog rising off the slow-moving river. He had been waiting for the sun to rise, to fill the eastern skyline with a taunting blood-red glow. And when it did, he raised the near-empty bottle to his lips in salute.

Zack didn't want to be a burden, although to whom he was no longer sure. He needed the alcohol to short-circuit his hard-wired instinct for survival, to make it easier to walk to the river's edge, fire a bullet into his brain and be washed out to sea. But all the whiskey seemed to do was numb his legs and churn his anger.

He rubbed his eyes, tilted the bottle to his lips once more, and drained the last of the amber liquid.

Switch

His body swayed unsteadily as he cocked his arm and threw the empty bottle in a high arc that soared over the low embankment. He lost sight of the bottle before it struck the water.

His head began to spin and he slid off the car and on to the ground, landing on his back. Cursing his own ineptitude, he struggled to rise once again, but the effort was too much and the damp grass felt oddly comforting.

He closed his eyes, meaning to rest for just a moment, and sank into welcoming blackness.

8

Sam was stopped one block from his house by a single police cruiser parked in the middle of the road. Its blinding bar of red and blue flashed in a slow, silent pulse.

In front of the car, one hand held up flat and rigid, the other hooked casually in his gun belt, a lone uniformed officer barely out of his teens waved him down.

As Sam pulled to a stop, he could see a commotion of cars and lights further down the block very near his own home.

'What's going on, officer?'

Sam unclasped his seatbelt to lean out of the Jeep.

'I'm afraid this area is closed off, sir.' The officer had a voice deeper than his age would imply. 'You'll need to drive around.'

'I live here,' Sam said. 'Just down the block, actually.'

He grabbed the edge of the windshield and

swung out of his seat to stand on the lip of the doorwell. From this heightened vantage point, he could see over the roofs of the neighbours' parked cars. The ambulance, fire and police lights looked to be practically in front of his house, although the street-lights were off and it was difficult to be sure.

'What's going on down there?'

'There's been an accident, sir. I'm afraid I can't let you through.'

Something cold and slippery uncoiled in his belly. 'What kind of accident?'

'A gas explosion of some kind.'

'Was anyone hurt? I live at one ninety-two.'

Sam saw it cross the rookie officer's face: a flinch followed by a short intake of breath.

'Was it my house?' Fear filled his chest. 'Hannah! MaryAnn! Are they OK?'

'Sir, if you would like to wait in your vehicle, I can contact my supervisor. I'm sure'

'ARE THEY OK?' Sam shouted.

The officer flinched again and took a backwards step, reaching for his radio.

Sam dropped into his seat and floored the gas. Before the officer could react, the Jeep swerved around the parked cruiser, crunched over a portable safety light, and tore down the street.

When Sam screeched to a halt near a cluster of official vehicles, no one seemed to be moving. It

41

was as if by tearing through the barrier, he had also stopped time.

Blind with panic, he pushed through the police and firemen, knocking away outstretched arms, unable to stop his own perpetual motion until he hit the immovable object – his house.

Only, it wasn't his house.

It was a smoldering hole filled with charred timbers, discarded bricks and misshapen steel. Nothing was recognizable as anything he owned. The smoking pit was more like something shown on TV on Veterans Day: *Scenes from the London Blitz*.

Sam looked to either side. The neighbours' homes still stood. The walls were scorched and large strips of vinyl siding had melted away to expose cheap, particle-board sheathing underneath. Fireproof glass-block bathroom windows had cracked and blackened, but the houses themselves remained unbreached.

This hole was where his home should have been.

Sam opened his mouth, but nothing came out except for a slippery hissing exhalation, which roiled across his tongue and vanished like mist through his lips. He inhaled and felt cold air climbing into his brain, numbing it further. It slid into his lungs, constricting them and making it harder to breathe.

He peed himself again, warmth trickling down his leg. But even that sensation lasted for only a short moment before the cold reclaimed it.

There were voices all around him, hands trying to pull him back from the edge of the hole where his house had stood, but no one could move him. His feet were part of the ground.

He remained frozen until a flicker of colour on the edge of his vision made him turn, and the flashing red and blue of an ambulance drew him forward.

The back door of the ambulance was open. Inside lay two large, zippered, white nylon bags. One was shorter than the other, but not by much. Sam walked to the bags and knew with heart-breaking certainty what they contained.

'Where's mine?' he asked numbly.

The ambulance attendant just looked at him.

'Where's my white bag?' Sam asked, louder this time.

And in that moment the bubble burst and time, noise and commotion rushed in to fill the vacuum. Sam felt the tugging pressure of a hundred pairs of hands. The hands were also screaming, a thousand sharp little mouths nipping at his skin and making incoherent noises that suddenly blended into one ear-piercing, agonized wail.

And just before he collapsed, Sam wished the hysterical fool making all the racket would shut the fuck up.

9

The world had stopped spinning.

Zack lay curled in a ball, his mind buzzing with a thousand radio stations all broadcasting at once.

'Sir?'

Zack felt a strong hand grip his shoulder and give a firm shake. His eyelids fluttered open, and the morning light pierced straight into his brain. He squeezed his eyes closed again and groaned.

He didn't want to be awake; he didn't want to be alive. Most of all, he didn't want to accept all he had lost.

'Sir, are you injured?'

'Fer Chrissake, Colin,' said a woman's voice, its smooth, sing-song centre edged with a faint Celtic burr. 'He's a bleedin' drunk. Either forget it or take him to the cage.'

'He's wearing a three-thousand-dollar suit, Mary. He probably owns the Merc.'

Zack lifted his hands to cover his eyes and slowly raised his eyelids again.

'What happened here, sir?'

Zack opened his fingers slightly to see a poster boy for police recruitment. The officer, who he presumed was Colin, stood six foot four with broad shoulders, a lantern-shaped jaw and skin the rich, velvety colour of medium-roast coffee.

Zack shifted his gaze to the woman. Officer Mary was a pale, sharp-faced brunette with thick, wiry hair that defied styling.

'Are you injured?' Officer Colin repeated.

'More than you know,' Zack mumbled.

The words felt too large for his mouth. He tried to lick his lips, but his tongue was thick and woolly and far too dry.

The officer produced a small plastic bottle of water from his jacket pocket, unscrewed the top and held it out.

The bottle was still cold and Zack rolled it across his forehead before tipping it forward and pouring a generous amount into his mouth.

He held the water for a few seconds before allowing it to trickle down his parched throat.

It hit like acid.

Zack tried to fight the sudden uprising, but his heart wasn't in it. With a lurch, he rolled on to his side and vomited watery green bile.

'Bloody hell.' Officer Mary shook her head and looked away. 'Nothing like a puking drunk to start the day off right.'

Zack continued to heave, his eyes bulging from the strain. Until finally, with watery eyes and dripping nose, he sucked in a deep breath and managed to relax his muscles, sending his body the message that there was nothing left to expel.

When he felt strong enough, he lifted the bottle again and took a swallow. This time his stomach retracted its claws and accepted the fluid with only a mild gurgle of protest.

Water had never tasted so good, and soon the bottle was empty.

'So what happened, sir?' Colin asked.

'Nothing.' Zack's tone was angrier than he intended. 'Just leave me be.'

Mary leaned forward and sniffed. 'You drink the booze or bathe in it?'

Zack rolled on to his back and stared at the sky. He wished he was dead. There were too many awful things to face and yet he had been unable to take the simplest first step. He felt the weight of the small gun in his pocket; it wasn't too late.

'You drive in that state?' Colin asked.

Zack shrugged, but answered, 'No.' His first reflex was still honesty; lying took concentration.

'Were you attacked? The car looks scorched and your clothes . . .'

Zack shrugged again. He didn't want to be himself right now. He wanted to be James Cagney in *Angels with Dirty Faces*: tough, defiant, abusive to screws and priests alike. He wanted to sit up straight and cold-cock the handsome son of a bitch. Maybe then the cop's partner would help him do what he couldn't. Hell, her act of heroism could get her on the fast path to the gold shield she coveted; maybe that would make her smile.

'What you grinnin' at?' Mary snarled impatiently.

Zack hadn't realized he was smiling. He turned to look at the woman. Her eyes were a rather remarkable shade of turquoise.

'You have pretty eyes.' The words flowed automatically from the one part of his brain he never needed to question, nor doubt. 'But you need to stop squinting. The deep wrinkles are the hardest to remove.'

Mary's face turned red. 'Who asked for your opinion, asshole?'

Her partner began to laugh. 'You know, I think he's right. You do have nice eyes—'

Mary stopped him with a cold stare.

Colin rested his hands on his hips and turned back to Zack. 'What's your name, sir?'

'Zack Parker.'

'This your car?'

Zack nodded.

'You want to report the damage?'

Zack shook his head.

'You hungry? There's a great pancake place just a block away.'

Mary sighed heavily.

Colin held out his hand until, hesitantly, Zack reached out and grasped it.

10

Sam stood on the edge of the crater that had been his home.

A thin ribbon of yellow crime-scene tape surrounded the pit. The tape rustled and rippled as a light breeze tested its temporary bonds. One section, near where Hannah's potted herb garden would have stood, had already ripped from its post and now fluttered in the wind like an elongated flag. Appropriately, it flew at half-mast.

A light rain turned the last smouldering embers to mud, and the dull sun, filtered through a veil of cloud, cast the scene in a softer glow than the emergency halogen lights of just hours before.

Neighbours peeked from behind curtained windows, keeping their distance, not daring to encroach on his space. For this, at least, Sam was thankful. He knew nobody wanted to contemplate how easily this could have happened to them, to their home, their family.

They would talk among themselves after he was

gone. Some would even visit the hole, mourn the loss of life and thank the universe for being spared. They would call it a tragedy and then begin to forget.

This realization made Sam feel even more distanced from the 'normal' community that Hannah had embraced. Before this, all he lacked was money to keep pace with the business-class neighbours and their rotating parade of shiny leased cars.

But now his family was gone and he had lost everything.

Sam began to cry again, salty tears painful against the raw skin around his eyes. The little blue pills the harried doctor at the hospital gave him had made him numb, but uncomfortably so, as if his brain was packed in cotton wool laced with slivers of crinkled tinfoil.

After giving him the pills, the doctor told him to leave. 'Go home' were his exact words. There were no beds available, except for the dying, and even then it helped if you knew someone.

Sam tried to explain that he no longer had a home and that death was an acceptable trade for somewhere to lay his head.

The doctor thought he was joking and laughed aloud as a police officer stepped forward to take Sam's arm and lead him away.

He had begun to shiver in the back of the police cruiser, his body convulsing savagely and his teeth chattering so loud, he worried they would break.

He popped two more of the blue pills and the young officer handed him a thick, woollen blanket to wrap around his shoulders.

When the shivering refused to stop, he asked the officer to drive by his home. The young man had looked at him with large, sad brown eyes before reluctantly agreeing.

As Sam walked the circumference of the pit, he felt as though he had turned to stone. The young officer cleared his throat. 'I need to get you downtown, Mr White,' he said. 'I wasn't really supposed to bring you back here.'

'What's your name?' Sam enquired softly.

He didn't turn around as he spoke and anyone passing would think he was talking to the crater rather than the young man who shifted nervously from foot to foot beside his cruiser.

'Dale, er, Officer Dale Ryan.'

'Thanks for everything, Dale.'

'You're welcome, sir, but we really need to get going. The detectives will want to talk to you.'

Sam turned his head slowly, as if his skull had grown too heavy for his shoulders. He looked down the street to where someone had moved his abandoned Jeep from the middle of the road and parked it against the kerb. Beside the mini-vans and family sedans, it looked more battered and forlorn than usual.

And, Sam realized, it was all he had left. 'Can I take my own vehicle?'

'Sorry, no,' Ryan said quickly. 'I'm supposed to make sure you get there.'

Sam snorted. 'You're to make sure I don't do anything stupid like drive my piece-of-shit Jeep into this fucking hole at 120 miles per hour, huh?'

'Um, yeah, I guess so, Mr White.'

Sam stared at the officer and a sudden wave of rage burst from within.

'Christ! When did I become so fucking old that twenty-somethings started calling me Mr and Sir, and watching over me like I was about to crap on their good seats?'

The officer stayed mute.

'I'm only forty-two.' Sam's anger crested and ebbed as rapidly as it had erupted. 'And I'm not planning to crap on your seats.'

'That's good to know,' Ryan said tentatively.

Sam stepped back from the crater's edge and walked to the cruiser.

'Tell them we're coming in.'

11

Zack picked at his plate of potato pancakes, slicing off a tiny bite with the side of his fork and pushing it around his plate.

'Are you going to eat that?' the male officer asked through a mouthful of waffle. 'Cause it looks delicious. I'm starting to wish I had ordered it.'

Zack put down his fork, the morsel uneaten. He opened his mouth to speak when the cellphone in his pocket chirped.

The two officers exchanged glances as Zack reached a trembling hand into his pocket, his fingers sliding over the tiny gun until they wrapped around the plastic phone. He flipped the phone open and held it to his ear.

'New friends?' asked the distorted voice.

'What of it?' Zack's voice was void of emotion as he automatically scanned the restaurant, searching the faces of the other diners, trying to find who didn't belong.

'You don't want to talk to them,' said the voice.
'Why not?'

Zack finished his scan of the restaurant, but didn't see anyone who stood out. Four people were on cellphones: two women, sitting across from each other at the same table and occasionally exchanging smiles even as they talked to other people; a skinny messenger with long, hairy legs squeezed into skin-tight bicycle shorts; and a grey-haired salesman in an out-dated check jacket who kept dabbing at his forehead with paper napkins.

Colin leaned across the table, his hand stretching to touch Zack's arm. 'Everything OK?'

Zack nodded, but twisted around in his chair to face away from the two cops.

'You still have something to lose,' said the voice.

Zack almost laughed. 'I have nothing.'

The line went silent for a moment and then another voice came on.

'Zack, is that you? I can't find Kalli. He won't tell me where she is.'

'Jasmine!' Zack jumped to his feet and walked away from the table. 'I thought you were—' His voice caught in his throat and his body began to tremble so badly he could barely stand.

Once he'd turned the corner to the washroom, out of sight of the cops, he sank to his knees on the dirty floor and grasped the concrete-block wall for support.

'Find her, Zack,' Jasmine pleaded. 'Do anything he asks.'

'I am. I will . . . anything.'

'Touching,' said the electronic voice.

Zack closed his eyes, not wanting the sound of Jasmine's voice to leave his head. She sounded so scared, and yet he knew it wasn't for herself. She was focused on Kalli, their fourteen-year-old daughter who loved to draw horses and still secretly sucked her thumb in her sleep.

The same daughter who, along with his wife, he believed had been blown to bits before his eyes.

'Don't hurt her,' Zack said. 'I'm begging you.'

'You know what I want.'

Zack held back a sob. 'I had most of it. I liquidated everything—'

'Did I ask for most?'

'No, but—'

'Stop snivelling. I can help you fulfil your obligation. Are you interested?'

'Yes,' Zack agreed instantly. 'Anything.'

'Here's what I need you to do . . .'

12

Officer Dale Ryan escorted Sam to the glass-and-steel lobby of the Portland Justice Center. Located in the heart of the city, the building housed not only the Portland Police Bureau, but also four courtrooms and the 676-bed maximum-security Multnomah County Detention Center. For criminals, that meant they could be booked, tried and locked up without travelling any further than the elevator.

Ryan signed him in at the reception desk, the relief of having turned over responsibility clear upon his face.

'Good luck, Mr White. I'm sorry for your loss.'

Sam nodded slowly. The effects of the blue pills had begun to wear off, making him feel tired and defeated. He wasn't even sure if his voice would still be audible if he opened his mouth to speak.

A slim, middle-aged Latino woman rose from behind a plastic desk as Ryan retreated.

'Would you follow me, please, Mr White? You're expected upstairs.'

The woman flashed him a quick smile – a rapid flexing of cheek muscles delivering minimum friendliness – before unlatching a security gate in the reception desk and inviting him in.

With his feet on automatic pilot, Sam followed her to a bank of elevators.

Inside one of the elevators, the woman waited for him to join her, then pushed the button for the thirteenth floor. Before the doors closed, however, she flashed him another false smile and exited without a word. Except for two security cameras with blinking red lights, Sam was left alone in the shiny metal box.

When the doors opened again, a woman with bright orange lipstick, a massive bosom and a mop of fiercely dyed peroxide-blonde hair gestured for him to come over to where she sat behind another ivory desk.

Sam didn't like the look of her or the floor's stark decor. He decided to stay where he was and closed his eyes.

A tug at his elbow jarred him awake. This time the blonde was directly beside him, and she looked even scarier than she had from a distance.

'You're expected, Mr White.'

The blonde tugged him out of the elevator and escorted him through a maze of desks to a small office against the far wall. The room contained two wooden chairs, a plain cafeteria-style table and a fake leather couch.

'Make yourself comfortable,' the blonde said. 'The detectives will be with you shortly.'

After the door closed behind him, Sam crossed to the floor-to-ceiling window that looked out on the city. He flinched when he saw his reflection floating in the tinted glass. The weary face that stared back at him had aged a dozen years in the last few hours.

Sam turned to the couch. It looked worn and soft and too inviting to ignore. He slumped on to the cushions and laid his head on the armrest. It was less comfortable than it looked, but his eyes were already closing.

Sam jumped when the door opened just moments later, the cacophony from the large room beyond crashing in.

Two detectives entered the room. They were both neatly dressed, but only one of them carried it with style.

The first detective looked almost effeminate. His golden-brown hair was perfectly shaped to complement his long, smooth face and his short sideburns were cut to a matched razor's edge. His fingernails had been manicured and buffed, and his shirtsleeves were fastened at the wrist by an expensive pair of gold cufflinks.

'Thanks for coming in, Mr White,' he began. 'I'm Detective Hogan and this is Detective Preston.'

In contrast to his partner, Preston wore a cheap

polyester suit and had a sharp crease around his forehead as if he had just removed a hat. He was the broader of the two, and his heavy gut was cinched behind an oversized western-style buckle. His height was enhanced by a pair of well-worn, alligator-skin cowboy boots.

Sam nodded hello.

'We understand you work armed security, so you'll know how this works,' Hogan said. Friendly, brother-in-arms, let-down-your-guard stuff.

When Sam finally spoke, his voice was weak and parched.

'No one has even confirmed that Hannah and MaryAnn are dead,' he said. 'All I saw were two white bags. Are you positive they didn't get out of the house before it exploded? We had a smoke detector. I checked the battery myself. Maybe they're at a hotel or—'

'I'm sorry to tell you—' began Hogan.

'The remains of two bodies were recovered from the ashes, Mr White,' interrupted Preston in a gruff Texan drawl. 'The coroner is working on them now.'

13

Chief Medical Examiner Randy Hogg looked more like a soft-rock crooner than a county coroner, and he liked it that way.

After slipping on a gangsta-style hairnet, Hogg snapped on a pair of disposable vinyl gloves and moved to the matching set of stainless-steel autopsy tables. Both bodies, blackened to the core, had been removed from their travel bags for his examination.

Hogg studied the corpses and felt a dull thrum deep in his belly. Even after all these years, there were some cases he had trouble distancing himself from and fire victims were at the top of that list. He hated how the heat melted away the fat and shrunk the muscles, scalp and skull into the stuff of nightmares.

Even though he knew they were just meat now, the look on what was left of their faces – a dying scream made flesh – sent a chill up his spine. The adult victim was the worst, as a heavy object, possibly a support beam from the collapsing ceiling, had landed on her head. The object had flattened the skull and cracked the eye sockets, but that wasn't all. The force of the blow had also crushed cheek and nasal bone, shattering the lower jaw and elongating the mouth to disturbing proportions. Investigators still hadn't found all her teeth.

As his assistant videotaped the cadavers with a palm-sized digital camcorder, Hogg began his cursory exam.

Looking at their charred, twisted exteriors, Hogg could guess what awaited him internally. Determining their sex was fairly straightforward as the hips were key giveaways. He could tell from their shape that the older victim had given birth at some time in her adult life. But he knew it would take close examination of the remains, plus comparisons to dental records, DNA and X-rays, to determine accurate identities. All of that would take time. Which, in turn, would annoy the hell out of the investigating officers.

Keep positive, Hogg reminded himself.

He took several deep breaths – inhaling through his nose and releasing it, hissing Cobra style, through his mouth – before returning to the bodies.

Both victims were locked in pugilistic poses, their fists and arms drawn up toward their chins. Skin and muscles tended to contract because of the intense dehydration caused by fire. This made entry to their internal organs (if they hadn't been completely cooked or liquefied in the blaze) difficult.

Not impossible, Hogg told himself, *just difficult.*

'Dr Hogg!'

Hogg turned to his cinematographing assistant. 'Yes, Sally, what is it?'

Sally was excited. 'This one's holding something. I think it's a doll or a – no, it's a bear, a stuffed bear.'

Hogg moved swiftly around the table to join Sally who was trying to get a better angle on the tiny object with her zoom-enabled camcorder.

To the naked eye, the scorched entity beneath the younger victim's blackened hands was barely discernible. Hogg lowered a magnifying glass from his macabre chandelier of tools to examine the object in closer detail.

'I think you're right,' he said. 'It is a bear. Its stuffing must have been made of fireproof material.'

With scalpel and tweezers, Hogg gently cut the top half of the toy bear from the child's rigid grasp. Beneath the animal's protective shadow, a tiny patch of unmarred skin, no larger than a matchbook cover, shone from the girl's chest like a tiny, perfect island in a rough charcoal sea.

The bear had protected a secret, and the revelation of it made Hogg gasp.

14

Sam reeled at the confirmation as if slapped in the face. Detective Hogan flashed his partner an angry scowl.

'Please excuse my partner's bluntness, Mr White.' Hogan settled into one of the chairs. 'He's better with crime scenes than people.'

Detective Preston snorted and, turning his back to the room, looked out of the window as though he had lost interest in the interview.

'Did they suffer?' Sam instantly wished he hadn't asked, as there was only one answer he could bear to hear.

'They wasn't laughin',' Preston muttered.

'We're sure they didn't,' interjected Hogan. 'The house went up like a bomb.'

Sam flinched.

'What caused it?'

'You tell us,' Preston said.

'The fire marshal suspects the furnace,' said Hogan. 'Gas leak—'

'And that ain't something that happens every-day,' interrupted Preston.

Sam spun to glare at the detective, a surge of rage bubbling within. 'What are you implying?'

Preston turned with arms folded tight across his barrel chest.

'This ain't my first rodeo, Mr White.' Preston's drawl made him sound both polite and condescending at the same time. 'And I find it damn suspicious that a modern furnace equipped with automatic shut-off valves would fail in such an almighty manner.'

The last modicum of colour drained from Sam's face.

'You don't know me,' he said weakly. 'To think I could even contemplate . . .' The sentence went unfinished.

'We've looked at your bank records,' Preston continued. 'You're not faring too well. Credit card debts, a large interest-only mortgage, furniture bought on one of those don't-pay-till-Judgement-Day plans. Need I go on?'

Sam ground his teeth. 'I would never hurt my family.'

'Maybe you didn't mean to,' Hogan jumped in. 'Maybe you just wanted to collect on the house, but something went wrong . . .' He left the theory hanging there, like live bait.

Sam closed his eyes for a moment, attempting to regain control of his emotions. 'What good does collecting on a house do if the bank owns it all?'

'Good point,' Hogan agreed, still trying to be friends.

Sam turned to Preston. 'And as you've investigated my finances, you also know that none of us had life insurance. So where's your fucking motive now?'

Preston snorted. 'Money is only one motive for killing a wife.'

'And child?' Sam's voice was ice.

'We're still looking into that.'

Sam rubbed his face with both hands. His palms were gritty and the friction pulled at his skin, causing tiny tracks of pain. The sensation was an unpleasant comfort.

'If it was my fault,' he said quietly, 'something I did or fucked up somehow, you won't even need a trial. I'll gladly slit my own throat.'

'We'll hold you to that,' Preston said.

Hogan flashed his partner another annoyed look before reassuring Sam.

'We know you were at work when this tragedy occurred,' he said. 'We're just trying to figure out how or why it happened.'

Sam picked at the corner of the tabletop with his thumbnail. Mute.

'Do you know anyone who drives a large Mercedes?' Hogan asked.

Sam looked up, eyes narrowing. 'No. Why?'

'A neighbour saw a four-door sedan parked across from your house at the time of the explosion. The neighbour believes it was a metallic Mercedes, although the explosion knocked out the street lights and it was difficult to see. A man in a dark suit drove it away before the police arrived. The witness says it's possible the man was injured in the blast. Naturally, we would like to talk to him.'

'You checked the hospitals?' Sam asked.

Behind him, Preston snorted.

Hogan nodded. 'Nothing yet.'

Sam chewed the lining of his inner cheek as he rolled the information around in his head to see where it fit.

'Anything you're not saying?' Preston asked.

'Like what?'

Preston walked forward until he was looming over Sam. 'Maybe this man was waiting for you to get home; collect on some outstanding debts. Gambling, drugs, underage women. You know, the kind of things you Hollywood types enjoy.'

If Sam hadn't been feeling so suicidal, he would have laughed. 'I never made enough to start pissing it away, Detective. You would know that if you read my bio.'

'I did,' Preston said. 'Even Googled your name.'

'Doubt I showed up.'

'Got a couple hits from when you played a scumbag on *Magnum*.'

'Long time ago.'

'That must rankle.'

Sam shrugged. 'You move on.'

'The wife make you give it up?' Preston pushed.

'It was mutual.'

'Yeah.' Preston grinned, showing teeth. 'Come on, man to man, it's never mutual. The wife barks and we either get in line or get the fuck out, right?'

Sam stayed silent, a building rage warming his cheeks.

'She made you give up your dream – lights, action, the works – and you fucking hated her for it. Everything changed because of the kid, right? Can't play dress-up any more when you got responsibilities.'

'Fuck you!' Sam's fist slammed on to the table-top. 'You know nothing about me or Hannah or MaryAnn . . .' His voice broke, anger turning to tears. 'You just . . . don't know.'

Sam lowered his face into the crook of his arms and began to sob.

Detective Hogan, his face impassive, glanced at his partner. Preston shrugged and slowly walked back to the window. He looked down on the scurrying ants in their colourful array of match-box cars.

A few drops of rain splashed against the glass as if in sympathy for the broken man weeping inside.

15

Sam stood on the sidewalk outside the Justice Center, unsure of where to go. The detectives had offered him a ride, but Sam declined. They had told him not to leave town, but didn't offer any alternatives for sticking around.

The fact he was homeless, penniless and in the worst state of mind he had ever known hadn't seemed to cross their minds.

He walked aimlessly around the building, filling his lungs with oxygen and fighting off a deep, clawing desire to step into a hole and sink for ever into its depths. Looking up, he noticed engravings of famous quotes about justice etched on the building's walls. He read them as he walked, seeking some message of comfort.

He finally stopped at the south-west corner beneath the words of Martin Luther King, a man who surely understood the unbearable weight of loss.

Injustice anywhere is a threat to justice everywhere.

Millions had found comfort or been rallied by those eight powerful words but, on this day, Sam didn't care about justice. What did justice have to do with something as senseless as losing your family?

'Hey, mister! Mr White! This is for you.'

Sam turned towards the voice and blinked his eyes into focus. He was surprised to find he was still standing outside the Justice Center even though he couldn't say where he thought he should be.

A bike messenger in a clunky, oversized helmet and cherry-tinted wrap-around sunglasses was shoving a brown padded envelope at him.

'There must be a mistake,' Sam said. 'I'm not the person you want.'

'Your name Sam White?'

'Yes, but—'

'It's for you, man.'

Sam accepted the envelope.

'But how . . . ?'

The messenger pushed off without a backward glance and began to peddle hard. After he turned the corner, there was a blare of car horn and the sharp screech of tyre, but no fleshy crunch to delay traffic.

Sam squeezed the envelope, feeling something small and hard nestled within. It was the size and shape of a bar of soap.

He looked around, studying the faces of passing strangers and cars in the street. He saw a silver Mercedes roll through an amber light at the corner, its back windows heavily tinted.

In Sam's hand, the envelope started to ring.

He hesitated only a moment before ripping open the envelope and removing a small flip phone from within. There was no note.

On the fifth ring, Sam answered.

'Hello?'

'Just listen, Mr White,' said a voice, its tone digitally scrambled to sound deeper and slower than normal speech. 'Your family is alive.'

'What?' Sam's voice rose in pitch.

'The dead woman and child,' continued the voice, its words slow and deliberate, 'aren't yours.'

Sam staggered backwards as if reeling from a physical blow. He leaned against the concrete and granite wall of the Justice Center, its six-storey foundation feeling barely strong enough to keep him upright.

'What are you talking about?'

'The bodies recovered from the fire this morning do not belong to your wife and child. Hannah and MaryAnn are still alive.'

Sam rubbed at his face. 'Who are you?' he whispered. 'What kind of sick game is this?'

'No game, Mr White,' said the calm monotone. 'If you don't want to lose them again, you'll need to do exactly what I say.'

'You bastard!'

'You are mine for three days. If you do all that I ask, you will see your loved ones again. If you disappoint me in any way, I will dispose of them.'

'Why are you doing this?' Sam's voice cracked on the edge of hysteria.

'Once the police discover the bodies aren't who they think they are, they'll be looking for answers. Since you have none, you'll want to avoid them. The choice is yours. If you do decide to involve the authorities and you are not available when I call, your family will die.'

'Can I talk to them? Please?'

The caller ignored his plea.

'You will be given a series of tasks, each one a further test of loyalty to your family. The final stage will be the delivery of one million dollars in cash.'

'But that's impossible. I don't have anything near that amount of money.'

'Your first task is a simple choice,' continued the voice. 'Either you can return to the detectives upstairs or you can disappear off their radar. I suggest the latter, but like everything I shall ask of you, the choice is entirely yours.'

Sam took a deep breath. 'Wait,' he said. 'If the bodies aren't my family's, who are they?'

16

Detective Hogan filled two mugs with oily black coffee from the communal pot in the tiny staff lunch room. Like most staff rooms, this one had its main corkboard wall decorated with notices for school raffles, garage sales, places for rent, and even a poster for local punk band The Rotten Johnnys, which one of the other detectives played drums for in his off-duty hours.

Hogan added powdered cream substitute to one of the coffees and carried the cups to the two-sided desk he shared with his partner.

Detective Preston tilted precariously on his office chair, balancing the $1^1/_2$-inch heels of his cowboy boots on the flimsy keyboard tray that jutted from the desk's underbelly. He accepted the murky coffee from his partner and took a large slurp.

'This is gawd awful,' he said with a grimace. 'How this became our great nation's most popular addiction, I'll never know.'

Hogan shrugged, took a sip and winced. It was awful. 'So what do you think of White?'

Preston tilted further back in his chair. 'I hate to say it, but I think he's OK. I rode him hard in there, but he got pissed at me for all the right reasons. His grief seems genuine. That said, I still think the situation is flaky. Just can't figure what he gets out of it.'

'I agree. There's no money angle. He won't see a penny from insurance. In fact, he's worse off. I like the frustrated-actor angle though. Maybe he wanted a clean slate so he could return to Hollywood unhindered.'

'Yeah, that's definitely worth pursuing. We should talk to the neighbours. See if there were marital problems.'

'There are always marital problems.'

'You got that right.' Preston grimaced again as he took another sip of coffee. 'If you got on the barkin' end of my wife, you'd wonder why I hadn't shot her already.'

Hogan's laughter was interrupted by the electronic chirp from his desk phone. He answered it with a chuckle. 'Hogan.'

'Ah, Detective Hogan,' said a voice tinged with excitement. 'Chief Medical Examiner Randy Hogg, here. I have an unusual finding to report.'

Hogan covered the mouthpiece. 'It's the coroner.'

Preston dropped his feet to the floor and picked up his phone. He connected to the same line.

'And what's that, Randy?' Hogan asked.

'I still have a lot of tests to do, you understand, but I discovered an anomaly with one of the bodies.'

'Speak English,' Preston jumped in.

Hogg changed tracks. 'Are you sure of the race of both victims?'

'The race?' Hogan was puzzled. 'Yeah, they're white.'

'Hmmm, that's what I have written down.'

'But?' Preston pushed.

'Yes, well, it seems the younger victim isn't Caucasian. We found some undamaged skin and it definitely appears to be African American. Naturally, I need to run more tests and compare skeletal and dental records, but on cursory exam, I would say your cadaver does not match your victim.'

17

They're alive!

Sam's vision began to swim as he lowered the cellphone. The flimsy plastic shell felt suddenly too heavy, as though its miniature electronics had been replaced by lead.

He looked around, his face a mask of pain. None of the scurrying strangers noticed. They moved in a blur, collars and umbrellas turned up against the spitting rain as they snuck a quick cigarette between meetings or grabbed coffee and steamed hotdogs from gleaming, chrome-accented carts on the corners.

Sam was a ghost to them.

They're alive!

The realization caused a wave of vertigo to wash over him, weakening his legs and making his stomach churn. He collapsed against the building, his face pressing into the cool damp of chiselled grey brick. Before he could catch himself, his knees buckled.

Switch

The rough concrete scraped his cheek as he tried to regain his footing, but his legs had no strength and his feet slid out from under him. He hit the ground with a smack and lay sprawled across the sidewalk.

An elderly couple with an umbrella built for two stepped on to the road to get by his inert form. The man scowled and the woman clucked her tongue in annoyance.

Sam broke into a guttural sob, his chest expanding and contracting with deep, shuddering breaths. No one came to his aid, and after several minutes, he felt drained and empty.

They're alive!

Sam wiped his nose on the back of his sleeve and pushed off the ground to rest on his knees. Curious faces quickly looked away. Nobody stepped forward to offer a hand. Either fear or indifference held them at bay.

When his thighs stopped shaking, Sam grasped the wall with both hands and climbed slowly to his feet. His legs continued to tremble and his bloody cheek stung, but he knew it was time to use that pain rather than collapse beneath it.

He shoved off from the wall and started to walk. He didn't have a plan, nor a destination, but he did have a reason to live.

Zack watched Sam stagger from the Justice Center. His movement was unsteady and Zack wondered if he was drunk or mentally unhinged.

He wouldn't have blamed him for being either. His own desire to climb inside a bottle hadn't diminished, and if he hadn't emptied the last one, he would be nipping at it now.

When Sam turned the corner, Zack swung the Mercedes into traffic to follow. He wondered if the two cops he had ditched at the restaurant were looking for him, or if they had decided to let him be. He couldn't afford to be arrested, not with the fate of his family on the line, but neither could he abandon his car. It contained everything he had left.

Zack picked up the cellphone, hit the pre-programmed speed dial and reported in.

18

Sam boarded a city transit bus and asked the driver how he could get back to his house. The driver told him to either take a taxi or ride the bus to the depot and transfer to a different line.

Sam dropped some coins into the box for his fare and sat on the bench by the door that was reserved for the elderly and handicapped.

Today, he felt qualified as both.

As the bus left central downtown and headed east, the houses began to lose their charm and the faces of the pedestrians became more clouded with defeat. A motel sign in pale blue neon blinked from a block ahead, and as Sam stared at it, he felt a deep weariness pulling at his mind.

Sam pulled the bell cord above his seat, alerting the driver he wanted to get off.

'This ain't the depot, bud,' the driver said.

'It'll do.'

Sam hauled himself to his feet and swung around to face the door. When the bus hissed to a stop, he stepped off, checked over his shoulder, and headed for the motel.

The same silver Mercedes he had spotted outside the Justice Center was idling half a block away.

The front-desk clerk at the Bluesman Motel was happy to have a daytime customer until Sam explained he had arrived without luggage or a vehicle.

'I don' want trouble,' said the man in a heavy Pakistani accent. 'No drugs, no guns, no whores, and absolutely no pornographic movies being filmed on the premises.'

'I'm just tired.' Sam handed over his credit card. 'Give me a bed with clean sheets and hot water for the shower.'

'We very clean,' explained the clerk. 'Very nice establishment. We not allow scum or pornographers.'

'That's a relief.'

The clerk narrowed his eyes into slits as he slid Sam's credit card through a small electronic card reader attached to his phone.

'You have room four. Very nice. Clean. Fresh. I personally unplug toilet myself.'

'Good to know.' Sam's mouth stretched open in a yawn. 'There a back door in the room?'

'No back door,' said the clerk, his eyes narrowing again. 'I see who come. I see who go.'

Sam tried to offer a friendly, reassuring smile, but ended up yawning again.

Switch

The clerk handed over the key. 'You want earplugs? They only four dollars extra.'

Sam waved him off and headed for his room, four doors down from the glass-enclosed front desk on the ground floor. As he put the key in the lock, he glanced over his shoulder towards the street.

The Mercedes had moved up a couple of car lengths to park beneath a scrawny tree that somehow survived amidst a steady fog of car exhaust and nightly sprinklings of recycled beer. The gloomy umbrella offered by the tree's patchwork canopy hid the interior of the car from Sam's view.

Turning his back on the car and its unknown occupant, he entered his room.

19

MaryAnn awoke in complete darkness, the sour smell of rot invading her nostrils.

She rubbed her eyes, sending tiny white and blue sparks dancing across her corneas, but when the sparks blinked out, the impenetrable darkness remained. She lifted her hand in front of her face and blinked to refocus, but her fingers remained invisible.

Fear made her heart beat faster and icy daggers of panic stabbed her brain.

She didn't like the dark.

The last thing she remembered was curling up in bed and writing in her diary. Paul had smiled at her in the hallway just before Biology class, and she could tell it wasn't his ordinary smile. This smile had been special – just for her. It had been a pleasant thought to fall asleep to.

A high-pitched squeak made her jump.

The squeak was followed by the sound of tiny, scurrying feet. MaryAnn pulled her knees in close to her chest. Wherever she was, the air was moist and cold. The floor felt solid, but if she dug in her nails, it could be flaked away. The walls were similar; cold and crumbly. It felt like a grave.

Another squeak made her strain her ears, trying to gauge its direction. A louder squeak answered and without warning the chamber erupted in duelling high-pitched squeals of pain.

MaryAnn cowered in her corner, pressing her back against the packed earth and humming a Coldplay song to drown out the noise.

When silence resumed, she inhaled deeply, holding the oxygen in her lungs for several seconds before releasing it. But then her ears picked up movement, the sound of a dozen tiny feet, sharp claws clicking on hard-pack floor.

She shivered and her lower lip trembled, then she began to hum again, determined to stay calm until she could figure out what was going on. The humming worked until one of the rats scurried across her bare foot.

MaryAnn screamed.

20

The clerk hadn't lied. The room was clean and the bed looked soft. It took all of Sam's willpower not to lie down and shut off the world – just for ten minutes. But he knew if he did, he would sleep for hours.

Instead, Sam stripped off his clothes and stepped into the shower stall. The water was hot and he let it pour over his back and shoulders, easing his tense muscles.

He placed his forearms against the tiled wall, rested his head upon them and closed his eyes as the soothing water spilled down his lower back, buttocks and aching thighs. He could feel acres of grit and the oily residue of smoke sweating from his pores as the stall filled with luxurious steam.

When he opened his eyes again, he was shivering; the steam long gone, the water a freezing spray.

Sam cursed himself for falling asleep, grabbed the complementary toy-sized bar of soap, ripped off its flimsy wrapper and scrubbed his shivering body from head to toe. When he finally stepped out of the shower, his lips were blue.

He dressed quickly – the smell of smoke clinging to his soiled clothes – and returned to the bathroom. A large frosted-glass window rested in an old wooden frame above the sink. There was no need for a lock as the years and layers of paint had sealed it tight.

Sam pulled a red-jacketed Swiss Army pocket-knife from his front pocket, opened the smaller of the two blades, and began to cut through the paint at the seams. It took ten minutes, some muscle and the rest of the soap to grease the tracks, but eventually the window slid up high enough for him to squeeze through.

Sam dropped to the ground. A narrow, two-foot-wide alley of broken bottles, discarded needles and scraggy weeds ran the length of the building. Being careful of where he stepped, Sam headed down the alley to the end of the block where a flimsy wire fence had been breached so many times it was practically a door.

Sam crossed the side street to the next block and walked to the corner. A quick check told him the Mercedes was still parked under the tree.

Sam took a deep breath, opened the larger blade on his knife until it locked into place, and moved forward.

21

MaryAnn's scream brought more movement: the shuffling of feet followed by the snap of a bolt and the sandpaper scrape of rusty metal.

The sounds were followed by a stabbing square of blue light that suddenly appeared as a floating mirage in the curtain of darkness.

MaryAnn shielded her eyes from the painful light, using her fingers to filter some of the glare.

'You're awake,' said a male voice. Its cadence was slow and husky. 'Feeling sick?'

MaryAnn swallowed, her throat dry.

'Who are you?' she asked timidly. 'Where am I?'

'Unimportant. How do you feel?'

MaryAnn bit back an indignant retort.

'I'm very thirsty and . . . there are rats in here.'

'I'll bring water.'

The square of light vanished and the darkness returned even deeper and more foreboding than before. MaryAnn struggled not to cry, fearing that if she started, she wouldn't know how to stop.

Soon, the square of light returned.

'Don't cause trouble,' said the voice, 'and you'll be fine.'

MaryAnn heard the metallic clunk of the lock.

'Where's my mom?' she asked.

'Don't worry about it.'

The square of light shifted and grew into a large rectangle. Inside the rectangle and blocking most of the light was a hulking silhouette.

The man ducked and entered the tiny cell. He had to remain bent over, as the ceiling was too low. Hunched over, his muscular body took on the shape of an ogre.

MaryAnn had difficulty taking her eyes off the man as he approached, but she forced herself to scan her surroundings while she had light.

The cell was a rough square carved out of the earth, barely six feet wide and around the same height. The four corners were supported by thick wooden beams, the rough lumber so dark and slick with creosote it looked like fossilized bone. Decaying panels of oil-soaked wood made a rough skirt around the base. Above the wood, the walls were nothing more than dried mud and flecks of rough stone.

MaryAnn glanced up and gulped. The dirt ceiling had so many cracks it reminded her of a giant spider's web.

The sudden thought that she might die there sent a steel spike through her carefully maintained control, and MaryAnn felt herself begin to crack.

The man handed her a bottle of water. He stood so close that she could smell his cloying after-shave. He had a square of plastic bandage on his neck, the centre of it spotted with dried blood.

'I want my mom and dad,' MaryAnn said weakly.

The man shrugged.

MaryAnn stared up at him, a sudden surge of anger igniting a fire in her pale green eyes. She unscrewed the cap on the bottle, took a deep drink of water to slake her thirst, and then un-expectedly sprang to her feet.

Before the man could react, MaryAnn's mouth opened and a high-pitched, ear-piercing scream punched from her throat using the full capacity of her adolescent lungs. The startled man lurched in surprise, his head smashing into the low ceiling.

He grunted as broken slabs of dried mud rained down in a dirty shower around him.

MaryAnn didn't hesitate. She ran for the light, breaking through the doorway into a narrow, dimly lit passage as ancient as the cell. The floor was the same hard-baked mud and occasional wooden board; the walls were cracked and crumbling, as if they might collapse at any second. The only light was from a string of bare bulbs attached to the ceiling.

MaryAnn followed the lights, her pace quicken-ing as an angry roar bellowed from behind.

Tears returned to her eyes as MaryAnn ran

down the endless tunnel, her anger quickly giving way to despair.

'Mom!' she cried loudly. 'Mom!'

A sound from up ahead almost made her stumble: *sobbing*.

'MOM!'

MaryAnn rushed to a series of cells identical to the one she had fled. Two of the cells were open and empty, but the next four were closed.

MaryAnn stopped at the first closed cell, desperately trying to quiet her breathing as she strained her ears. The sobbing was coming from within.

'Mom?' MaryAnn called. 'Mom, is that you?'

The woman inside whimpered and her sobbing grew in volume. MaryAnn reached for the square window cut in the door, her fingers fumbling with a sliding bolt that hadn't been oiled in decades.

But before she could get it free, a giant fist grabbed her by the hair and yanked her off the ground.

'You little bitch!'

MaryAnn couldn't believe the pain. It felt like her entire scalp was about to be ripped from her skull.

'I was being nice to you.'

MaryAnn tried to talk, to beg to see her mom, but the agony was so great she couldn't move her mouth.

'Put her in cell three,' said a second voice. 'Maybe the company will settle her down.'

MaryAnn tried to see the second man's face, but tears from the pain were blinding her.

The large man lifted her higher and leaned in close to her ear. His face was flushed red and a thin sheen of sweat made his flesh glisten.

'You just lost a friend,' he whispered menacingly. 'Bad move.'

MaryAnn whimpered and then, overcome with pain and fear, promptly fainted.

22

Moving towards the Mercedes, Sam slipped in beside a group of three men ambling past the corner. Their bodies acted as a shield in case the driver's gaze drifted from the motel. Once he was beside the car, Sam moved out of the trio's slipstream and reached for the passenger door. It was unlocked.

By the time the driver noticed him, it was too late. Sam had a knife to his throat and the car door was swinging closed to lock out the prying eyes of passers-by.

The man yelped in surprise, his head cracking against the side window as he recoiled from the knife. Sam moved with him, the sharp blade drawing a trickle of blood as he applied pressure.

'I'm a friend,' the man cried. 'I want to help.'

'Where's my family?' Sam asked, his voice cutting a sharper edge than the blade.

'I don't know. I swear.'

Sam applied more pressure to the knife and

the trickle widened into a three-inch gash.

'I'm telling the truth,' the man pleaded. 'My name is Zack Parker and my family's been kidnapped.'

'Bullshit!'

'I wish it was,' Zack groaned. 'By Christ, I wish it was.'

'You were outside my house before the explosion.'

'Yes.'

'Why?'

'He said my family was there.'

'At my home?'

'Yes.'

'Who said it?'

'The kidnapper. I don't know who he is.'

Sam growled, baring his teeth like a feral dog.

'I swear to you,' Zack said, 'I don't know who's doing this.'

'The explosion?'

'I didn't do it. I . . .' Zack winced. 'How could I? My wife and daughter were inside.'

'*Your* wife?'

'Yes. My family was switched for yours.'

Sam felt fingers of madness clawing into his mind. 'Bullshit!'

Zack exploded. 'You think I don't want to believe that? You think I wouldn't give anything for it not to be true?'

'I don't know you,' Sam snapped back. 'You could be the one who phoned me.'

Zack leaned into the knife, allowing it to slice deeper into his flesh as he forced his face closer to Sam's.

'My family died in your house. The man who called you has already destroyed me.' Zack's eyes glistened. 'I don't know why he let me live. I wish he hadn't. But since I'm here, I want to help.'

Sam stared deep into Zack's eyes and felt the man's warm blood begin to flow over his fingers.

'Why should I believe you?'

Zack gritted his teeth as the blood from his wound continued to flow freely down his neck.

'Two bodies were removed from your house this morning. They belonged either to you or to me. What scenario do you want to believe?'

'I want the truth.'

Zack snorted and moved his head back to rest it against the window. Sam didn't move with him and the knife lost contact with the wound. Blood soaked into the collar of Zack's white shirt.

After a moment, Zack sighed. 'The truth is that I fucked up and paid with the lives of my wife and baby girl.' Zack's voice broke and his eyes filled with more tears. 'I did everything he asked. I just . . .'

'Just?' Sam prodded.

Zack raised his chin to stare at Sam through bloodshot espresso-brown eyes.

'I thought it was about money,' he said slowly, as though still trying to piece it together in his own brain. 'I brought what I could. It wasn't every dollar he asked for, but everything I could get my hands on. I hoped it would be enough.

'I waited on the street outside your house. He chose the meeting place. He said it was the final step: the money in exchange for my family. Instead, your house exploded with my family inside.'

'Jesus!'

Zack continued, his voice so soft it was nearly lost in the buzz of light traffic.

'I thought I caught a glimpse of Kalli, my baby, standing at the window, waiting for me, alive and trusting I would save her.'

Zack's eyes were so full of pain, Sam nearly forgot his own.

'Why did you leave the scene?'

Zack rubbed at his eyes. 'To do to myself the same thing you wanted to.'

'What stopped you?'

'Courage. Or lack of. I got drunk instead.' Zack sighed heavily. 'Couldn't even do that right.'

Sam took a closer look at the face of the man across from him. He looked how Sam felt. His chocolate-coloured skin was sallow with a tinge of grey. His eyes, sunken with weariness, looked even deeper-set against hollow, sucked-in cheeks. He was dangerously thin and it was difficult to gauge his age as his thick, close-cropped hair wavered on the cusp of adding cream to its coffee.

The only feature that hinted at a prosperous normality was his wardrobe. The suit alone, despite its rumpled state, must have cost more than Sam's entire liquidated worth.

'How do you know me?' Sam asked.

'I don't,' Zack answered. 'Not really. I guessed you were the owner of the house. I've been following to see if you shared the blame.'

'For the death of your family?'

Zack nodded.

'And if I did?' Sam asked.

Zack inclined his head with a subtle nod.

Sam looked down and saw a small silver pistol clutched in Zack's right hand. He relaxed his arm, bringing the knife down to his lap.

'You've got the better hand,' he said.

'But I didn't use it.'

'Why should I believe you?' he asked again.

'Do you need to?' Zack removed a linen handkerchief from his pocket and used it to staunch the blood still flowing from his neck. 'If I'm lying, you'll find out when the police identify the bodies. If I'm not, I'm the only friend you've got.'

Sam rubbed his chin, feeling the sandpaper stubble that had grown over the last few hours. He needed an avenue for his anger; a vent for the burning madness filling his mind, but as he studied the distraught man in front of him, he came to the decision that Zack wasn't it.

He held out his hand. 'Sam White.'

Zack's gaze flicked down at the offered hand before locking with Sam's rigid stare. The air inside the car was thick and rigid. The moment lasted less than an eye-blink, but in that flash a bond was formed. Zack returned his gun to his pocket and accepted Sam's hand.

'What do we do now?' Sam asked.

'Did you pay cash for your room?'

'Visa.'

'The police can track it.'

'So?'

'The bodies aren't who they're expecting. Can you explain that?'

'I can now.'

'Will they believe you?'

Sam pondered the question. 'I wouldn't.'

'That's exactly what he does: puts you in a position where you've nowhere to turn. You have to keep running, and when you're running, you don't have time to think.'

'Or to sleep,' Sam added, but instantly felt guilty for his own weakness.

'Sleep gives you strength,' Zack said. 'I never realized what an important tool it was until I tried to go without. Look at me.'

Sam lifted his gaze.

'I wore myself to the quick trying to stay ahead of this fucker, but he's sleeping and plotting and laughing himself sick. If I had to start again, I would take better care of myself so that maybe I would be faster and more alert when it counted.'

Sam lowered his gaze again, his guilt over the weariness he felt undiminished.

'I have a room we can use,' Zack continued.

'The clerk takes cash and doesn't give a damn what name we give.'

'We?' Sam asked.

'Whoever's behind this is done with me now,' Zack said. 'You're his new plaything. You may not believe me, but I don't want anyone to go through what I did, to lose what I've lost. I'll do everything I can to help, but there's one condition.'

'Go on.'

'Once your family is safe, I get to pull the trigger that sends this bastard straight to hell.'

23

MaryAnn opened her eyes to darkness once again, the clunk of a closing door so quickly absorbed by thick walls it could have been a tendril of dream.

She tenderly touched the top of her head, wincing at the pain that pricked her scalp. She smoothed her hair and imagined it was her mother's hand.

'Who's there?' asked a woman's voice, just barely above a whisper.

MaryAnn froze. The voice didn't belong to her mother.

'I know someone's there,' said the voice. 'I saw them throw you inside.'

MaryAnn sniffled, barely holding on to what little control she had left.

'I'm MaryAnn.'

'Are you alone?'

'I – I think so.'

'How did you get here?'

'I don't know. I was asleep in bed, and then . . . I woke up here.'

The woman's voice softened, but only slightly.

'How old are you?'

'Thirteen.'

'Have you seen anyone else?'

'No. I heard someone sobbing in another cell, but I didn't get to see her. I . . . I think it might be my mom.'

The voice hesitated. 'She's been weeping for hours. I think she may have gone a little crazy down here. Not that I blame her.'

'Where are we?'

'I don't know, child. They're not forthcoming with answers, though I've tried.'

MaryAnn's voice began to crack. 'I'm so scared.'

'I know, baby.' The woman's voice melted into a soothing tone. 'Come on over towards my voice. There's a cot and a couple blankets. It's not much, but it's better than that filthy floor.'

MaryAnn picked herself off the floor and slowly moved in the direction of the voice. When her legs bumped into the metal frame of an army cot, she reached down and felt a pair of bare legs, rough stubble marring smooth skin.

She recoiled.

'It's OK, child,' assured the voice. 'We're in this together.'

MaryAnn fought against her instincts not to trust strangers, but she was so scared and missed her mom so much, she sat on the cot and rested her back against the woman's legs.

The woman stroked her hair, cooing softly in a quiet sing-song voice. MaryAnn began to relax, tucking her feet under her and curling closer to the warmth of the woman's body.

'You rest now, baby,' said the voice. 'I won't let anyone hurt you. That's a promise.'

MaryAnn's emotions bubbled to the surface and she cried herself to sleep.

24

Neither driver nor passenger absorbed the heated-leather comfort of the Mercedes as they struggled to stay afloat in an ocean of troubling thoughts.

'He wants a million dollars,' Sam said, thinking aloud. 'Doesn't he know I'm a security guard at a shopping mall, for Christ sake?'

'He asked me for the same,' Zack said. 'I thought I could raise it, but there just wasn't enough time. I managed to get most of it by liquidating everything I owned . . . If only he had given me more time . . .'

Sam looked over, his eyes scanning Zack's thin frame. There was a lighter band of skin on his wrist where a watch would normally reside. His fingers were also bare of any jewellery except for a simple gold wedding band that wouldn't have cost more than a grand at even an exclusive jeweller's.

'What about the car?' said Sam. 'The suit?'

Zack's eyes flared with anger. 'I would have

crawled naked to him to save my family. I offered the car. I offered the money. I offered my life in exchange for theirs, but it wasn't enough.'

Zack's knuckles turned white as he squeezed the steering wheel. 'Do you know what a car's worth when you need fast cash?'

Sam shrugged. He had never owned a new car.

'Nothing,' spat Zack. 'Friends don't want it because it's not next year's model. The thieves and chop shops don't want it because it's cheaper to steal their own. I offered up the car, hoping he would add its value to the cash. He didn't take either.'

Sam was startled. 'He didn't take the money?'

'There's over $750,000 in the trunk. It's worthless to me now.'

Sam glanced over his shoulder, eyes burrowing through the back seat into the cavity beyond as a terrifying spark of violent imagery flashed before him.

'You don't need to rob me,' Zack said, plainly reading Sam's mind. 'You can have it. My family is dead, killed by my failure. If I can help yours . . .' His voice faded.

Sam was dumbstruck. 'I don't know what to say.'

'Say you'll trust me.'

Sam looked down at his lap, the fingers of one hand absently crushing and pinching the others. The jabs of pain did nothing to reassure him that he was awake and that this wasn't just one long, horrible nightmare.

'Trust is earned, not given,' he said finally.

The man raised an eyebrow. 'Not even with a trunk full of cash?'

'Not even.'

Zack pondered the statement. 'OK. Until I earn your trust, how about you promise not to slit my throat when my eyes are closed?'

'If you lie to me, or I discover you're involved with this, it won't matter if you're asleep or awake.'

A thin smile flickered over Zack's face, momentarily lifting the sadness from his eyes. 'I can live with that.'

Sam liked the man, and for a moment he could picture the friendship they might have had: laughter and backyard barbecues; two families sharing a meal . . .

Sam shook the vision from his head, knowing his mind was searching for an escape from the reality before him. It was one of the things Hannah would constantly admonish him for.

What planet you on now, Sam? she would say, her hands jabbing into hips, elbows cocked at a jaunty angle as she rose on her toes in a weak attempt to make herself look larger and more menacing. *Problems don't go away just because you close your eyes and pretend they're not there.*

Sam looked out of the side window, watching the blur of storefronts, their signs unreadable as though his mind could no longer comprehend the language. He wiped at his eyes, clearing a damp curtain of fog, and ran two dry knuckles under his dripping nose.

'How do we get my family back?' he asked.

'I don't have that answer,' Zack said carefully. 'But I know you must be exhausted. He wants us tired, not thinking, making mistakes. Like I said, that's where I went wrong. I was so tired I became blind to his game. He gives you time to torture yourself with guilt between assignments, or "choices" as he calls them. Before he calls you again, we need to rest. Then, we'll figure out how to hunt.'

25

Detective Preston struggled to get comfortable in the passenger seat of a department-issue Nissan. He often cursed whoever had designed the car's form-fitting bucket seats, knowing it was likely some smartass Asian computer that had never heard of Big & Tall stores or corn-fed cowboys from Texas.

'Where do you think he would have gone?' he grumbled to his partner.

'I expected he'd end up back here.' Hogan glanced out of the windshield at the navy blue Jeep parked against the kerb less than a half-block from their position. 'It's the only damn thing left he owns.'

'What about parents?' Preston asked. 'You look into them?'

'The wife's folks live in Florida,' Hogan replied. 'But the housekeeper says they're on stress reduction in Italy. Cycling and wine-tasting in the country, no cellphones or email allowed, and she didn't have a contact number. I issued an alert to the consulate in case they check in. His parents are AWOL, too. Seems they sold up last year and bought a land yacht to tour the desert states. Modern gypsies of the road.'

'What a nightmare,' Preston muttered. 'Can you imagine being stuck with the wife twenty-four/seven in a tiny box on wheels? The Arizona boys must be bleepin' swamped. I bet they get more bludgeoned codgers by the side of the free-way than we have splattered varmints.'

'I enjoy spending time with my wife,' Hogan protested.

'Oh, I like mine fine, too, don't get me wrong, but you wait and see.'

Preston reached for the dashboard handset and pressed the transmit button.

'Darlene, you there, honey? Come on back.'

'I'm here, cowboy,' replied the unit dispatcher. 'What's your twenty?'

'Are you flirting with me, darlin'? I am a large man, but twenty may be pushing it.'

Darlene's cackle sent a shiver down Hogan's spine. How she could possibly believe his partner's B.S., he didn't know. Darlene had a face like a Louisiana alligator and, to every officer but Preston, the personality to match.

'What you needin', cowboy?'

'Patch me through to Cosmo, will you, honey?' Preston winked at his partner.

'I took a look through the actor's wallet,' he

explained. 'Then had Cosmo run a few numbers and keep them active.'

The radio squawked and a clipped voice announced, 'Kostyuchenko.'

'Cosmo, any new hits on the Visa I gave you?'

'Hold.'

Preston turned to his partner. 'Real chatterbox, huh?'

Hogan shrugged. 'He doesn't like you.'

'You kiddin'? The geek worships me.'

'You call him Cosmo. He hates that.'

'If I used that Russian handle, I'd be so tongue-tied I'd need to arrest him for assault.'

The radio hissed. 'Hello? You are there?'

'Talk to me, Cosmo.'

'Card used to check into Bluesman Motel. It's located at—'

'Yeah, we know it,' Preston interrupted. 'Good work, Cos. I'll talk to the captain about those sheep you wanted.'

'Sheep?' Kostyuchenko blurted in a panic. 'Not sheep. RAM! I need more RAM.'

26

Sam woke with a jolt and swept a thin polyester blanket from his shoulders. His skin was flushed and damp, his mind instantly abuzz with anxiety and guilt.

He sat up in the small bed set adjacent to the only window. Through sleepy eyes, he took in his surroundings: one medium-size room decorated in basic primer white with a wash of nicotine. Twin beds, their bare metal frames bolted to the floor; and two narrow, sawdust-board nightstands.

A 24-inch colour TV, its remote firmly connected to its side with a two-foot-long curly telephone cord, sat atop a solid three-drawer dresser. A black Bakelite phone, from which he had made frantic but fruitless calls to Hannah's parents and his own, rested on the nightstand beside Zack's bed.

On the far wall, a hollow-core door led to the tiny bathroom.

Zack stirred on the matching bed and opened

one eye, the way a house cat might just to see if it was worth opening the other.

'You sleep?' he asked.

Sam shrugged. 'A bit.'

'Sleep helps you deal, Sam, and either you deal or you lie down and die. Personally, I don't mind the dying.' Zack's face grew dark. 'But you don't have that option, and I don't want that asshole walking around on the planet when I'm gone.'

Sam swung his legs off the side of the bed and reached for his clothes. He understood that, unlike Zack, he at least had been given a little hope, but it didn't make him feel any less afraid.

As he dressed, he looked through the gap in the curtains to see Zack's Mercedes parked in the asphalt lot one floor below. Its polished metallic surface reflected the early-evening light.

'You sure the money's OK in the car?' Sam asked.

Zack nodded as he slipped into his own clothes. The silk suit had lost some of its wrinkles from hanging in the shower stall while he slept, but the humidity had done nothing for the blood, dirt and grass stains.

'Mercedes build their cars like tanks,' he explained. 'I also paid a little extra for the Diplomat package, which adds fireproofing and a secondary deadbolt on the trunk. You would need some real special tools to get that money, and even then you wouldn't waste your time unless you knew it was there.'

'Mmmm, OK, it's just . . .' Sam searched for the word, 'unsettling, I guess.'

'You want the keys?' Zack asked.

'What?'

'Would you feel better if you had the keys, instead of me?'

Sam shook off the suggestion. 'Nah. Forget it. I'm so jittery I'd probably lose the damn things.'

'Any time you change your mind . . .'

Sam nodded to show he appreciated the offer. 'So what now?'

As if in answer, the cellphone rang.

27

'You know,' Detective Preston said, 'it's not that I don't appreciate spending extra time with you, but my stomach is telling me to go home, get something to eat, curl up with the wife and watch a little *Jeopardy*. Maybe even crack a cold Texas beer.'

Hogan ignored him and continued to search the abandoned room.

The motel clerk stood at the open door to Room 4, his hands on hips and a frown creasing his face.

'He not check out,' he said for the fourth time in under a minute. 'I see who come, I see who go. He not go.'

'Snuck out.' Preston jabbed his thumb in the direction of the small washroom at the rear. 'Open window.'

'He not to do that,' said the clerk. 'Window not to be opened. We run very clean place here. Very nice. No pornographers.'

'Pity,' Preston quipped. 'Those are always fun doors to kick down.'

Hogan sighed and scratched his chin. 'You think White planned this?'

'Misdirection?' Preston shrugged. 'He didn't strike me as being that clever, but . . .'

'If the explosion was a cover-up . . .' Hogan voiced aloud.

'Of the black girl's murder . . .' Preston continued.

'Then he could be on the run,' Hogan finished.

'Which makes us look like dopes for letting him walk,' Preston added.

Hogan turned to the clerk. 'How was he acting when he checked in?'

The clerk's eyes grew large. 'He very tired and yawning. Did not strike me as scumbag or pornographer. I very careful, but not perfect. Only human.'

'Any visitors?' Preston asked.

'No. I see who come. I see who—' He stopped himself and looked a touch embarrassed. 'I did not believe window could be opening.'

'Well, it did take a bit of elbow grease,' Preston agreed. 'And he certainly didn't do it for the fresh air.'

Hogan sighed. 'Doesn't look good, does it?'

'Maybe he's a better actor than we gave him credit for.'

Hogan flipped open his cellphone.

'I'll get approval for patrol to watch his Jeep,

and get the coroner to make identifying the victims a priority. Once we know who was killed, we can figure out why.'

Preston pulled out his own phone. 'I'll make sure Cosmo alerts us if any new charges pop up on the card.'

'I will be closing window now,' said the clerk, and vanished into the bathroom.

28

Sam forced himself to breathe as he answered the cellphone.

'Mr White. Just listen,' said the altered voice. 'There is a liquor store, Toler's Tonics, on Tenth Avenue and North Street. I want you to go there and pick up two forty-ounce bottles of hard liquor. I don't care what brand or what type of alcohol you choose. Do you understand?'

'Yes.' Sam glanced over at Zack, frowning.

The voice continued. 'I know you consider yourself to be an honest man, Sam. It's one of the little things you take pride in. That's about to change.'

'What are you talking about?' Sam asked, frustration clear in his voice.

'Pride is a sin, Sam.'

'I apologize,' Sam snapped. 'There! Can we end this now?'

'I told you to listen. Do not test me. You won't like where it leads.'

Sam took another deep breath. 'OK, I'm sorry. I'm listening.'

'You are not to pay for the alcohol,' the voice continued. 'The owner of that store has been robbed four times in the last six weeks. During the last attempt, the thief's head was removed from his shoulders by shotgun. You may have read about it. The unrepentant store owner was hailed by media and police as a local hero. Along with relishing the glory, he now has a taste for blood.'

Sam groaned. 'Christ.'

'You may wish to retrieve your weapon from its locker at the mall before entering the store. I will call again in two hours. If you have not accomplished this task, I will execute your wife. The choice, as always, is entirely yours.'

Sam blurted, 'Can we meet—' but the phone went dead before he could complete the plea.

Sam let the phone fall on to the bed, his face ashen.

'Your first assignment,' Zack said, his voice barely above a whisper.

29

Alan Robertson picked at his supper, his fork slicing through a baby red-skinned potato. He moved the half-moon pieces to one side where they would wait to be sliced again.

He didn't notice his wife's worried stare radiating from the other end of the oblong table. Nor did he hear the escalating squabble between his two children as they argued over whose turn it was on the PlayStation 3 after supper.

When the phone rang, Alan rose automatically and walked to the front hall where his wife had fashioned an elegant alcove. A cordless phone sat on an antique roll-top desk beside a red-velvet bench.

Alan remained standing as he answered the ringing receiver.

'Did you read the email?' asked a voice that Alan knew too well.

'Yes.'

'And watch the news?'

'Yes.'

'Shame about his family.'

'Y–yes.' Alan's voice cracked.

'It must have been horrible.'

'Y–yes.'

'What would you do to save yours?'

'Anything. I would do anything.'

'I believe you.'

Alan sunk to his knees with the phone still pressed against his ear. The ceramic tiles were hard, but comfortably warm from the under-floor heating. He had sacrificed no expense to give his family the best of everything, and yet when they needed him most, his money was worthless.

'Isn't there something else I can do to show how sorry I am?' Alan asked.

There was a long pause, and then, 'You should have thought about that before, Alan, when it would have mattered.'

'But I never lied. I . . . I . . .'

'You told what you saw, Alan, not what you knew. You were in that room, too.'

'It was the lawyers. They only asked—'

'Too late!' the voice screamed. 'Far too fucking late, Alan.' He was breathing heavy now. 'Do you love your family?'

'Yes.'

'Do you want them to suffer?'

'No. God, no.'

'Then prepare yourself and wait for my call.

You'll have one chance and one chance only. Do you understand?'

Alan's voice was barely audible. 'Yes.'

The phone went dead in his hand and Alan began to weep.

30

'I'll need your keys,' Sam said.

Zack held them up so the laser-etched Mercedes logo caught the light.

'They're yours,' he said. 'But stop for a second and hear me out.'

Sam frowned.

'I know this is difficult,' Zack continued. 'Hell, it's impossible, but this is exactly what he did to me. He kept me running around so much that I didn't take the time to think. I just reacted, like you're doing. But there are two of us now. What did he ask you to do?'

Sam hesitated, and then explained.

Zack thought for a moment. 'He'll need to be watching somehow – to make sure you don't cheat and just pay.'

'Christ,' Sam groaned. 'I didn't even think about paying.'

'Amazing how quickly we change, huh? In different circumstances, we're all different men.

This is what he wants, to break us down, bit by bit. We have to out-think him.'

'How?'

'I'll go with you,' Zack said. 'But drop me off around the block. Maybe I can catch him watching you. If we can get a licence plate, a face, a name, something that will tell us why he's picked us, then maybe we can end this before your family pays the same price as mine.'

Sam thought about it. 'He said I should get my gun.'

Zack raised an eyebrow. 'I'm in no position to judge anything you do.'

Sam chewed on a fingernail, quickly ripping it down to the quick.

'If he wants me to get the gun, I should do it. It doesn't mean I have to use it, but if I defy him on this, he may take that as a challenge.'

'Let's do it, then.' Zack got to his feet and held out the car keys. 'You want to drive?'

Sam waved him off. 'Like you said before, I need to think.'

31

On the way to the mall, Sam stared at Zack, his mind chugging through its gears. Underneath the exhaustion, he had a good face, handsome, sharp and obviously intelligent. It even seemed vaguely familiar, but Sam doubted he was part of the acting brigade. He was good at remembering the competition.

'What did he make you do?' Sam asked.

'My first assignment?' said Zack.

Sam nodded.

'Nothing like this,' Zack said. 'I was to run five red lights in different parts of San Diego.'

'San Diego?'

'That's where I live . . . lived.' Zack paused. 'Nothing left there for me now.'

'Why the red lights?'

'Until that point in my life, I'd never even had a speeding ticket. Squeaky clean, I was.' Zack grimaced. 'My palms were sweating so badly I could hardly hold the steering wheel. Nearly crashed at two of the intersections, too. Cars everywhere, honking and screeching tyres. He was timing me between lights. I only had so much time.'

'What did he get out of making you do that?'

Zack shrugged. 'Got me an arrest warrant, I suppose. Each of the lights he chose had one of those automatic cameras installed. I don't know how long it takes for the cops to download the photos or whatever, but I knew when they saw my car running five lights in one afternoon, they would be tracking me down. That alone made me paranoid about every cruiser I saw, wondering when they were going to pull me over, take me out of the game.'

'That's what he threatened me with. If the cops became involved and I couldn't respond to his calls, my family was dead.'

'Yeah,' Zack sighed. 'Bastard holds a short leash.'

At the mall, Sam slid out of the Mercedes and raced inside, snaking his way through the unruly dinner crowds.

When he reached the escalators, he cut off from the main walkway and headed up the side corridor that led to the washrooms. Entering the *Authorized Personnel Only* doors, he took a sharp left to reach a single blue door labelled *Security*.

He unlocked the door and slipped inside.

Sitting on the bench facing the lockers, Sam spun the dial on his padlock and yanked it open. Since he had removed his uniform, the inside was practically bare, containing only his black leather shoes, leather holster and belt, and the small blue plastic gun box.

He lifted out the box and unlocked it.

From inside, Sam withdrew his company-issue Smith & Wesson Model 25 revolver in blued carbon steel and Cocobolo finger-groove grips. It was the kind of gun designed to look intimidating when worn on the hip, yet at 39 ounces it was still light enough to carry around for an eight-hour shift.

Sam's permit only allowed him to carry the gun while on duty within the confines of the mall. The company issued additional temporary permits whenever he needed to transport the gun to the shooting range for his monthly practice sessions. But those permits had to be ordered at least two days in advance.

Sam slipped the gun into his belt at the small of his back and stuffed a box of standard .45 cartridges into his pocket. He returned the gun case to the locker and re-spun the lock.

Just as he stood, the door opened and Harry Coombs, one of four day-shift guards, entered.

'Oh, hey, Sam,' Harry bellowed good-naturedly. 'Awful keen today, ain't ya?'

Harry was six foot five, with wide shoulders, so he had to slip in through the doorway sideways.

Despite his bulky size, Harry's head still looked too large for his body and sported a meaty, shovel-flat face. If they ever made another *Flintstones* movie, Sam was sure Harry could land a good part.

Sam smiled nervously as his hand slipped behind his back to make sure the gun was secure in his belt and hidden from sight by his grey vest.

'I forgot something in my locker last night,' Sam said, thinking quickly. 'Didn't want it stinking up the place.'

Harry laughed, exposing a set of crooked, yellow teeth.

'Fuck, yeah, I hear ya,' he said. 'Remember when that English dude – was it Winston or Cecil? Something sissy like that, anyway – when he left some of his weird cheese here? Chrrrist, did that stink.'

'He never lived it down,' Sam added. 'You called him Cheese Head until the day he packed it in.'

Harry roared and slapped the wall so hard, Sam could hear plaster breaking.

'I called him Stinky Fuckin' Cheese Head till the day he quit. Served him right, too. Some days I think I can still smell it.' Harry lifted his nose towards the ceiling and sniffed loudly.

'Nah, that's your giant feet you smell, Harry.'

Harry laughed again and swung one of his size 18 Wingtip Oxfords in a mock kick.

'So what did you forget?' he asked.

'Err, tuna sandwich,' Sam said. 'Just starting to go ripe, too.'

Harry wrinkled his nose.

'Well, get it the fuck out of here, then. I think I'm beginning to smell it.' He grinned. 'Fish Head.'

Sam groaned, but took the excuse to leave the tiny room and Harry's curiosity behind.

Back in the corridor, Sam readjusted the gun and moved quickly through the staff doors to rejoin the noisy stream of busy shoppers.

As soon as Sam exited the mall, Zack pulled the Mercedes to the kerb and picked him up.

'Any problem?' Zack asked.

'Nothing I couldn't handle.'

The two men travelled in silence as Zack negotiated the traffic to take them downtown. Sam watched, his curiosity engaged, as Zack expertly switched out of congested lanes to swing down side roads and merge back with traffic in places where the lights weren't so stubborn.

'You know the roads well,' Sam said. 'I thought you lived in San Diego.'

'I've spent the last twenty years down south, but I grew up here. I used to cruise these streets at all hours in my teens. My first car was a beauty, too. '73 Mustang rag-top in mustard yellow with black trim, loaded with a gas-guzzlin' V8 pushing 266 horses.'

'Get out.'

'My father gave it to me when I passed my driver's test, but I think he was disappointed.'

'Disappointed?'

'He really liked the idea of a chick magnet in his driveway. But when I came home with my gang of Science Club nerds rather than the cheerleading squad, I had the feeling he felt he had wasted his money.'

'He wanted to recapture his youth through you,' Sam suggested.

'He was as big a nerd as I was and always had been. I think he wanted me to be different.' Zack paused. 'To be the cool kid he never got a chance to be.'

'Wasn't in the genes,' Sam added.

'You got that right.'

32

One block from the liquor store, Zack pulled in to the kerb. 'You want to walk or drive from here?'

'Think he knows about you?' Sam asked. 'That you're helping me?'

'I couldn't say. He knows more than he should, but I've never caught anyone tailing us.'

Sam looked around reflexively, scanning the light traffic. He licked his lips. 'If he wants to make sure I don't pay, he would need to be watching from inside the store, right?'

'Makes sense.'

'At the mall,' Sam continued, 'we can watch each store from the security booth on close-circuit cameras. If this liquor store has them, and he's somehow tapped in from the outside, then he could watch everything without exposing himself.'

'Shit!' Zack rubbed his face with his hands. 'If that's the case, he won't be lurking around for me to spot.'

Sam sighed. 'May as well drop me at the front door, then. Until we know more, this fucker holds all the cards.'

Sam approached the reinforced steel door of the liquor store with his stomach in knots. It was like stepping on stage, a feeling that you were going to forget all your lines and vomit on your shoes.

As he walked, he went over the preparations he had made in the car. He'd used a small key to unlock the Smith & Wesson's internal safety mechanism and loaded it with five, 200-grain, copper-jacketed .45 Colts. He left the sixth-chamber empty, as he had been trained to do, to prevent an accidental discharge.

After just a few steps, he had to discreetly move the revolver to the pocket of his vest as its steel had grown inexplicably hot against his skin. The loaded weight of it, instead of bringing comfort, made him feel noticeably lopsided.

A single window broke the store's solid brick façade, but even that source of light was heavily barred in black steel. The store looked so un-inviting, Sam wondered if the owner wasn't selling drugs and under-the-counter Thai porn rather than booze.

When he entered through the heavy door, a buzzer sounded, its tone a startlingly rude burp.

Sam scanned the interior, noticing several cameras in the corners of the ceiling. The store was packed with solid wooden shelves crammed with spirits. Large, glass-fronted coolers along the rear walls also carried a generous selection of beer, wine and sugary alco-pops.

'Can I help you?' asked a gruff voice.

Sam turned to see a balding man with tumbleweed salt-and-ginger eyebrows and a colour-coordinated, walrus-style moustache. Standing at barely five foot four, and just about as wide, the man looked like a solid square of muscle and fat.

'Just orienting myself,' Sam said. 'Need to pick up a couple forties.'

'Fishing trip?' the walrus asked with a slight grin.

'Block party,' Sam replied.

The irony of his improvised answer struck him. Sam barely knew his neighbours because he worked nights and slept days, but also because he selfishly hadn't wanted people to know him as just a security guard. When he was an actor, even a struggling one, people looked at him differently than they did when he said he worked nights in a deserted mall, drinking coffee and dreaming of things he couldn't afford.

'The larger bottles are on the bottom rows,' the walrus explained. 'Help yourself.'

Sam nodded his thanks and walked up the aisles, picking a large bottle of vodka and one of rum. He reminded himself that whatever happened, he was doing this for his family. His palms were sweating when he returned to the front of the store and laid them on the counter beside the cash register.

As the owner rang them in, Sam cleared his throat and tensed his muscles.

'I need to tell you a story,' he said carefully.

The walrus looked at him, one eye cocked warily.

'My family has been kidnapped,' Sam explained. 'In order to free them I need to take these bottles from you without payment.'

The walrus snorted and cocked the other eye. 'That's the stupidest ruse I ever heard.'

Sam nodded. 'I know, but it's the truth.' Sam reached down to the pocket of his vest. 'I need to take these.'

The walrus puckered his lips in an unfriendly grin. 'Tell you what, pal,' he growled, 'fuck you and whatever horse you rode in on. You either pay or get the fuck out. You think because I own a liquor store, I'm made of money. It's a business, like any other, and I can't give booze away to hard-up losers like it's Scrooge's fuckin' Christmas.'

Sam stepped back and pulled his gun in one fluid motion, levelling it at the man's face. The hole of the barrel was positioned directly between his eyes.

'Put the bottles in a bag,' he ordered.

The walrus tensed, the stringy muscles in his neck bulging.

'You think a gun scares me?' His face turned an angry shade of red. 'You don't think I've had more steel pushed in my face than fuckin' *Jaws*?'

Sam grit his teeth. 'Put the bottles in a bag or, I swear, I'll do damage. My wife and child—'

'Don't give me some bullshit story.' The walrus leaned forward, his weight balanced on heavy knuckles. 'You're just another fuckin' booze hound who can't keep a steady job.'

Sam cocked the hammer, the sound louder than he ever remembered from the shooting range.

The walrus didn't even blink; his eyes remained locked on Sam's face.

'You look familiar,' he said.

'What?'

'Yeah, I've seen you somewhere before.'

'Who cares? Just do what I ask.'

The walrus flicked his gaze to a camera above the door. 'You know I have all this on tape.'

Sam stepped forward and waved the gun in the owner's face.

'Pack the bottles now!'

'Sure, sure,' the walrus said, his voice sliding into an unnatural calm. As he talked, he dropped both hands below the counter and returned with a white, plastic bag clutched in his left.

Sam began to relax until he saw the walrus's right hand twitch below the counter and the butt of a pistol-grip shotgun appeared. With a snarl, Sam lunged forward and whipped the barrel of his gun across the man's face. The barrel caught the man's bulbous nose, splitting it open in a gush of blood.

The walrus reeled backwards and struck the opposite counter, but it didn't slow him down. He continued to lift the shotgun. Panicking, Sam swung his revolver back, cracking the butt hard against the man's temple. The walrus staggered again, his knees seeming to buckle as his left eye filled with blood. But then he straightened and brought the shotgun level with the counter.

With a primal scream, Sam swept up the large bottle of rum and brought it crashing on to the side of the man's head. The bottle shattered and the sickening crack of bone was like a thunderclap in the middle of a rainstorm of glass.

The walrus's eyes rolled white and he sank back to his knees. Not wanting him to rise again, Sam grabbed the other bottle, but the walrus had endured enough. The shotgun fell from his grasp and he collapsed to the floor in a heap. A thick river of blood flowed from his wounded scalp.

Gasping for breath, Sam grabbed a second bottle of booze and rushed out of the store.

Zack had only driven two blocks before Sam told him to pull over.

At the kerb, Sam opened the door, leaned out and vomited into the gutter.

'You OK?' Zack asked.

Sam shook his head. 'You should have seen him. Christ, he could be dead.'

'You did what you had to.'

'Did I?' Sam asked. 'How do I even know my

family is alive? I could be doing this for no reason at all.'

'Maybe he'll give you some proof, now that you've completed the assignment.'

Sam wiped drool from his lips on to the back of his hand. 'Did you ever get any?'

Zack flinched. 'Not till it was too late.'

Sam swallowed hard. 'That's what I'm afraid of.'

33

MaryAnn lifted her head and listened. Through the thick walls separating their cells, she could hear the third prisoner sobbing. It felt like she was miles away.

'It sounds like a ghost, doesn't it?' said MaryAnn's cellmate. 'Like it's not really human.'

'But it's not a ghost,' MaryAnn said sharply. 'I was right by her cell. She's another prisoner. I think it's my mom, but she hardly ever cries. Not like this, anyhow.'

'That woman is in pain, all right.'

'If it's my mom, maybe she thinks I'm dead.'

'No deeper hurt than the loss of a child,' the woman agreed, the smoke in her voice turning heavier, as if each new word weighed more than the last.

MaryAnn stood up on the cot, cupped her hands over her mouth to form a megaphone and pressed against the dirt wall.

'Mom!' she yelled loudly. 'Mom! It's me, MaryAnn. Can you hear me?'

MaryAnn paused and listened. The woman's sobs sounded louder now and, if possible, even more distraught.

'I don't think she can hear me,' MaryAnn said quietly.

'These walls are thick, too thick for words to pass through maybe. Could be all she hears is her own despair.'

MaryAnn spun. 'My mom's not like that,' she snapped. 'She would do anything for me.'

'I'm not saying she wouldn't, baby,' the woman said. 'It's just what I was saying before about her sounding like a ghost. If she believes you're dead, she might not trust that the sound of your voice is real.'

'Oh?' MaryAnn dropped back on to the cot. After a moment of silence, she asked, 'Do you think they'll feed us? I'm getting real thirsty again.'

The woman reached out and stroked the girl's hair.

'The big one usually brings food and water once a day, but I've been losing track of time in the dark. Not sure when he came last.'

MaryAnn sniffled and leaned back until her weight pressed against the woman's legs.

'Are we going to die down here?'

The woman sat up, opened her arms and pulled the child against her chest.

'I'm not going to lie to you, baby. There is a chance we'll die here, but I don't plan to go without one hell of a fight. You gonna stand with me?'

MaryAnn burrowed deeper into the woman's embrace. She nodded.

34

'He recognized you?' Zack asked, breaking a heavy silence.

'He said he did, but that could be from anywhere.'

'Oh?'

'I've been on TV some,' Sam explained. 'A few commercials here locally; a couple crime drama walk-ons; played a corpse twice on *C.S.I.* My biggest break was a spot on *Magnum P.I.* back in 'eighty-six.'

'No shit?'

'They flew me to Hawaii for two episodes. Speaking part, name in the credits, the whole deal.'

'Who did you play?'

Sam relaxed a little as he remembered happier days. 'I was Magnum's punk nephew who just happens to drop by without mentioning a nasty cocaine habit and some debt problems with one of the local drug lords.'

'Sounds good,' Zack said.

'Yeah,' Sam sighed. 'Thought it was my ticket to a regular gig, but . . .' He let the thought trail off into the past where it belonged.

'It's crazy where we end up sometimes,' Zack said to fill the silence. 'Just no planning for it.'

35

Detective Preston was irritated with his partner.

'Why are we here? It's past eight and I'm supposed to be home watching *Jeopardy* with the wife. She promised to make popcorn with melted butter and just a sprinkle of cracked sea salt.'

He kissed the tips of his fingers.

'And what have you got on offer?' He raised his hands to encompass the store. 'Shoplifting.'

'I wanted to get you a gift,' Hogan said drily. 'But I couldn't remember: do you prefer your vodka with or without bloodstains?'

'Hell.' Preston grinned, tucking both thumbs into his belt loops and sticking out his belly in mock salute to his good-ol'-boy heritage. 'Booze is booze. I'll take it in any shade you like.'

Still grinning, Preston turned to look at the floor behind the cash register. The spilled rum had diluted the victim's blood and formed a crimson pool. It was dotted with lethal shards of glass that reflected the store's fluorescent lights.

Preston turned serious. 'You expecting him to die?'

Hogan shook his head. 'This guy's got a skull like a bull moose. They took him to Martha's for an X-ray, but he was already bitching about lost trade in the ambulance.'

'So I ask again. Why are we here?'

Hogan grinned. 'Follow me.'

Hogan led his partner into a back room piled with crates of wines and spirits. The room led off into a small office stuffed with overflowing boxes of paper receipts, a toilet that could inspire a *Trainspotting* sequel, and an even smaller closet that housed three VCRs and three thirteen-inch, black and white monitors.

With his partner leaning over his shoulder, Hogan hit the Play buttons on all three VCRs. As the robbery and assault progressed from different angles, Hogan hit the Pause and Zoom button on the middle machine. Sam's face filled the screen. His eyes, narrowed in anger, stared directly into the camera.

'Well, dip me in clover and invite the cattle over for tea,' Preston muttered. 'What the heck is he doing robbing a liquor store? Didn't I tell you there was something flaky about him?'

'It gets flakier. According to the vic, White claimed his family had been kidnapped and he had to steal the booze to get them back.'

'Bleepin' actors,' Preston grumbled. 'They all go off the deep end sometime.'

138

'Maybe so,' Hogan agreed. 'But that could offer an explanation for his erratic behaviour.'

'It's bull,' Preston said gruffly. 'Kidnappers don't blow the crap out of your house, and they sure as shit don't leave extra bodies behind when they leave.'

'So what's your theory?' Hogan asked.

'He's a whack job. Plain and simple. He decided to kill his wife and take off with his daughter back to L.A. To cover his tracks, he switched his daughter for some other kid before blowing up the house.'

'So we should be looking into missing black kids?'

'Or disturbed graves,' Preston said. 'No reason to use a live one when you're planning to burn 'em.'

'Christ! You've got some warped imagination.'

Preston shrugged. 'Show me a cop who doesn't and I'll show you his lobotomy scars.'

36

In the motel room, Sam sat on the bed and stared at the two liquor bottles perched on the table. Twin sentinels of oblivion and they sang out his name.

A similar song called from his vest pocket where a tiny Ziploc bag still contained a half-dozen blue pills. He knew the combination could send him to a place where problems didn't exist, but, for the sake of his family, he fought the urge.

Alone with his thoughts, Zack having walked to a deli around the corner, Sam wondered just what he had started and if he would ever be able to justify his actions to his family and to himself when it was over.

Zack stood outside the deli with the cellphone pressed to his ear.

'The guy in the liquor store recognized him. Why?'

'I don't know,' said the altered voice. 'Maybe he saw his commercial on TV.'

'Bullshit. I want to know what game—'

'Careful, Dr Parker. You don't want me angry. Jasmine wouldn't like it. Now, the important question is, does Sam remember *you*?'

'No. And there's no reason he should. We never spoke back then.'

'Keep it that way.'

The cellphone rang and Sam snatched it up.

'A job well done, Mr White,' said the digitally altered voice. 'A touch messier than I expected from an upstanding citizen, but you've always had that dark side, haven't you? It shows your potential.'

'Potential for what?' Sam asked carefully.

'Have you thought about the money?'

'Can I talk to my family?' Sam interjected. 'How do I know they're alive?'

'If they were dead, you would know,' said the voice. 'I don't want to disturb them, but if you choose, I could make them scream.'

'No!' Sam blurted. 'No, just let them be. Please.'

'As you wish.' A pause. 'Now, as I asked before, have you thought about the money?'

'Yes. I mean, I'll get it, I just don't—'

'I know you can work it out, Sam. You'll hear from me soon.'

The caller hung up.

To deliver a million, Sam still needed to come up with two hundred and fifty thousand dollars. The thought of it made him want to weep.

He had left a message for Hannah's parents, but they were travelling without cellphones. If they mortgaged the house, they could maybe raise that much. But how long would that process take? His own parents were useless. They had sold their house and bought that stupid RV. As for friends, that was something he had failed to nurture. The last true friends he could remember had vanished from his life a long time ago.

When he'd suffered moments of despair in the past, usually over something that now seemed meaningless like blowing an audition or being insulted by a director half his age, Hannah was always there to offer comfort. He had depended on her.

Christ, he missed her.

The door opened before Sam could sink any further, and Zack entered the room bearing hot Vietnamese subs and chilled cans of Diet Dr Pepper. Sam accepted the food with a nod of thanks and sat on the edge of the bed to eat. His mouth worked on autopilot, but he didn't notice the taste.

'He called again,' Sam said after a few bites.

Zack stopped chewing. 'What did he want?'

'Asked about the money.'

Zack nodded slowly. 'I've been thinking on

that, too,' he said. 'I need to make a few calls first. See if I can locate someone.'

Sam's eyes widened. 'I appreciate that because I'm drawing a blank.'

'Don't get excited yet,' Zack cautioned. 'It's just an idea.' He went quiet. 'Did he mention your family?'

Sam's face grew hard. 'Yeah.' He exhaled through his nose. 'Said if I really wanted proof, he could make them scream.'

37

'You're going the wrong way,' protested Detective Preston. 'I live in the other direction.'

'I just want to check something,' Hogan said.

'And you can't check it after you drop me at home?'

'Relax. *Jeopardy* is over. You're not missing anything.'

'The wife tapes it.'

'You're kidding.'

'What?' Preston protested. 'We like to watch it together. See who can answer the most questions.'

'How do you know she doesn't cheat?'

'Cheat?' Preston furrowed his brow. 'What do you mean?'

Hogan grinned. 'How do you know she doesn't watch the show while she tapes it? Then when you get home, she already knows the answers.'

Preston thought about that for a moment. 'No, she wouldn't do that.'

Hogan laughed. 'You're the one who's always

telling me how deceptive women can be.'

'True, but . . . nah! You really think she'd do that?'

'Why not?'

'So the nights when I win,' Preston pondered.

'She's just letting you . . .'

'So I don't get suspicious,' Preston finished.

'Exactly. If she won every game, you'd be bound to twig.'

'The sneaky . . .' Preston shook his head and left the sentence adrift.

Hogan turned the car on to Sam's street and parked in front of the crater where the two bodies were recovered. He switched off the engine and climbed out. With an irritated sigh, Preston joined him.

Hogan walked to the edge of the crater and looked around. Broken pipes, electrical wires, chunks of concrete, burned timbers, twisted metal, bricks and the occasional bright sparkle of something that could have been a destroyed toaster, stereo or a hundred other everyday items.

He turned his back to the pit and surveyed the street.

'What?' Preston asked.

'I'm not sure, but White deliberately looked into that camera back at the liquor store. It was like he knew someone would be watching. He needed to show what he had done.'

'That could have been for us,' Preston argued. 'A little eff-you from a killer on the run.'

Hogan's eyes locked on the garage of the house across the street. He walked towards it, the quiet residential road empty of traffic.

Preston joined him on the other side to stand on the sidewalk in front of a two-storey white house with brown trim.

He followed his partner's gaze to see a three-headed security light attached to the peak of the double garage.

Hogan walked to the driveway, his movement activating the lights. Aimed unusually high, the lights shone across the road to flood the edge of the pit. But what intrigued Hogan the most was that only two of the lights appeared to be working.

'You notice something odd about that middle light?' Hogan asked.

'Apart from it being burned out?'

'Apart from that, yeah.'

Preston walked closer and looked up.

'It doesn't match the other two,' he said. 'In fact, I don't think it's a light. It looks like a lens. Security camera maybe?'

Hogan walked up the garden path to the front door of the house and rapped on it with his knuckles. A cutesy hand-carved nameplate on the door read: *Shepherd's Flock*.

The door was answered by a redheaded man in his early fifties. He was still dressed for the office in striped shirt and tie.

Hogan showed his badge and the man's face instantly took on a resigned look.

'Is it the boy?' he asked with a slight Scottish lilt. 'What's he done now?'

'We're here about the house across the street,' Hogan said.

The man winced and his voice took on a concerned tone. 'What a shame, eh? That poor family.'

'Were you home when the house exploded?' Preston asked.

'Aye, I was still sleeping. Scared the crap out of me, I don't mind sayin'.'

'We were wondering if you still have the security footage?' Hogan asked.

The man wrinkled his brow. 'I don't get you.'

'Security footage from your camera?' Hogan jabbed his thumb in the direction of the garage. 'It's aimed across the street.'

'I don't have a camera,' he said. 'Just the automatic lights there.'

'Could you come and have a look?' Hogan asked.

'Aye, sure.'

The three men walked to the driveway and looked up at the lights. The owner scratched his head.

'That's odd. I don't know what that middle one is. Can't say I've ever clapped eyes on it before.'

Hogan frowned. 'Do you mind if we take it with us?'

'Not at all. Let me get a ladder and a spanner.'

The man disappeared into the house.

Preston looked at Hogan, his eyes pained.

'What?' Hogan asked.

'Clapped eyes? Spanner? You have any idea what the frig he's talking about?'

Hogan grinned. 'I get the gist.'

38

After finishing his sandwich, Sam curled the waxed paper into a ball and tossed it towards a small wicker basket in the corner. It fell short and skidded across the carpet to rest under the table.

He picked up the phone. 'I'd better call work. They'll be expecting me to show at ten.'

It had just turned nine thirty.

After explaining to his boss that his house had been destroyed in a fire and his family was missing, Sam listened for a minute and hung up.

'He said I can take a couple days, but I shouldn't make a habit of it.'

'Prick,' Zack muttered.

'Aren't they all?'

'I try not to be,' Zack said.

'You're a manager? Of what?'

'I'm a plastic surgeon, actually. I run . . .' He paused. 'I ran my own private practice in San Diego.'

'Boob jobs and Botox?'

Zack shrugged. 'Yeah, mostly cosmetic, but I also spent two days a week in the children's hospital. They were some of the most heart-breaking and rewarding cases.' He paused again. 'I'll miss that.'

'Can't you go back?' Sam asked. 'Once this is all over, I mean.'

Zack shook his head. 'My second assignment took care of that.'

'What did you do?' Sam's voice was filled with both sympathy and dread.

Zack wiped his hands on a paper napkin and dabbed a dribble of sauce from the corner of his mouth.

'It was a day or so after running the red lights,' Zack began. 'I had been neglecting my practice as I was selling everything I owned to raise the money, when he called and said I had a special client that I couldn't disappoint . . .'

Zack hesitated briefly, his face showing the memory was still painfully fresh.

'She was a regular patient, someone I had per-formed several procedures on over the years. Gravitational tune-ups, we called them. She had been in the soaps in New York for a while. A beautiful woman with amazing bone structure. . . Of course, she was vain about her looks, but underneath the paint and varnish, there was a sweetness and vulnerability to her that I liked.'

'Liked?' Sam asked, thinking the worse.

Zack flinched.

'Like,' he corrected. 'She's alive. He didn't make me kill her.'

'What did he make you do?'

Zack took a deep breath. 'I was to disfigure and then rape her.'

'Oh, Christ!'

'My wife and daughter are kidnapped,' Zack continued, his voice pained. 'I haven't slept in days, and then I'm to go against everything that makes up the core of who I am.' He looked at Sam with pleading eyes. 'Since Kalli was born, I've thought sometimes about how much I'd sacrifice for my family. I imagined how I would throw myself in front of a charging elephant, or give up my spot in a lifeboat to make sure they survived a sinking ship. But this man doesn't want sacrifice. He doesn't want us to be heroes or martyrs or anything remotely noble. He wants to eat away our souls – to make us monsters.'

Sam found it difficult to speak. 'What did you do?'

Zack glared at him. 'What do you think?'

Sam looked away, knowing he couldn't judge, and fearing what lay ahead on his own path.

Zack reached out and grabbed Sam's arm. He pulled him in close until their faces almost touched. His voice was barely audible; his breath spicy sweet.

'I faked it,' he whispered.

Sam's eyes grew wide. 'How?'

'Cosmetic surgery is all about precision. Tiny,

151

microscopic stitches performed in a delicate manner. With good tissue and muscle, we can perform miracles. In skilled hands, we can also do the reverse.'

'I don't understand.'

'Small cuts under the skin, muscle separated from subcutaneous fat and folds of flesh, the results are instantaneous and rather hideous. Like an old man whose face collapses when he takes out his false teeth. The bruising alone makes it look like a Mac truck has hit you. But if no permanent damage is done, if the underlying structure remains intact, it can also be repaired. We're a small community. When she was rushed to the hospital, the surgeon would have recognized my work and known what to do.'

'And the rape?'

Zack looked off into the distance. 'There were no cameras in my operating room. I was certain of that. All I needed was to set the scene and everyone would jump to the easiest and most sordid conclusion. After all, I'd just mutilated the poor woman. Why would anyone doubt that I'd raped her as well?' Zack's eyes were pained. 'No one even questioned my guilt.'

'You cheated,' Sam said admiringly.

'But at what cost?' Zack asked.

'You think he found out?'

Zack shook the question off. 'I've thought about that, but why would he care? That woman's life didn't mean a goddamn thing to him. He wanted to ruin *my* reputation, *my* career. He wanted to turn me into a man on the run. She was just a means to break me.'

'But he didn't,' Sam said. 'You're still fighting.'

Zack wiped at his eyes as tears leaked from the corners. 'If you don't think I'm broken, Sam, you're not looking hard enough.'

39

Perched on an aluminium ladder, Hogan discovered he didn't need tools to remove the tiny camera. Unlike the lights, which were hardwired into the house's electrical system, the camera had no wires. Instead, it was powered by an internal battery and was attached to the circular metal plate anchoring the twin security lights by a small, yet powerful magnet.

Hogan pulled the camera from its perch and turned it over gently in his hands. Barely the size of his fist, it was a sealed, nondescript white plastic box with a small lens on the front and a short metal antenna protruding from its side. The tiny writing around the edge of the lens showed it boasted a powerful zoom lens and sophisticated wireless technology.

'Does it have tape?' Preston called up.

'I've never seen this make before, but I'm pretty sure it's a remote feed. If I'm right, the camera is controlled by a computer that can send and retrieve data via a wireless network.'

'The operator must live close by,' Preston said.

'Not necessarily. With the right relay stations, the operator could be virtually anywhere in the city. Or, more likely, he controls it from a laptop in a car parked near by. It probably has a sleep mode to conserve power when it's not being used.'

'So there's no way to know what it saw?'

Hogan climbed down the ladder. 'I doubt it. I can't see a slot for a back-up drive or Flash card, but we'll get the techies to dust it for prints and take a look inside.' He dropped the camera into a clear plastic evidence bag that he pulled from his jacket pocket. 'If they come up with a serial number, maybe we can track down who bought it.'

'Oh, boy,' Preston said with mock glee. 'But do you think we could do that tomorrow? I'm starting to get real tired of your face.'

Hogan laughed aloud. 'You're just dying to get home to see if your wife is cheating on *Jeopardy*.'

Preston frowned. 'Yeah, you may have ruined that one simple pleasure in my life, too. Jerk.'

40

MaryAnn heard the creak of rusted hinges as the door to the cell began to swing open.

She sat up in panic, her whole body tensing.

'Easy, child.' The woman placed a hand on the girl's shoulder.

MaryAnn stared at the door, the widening rectangle of light blinding her after so many hours in pitch-blackness.

'I have to know.' She whispered so quietly that her lips barely moved.

Once the rectangle was completely bathed in light, the giant moved to blot out all but the edges. The halo effect made him look two-dimensional, like a cardboard cut-out.

'Don't move.' His voice was slow and steady. 'I brought water and food.'

'Thank you,' said the woman.

MaryAnn glanced at her and frowned. She didn't like the woman's tone – it was too grateful.

'MaryAnn and I appreciate it,' she continued. 'Don't we, MaryAnn?'

MaryAnn continued to frown.

'Don't talk.' The man entered the cell. In his hands was a small tray containing two bottles of water and two plastic-wrapped sandwiches.

'I'm sorry, David.' The woman kept her voice subservient. 'We just get lonely. It's nice to—'

'My name isn't David.'

'Oh, sorry, I thought it was. I'm—'

'I don't want to know!'

The man halted in the middle of the cell with his back bent, the plastic tray halfway to the floor. He tilted his head to look at the woman, his face plainly showing the laboured computations of his brain.

That's when MaryAnn bolted.

'No, MaryAnn!' the woman screamed.

The man roared with anger, dropping the tray on the floor as he spun in pursuit.

He had only gone two steps when the woman landed on his back, her sharp nails clawing at his eyes and sharper teeth sinking into his neck.

MaryAnn ran down the corridor, her eyes watering from the brightness of the lights, every shape a blur. This time, however, she wasn't running to escape. She had a new purpose.

Skidding to a halt outside the cell where she had

stood before, MaryAnn pressed her ear to the wood. A tortured sobbing came from within.

MaryAnn pounded on the door with her fists.

'Mom!' she cried. 'Mom, I'm alive. I'm OK. Stop crying, please. I'll get you out. Dad will be looking for us. You know he will.'

A sharp scream of pain from within the cell stopped MaryAnn cold.

'M–mom?' she called.

MaryAnn grabbed the handle to the cell door and was surprised to find it wasn't locked. She pushed against it and felt the door begin to open, its ancient hinges groaning.

When the door was open partway, light from the hallway revealed the outline of someone lying on a cot in the corner. A blanket covered everything except for an arm that had slipped out of the cocoon and dangled over the edge. The arm was obviously a woman's, thin and pale, almost elegant in its limp state. The hand, however, had been digging in the dirt, all five nails broken, the knuckles bloody and bruised.

MaryAnn stifled a sob.

'M–mom, is . . . is that you? Are you OK?'

The arm twitched.

'She's just fine,' said a cold voice from the darkness behind the door.

MaryAnn spun just as a closed fist smashed into the side of her face. The force of the blow knocked her off her feet and sent her crashing into the solid doorframe. Her head cracked against stone and she collapsed to the ground in an unconscious heap.

The woman screamed as she was thrown off the monster's back.

She landed hard, but ignored the pain to roll into a wrestler's crouch. She bared her teeth, preparing to do whatever it took to protect the child.

The giant clutched at his bloody neck where his bandage had been ripped off and howled in rage.

'You bitch!'

'Leave the child be,' she hissed.

'Fuck you!'

The woman sprang forward, but the giant wasn't an amateur. Moving faster than his bulk would have suggested possible, the man used her own momentum to spin her and wrap one of his large arms around her throat. His other arm quickly snapped up to lock the flesh and bone vice, and then he began to squeeze.

The woman's eyes bulged as the increasing pressure began to close her windpipe. She kicked at him, but the giant just laughed and leaned backwards, lifting her feet off the ground.

'Don't kill her,' said a voice from the doorway. 'She could still be useful.'

The pressure on her throat didn't ease and the woman felt on the brink of losing consciousness. Bright sparks exploded behind her eyes.

'I said let her go, Richard. You've already fucked up once.'

Before the darkness claimed her, she saw the limp body of MaryAnn dropped onto the cot. Her face was misshapen and coated in blood.

41

The cellphone rang and Sam felt his heart stutter like an engine choking on thin gasoline.

He answered it.

'Mr White,' said the altered voice, 'I would like you to make a delivery.'

'OK.' Sam felt his stomach churn.

'You are to take the liquor bottles to the exact centre of the city. You will receive further instructions upon arrival. You have one hour.'

'Where is—'

The line went dead.

'Shit!'

Zack looked at him expectantly, his face reflecting the same pallid fear and churning anger as Sam's.

'Where's the exact centre of town?' Sam asked.

'Burnside Bridge,' Zack replied without hesitation. 'It divides the city north and south; the Willamette River divides east and west.'

'So the middle of the bridge . . .'

'Is the exact centre of town,' Zack finished.

'That rings a bell,' Sam said. 'Probably something I was taught in school if I had been paying attention. Anything special about the bridge?'

Zack thought for a second and shrugged. 'It's a drawspan. It can be raised for river traffic.'

'I'll need to do this alone,' Sam said.

Zack nodded in agreement. 'That's probably why he chose that spot. He can watch from either end of the bridge to make sure you don't have company.'

'And if I try anything,' Sam added bitterly, 'he'll open the bridge and dump me in the damn river.'

Zack held out the car keys, but Sam shook him off.

'We should pick up my Jeep. If he doesn't know you're helping me, that's what he'll expect to see.'

'What if the police are looking for you?' Zack asked. 'If the liquor guy did recognize you, your Jeep could be on a watch list.'

'Shit! OK, let's find out.'

Zack drove into the quiet residential neighbourhood and parked behind a Suburban 4x4 that was the size of a small bus.

Sam's house, or the crater that had been his house, was a full block further down.

'You see anything?' Zack asked.

Sam shook his head. 'I can't see them paying for a stake-out over a couple bottles of booze. If

162

anything, they'll have a patrol car driving by a few times a night.'

'Still?'

'I'll dump it tonight,' Sam said. 'Just one last trip.' The last thing in this world he owned and now even it had to be thrown aside.

Sam left the Mercedes with the stolen liquor bottles under his arm and cautiously moved down the block. His senses were keen for any movement or idling cars, but the street was quiet and he made it to the Jeep without incident.

He slipped inside and placed the two liquor bottles on the passenger seat. A plastic bag resting on the bare metal floor caught his eye. Curious, he bent down to open it. Inside, was his guard's uniform that he had meant to take to the cleaner's, his red thermos and the DVD of his commercial that Ken had made.

Working at the mall and being shot at by sugar-high kids with paint guns seemed a lifetime ago; a lifetime when his biggest problems were a soiled uniform and bruised ego.

With a deep breath, Sam sat up, slid the key into the ignition and pressed down on the clutch to move the gearbox into neutral. The engine roared to life and quickly settled into a steady purr.

Zack pulled up beside him and looked across the Jeep's open doorwell.

'I'll work on that idea for the money while you're gone,' he said. 'There's an old acquaintance I need to contact.'

Sam nodded his thanks and, with steely determination, headed for the bridge.

After Sam was gone, Zack opened his cellphone and reported in. The fate of his wife made the betrayal a necessity, but Zack was finding it more difficult than he ever imagined.

Sam wasn't the same person he remembered hating so many years ago.

42

Burnside Bridge is an impressive structure. From the river path, the operator cabins on either side of the rising leaves look like fairytale turrets. From the road, however, it's just another narrow stretch of blacktop that joins two halves of a city.

As he approached the centre seam, directly between the two turrets, Sam flicked on his hazard lights and pulled off to the side. The small Jeep blocked the bike path and a thin sliver of one lane.

Traffic was light, but several impatient drivers still honked their horns in protest as they swerved past.

With the cellphone resting on the dash, Sam dug out his Zippo and tin case of small cigars. He chose a cigar, moistened the outer leaf, took a moment to toast the tip, and then rotated it just outside the lighter's flame until the tobacco glowed evenly. He found the ritual, although unnecessary, calming.

As he exhaled the pungent smoke, Sam watched the bridge operator become agitated inside his glassed-in cabin. He made angry gestures at the Jeep from his chair, shaking a finger and three knuckles, thumb cocked like the hammer on a gun. When Sam continued to ignore him, he reached for his phone.

At the same instant, the cellphone rang.

'Where next?' Sam asked.

'Anxious, are we?' said the voice.

'Just to see my family,' Sam answered coldly.

'Soon,' said the voice. 'At the east end of the bridge, there's a village underneath. There you will meet Davey O. At the south end of the river path, there is a warehouse. The fence has many gaps. When I see you both in the yard, I'll call back.'

'What does—'

The caller was gone.

Sam tossed the half-finished cigar aside and eased the Jeep into gear. The bridge operator raised his arms in an unmistakable *What the Fuck?* gesture. Sam ignored him.

At the east end of the bridge, Sam pulled off the main drag and took the back streets to a gravel lot guarded by a broken chain-link fence.

Unlike the west side of the river, which attracted tourists and residents to Old Town, Chinatown and Waterfront Park, the east side was still waiting for its regeneration. Until that happened, speculators had left parcels of prime land to lie fallow, biding their time for the right moment to reap the profits.

Sam parked the Jeep and walked around to the back. He opened the tailgate and pulled back a thin square of black rubber to expose a recessed, stainless-steel latch locked with a heavy-duty padlock. He spun the lock to the right combination and opened the latch. He pushed aside the wheel jack and emergency road kit to lift out a small canvas knapsack that contained a black metal flashlight with a weak but usable beam.

After a moment's hesitation, Sam removed the revolver from his vest pocket and placed it inside the hold beside a small black toolbox that held his emergency supply of stage make-up, wig parts and false teeth. Hannah often teased him about it, saying he was worse than a woman with an overstuffed handbag. But twice the kit had allowed him to snag a small speaking part because the actor that the director really wanted couldn't be tracked down in time.

After locking the hold and replacing the mat, Sam wrapped one of the liquor bottles in an oil-stained rag to stop it clanking against the other, and stuffed them both in the knapsack. Then, with flashlight in hand and knapsack over his shoulder, he made his way to the river.

43

After crossing the freeway, Sam descended a long flight of stairs. The wooden treads were slick with evening fog and the metal handrails were corroded by use and decades of bird crap.

At the bottom, Sam peered into the misty darkness beneath the bridge. Gradually, as his eyes became accustomed, the shambling activity of the homeless congregation took form. These were people who had turned their backs on the city shelters and either didn't want to follow the sober rules of Portland's ever-growing tent city, Dignity Village, or couldn't make the seven-mile trek to get there.

Sam walked closer, his body tense, eyes scanning makeshift tents and cardboard shelters in search of a man he didn't know. He was surprised not only by the number of homeless who huddled beneath and within the ancient bridge, but by their composition: youths, dozens of them, with feral eyes and stern faces; single women and men, their chatter bubbling with anger, laughter and madness; even whole families, the loss upon their faces palpable.

Sam stopped just a few yards beneath the shadow of the bridge as a bearded man, not much taller than an average eight-year-old, approached. In a dusty-brown slicker that stretched behind him like a wedding train, and a pair of oversized cowboy boots, he looked like a misplaced Hobbit who had leapt from the pages of Tolkien into a chapter by Zane Grey.

The man stopped less than a foot away and looked up with such intense concentration, Sam found it difficult not to flinch.

'What d'yer want?' the man demanded in a low growl.

'Er, I'm looking for someone . . . a man.'

'Plenty of those. Name?'

'Davey O.'

The man nodded and turned to scan the darker recesses of the makeshift village.

'Second burning barrel,' he said after a moment. 'White hair, green coat. Watch how you step. Men have died for less than the weight you carry.'

Before Sam could ask for an explanation, the man disappeared into the bridge's deep, dark embrace.

Sam approached the burning barrel. Two men and a pug-nosed woman stood around it, sharing tall tales and a bottle of wine without a label. In the flickering light, the wine was the colour of an unripe lemon: pale yellow with just a tinge of green.

'Davey O?' Sam asked.

A man with white hair, his back stooped beneath a pea-green coat, turned around slowly. His steel-grey eyes locked on to Sam's face with a similar intensity as the guardian, but then they inexplicably softened and his face became more youthful than his worn physicality implied.

'I know you,' Davey said.

'We need to talk,' Sam said uneasily. 'I have something for you, but I can't give it to you here.'

'Sure, sure. Let me grab my bag.'

Sam waited as Davey disappeared inside a makeshift lean-to made from scrap lumber and cardboard, the pieces held together by an intricate web of orange and green fishing net. From within, he produced a bulging, blue denim backpack.

Everything he owned was probably inside that backpack, Sam thought. And for the first time in his life, he actually understood how that felt.

With great effort, Davey swung the heavy pack on to his shoulders and followed Sam downstream, away from the cover of the bridge, away from prying eyes.

'You're Sam.'

'You were expecting me?' Sam asked in surprise.

'No, but I remember you.'

Sam stopped. 'Remember me?'

'Yeah, yeah. All those plays, man. They were really cool.'

Sam started walking again. 'I haven't been in a play since high school.'

'That's a shame,' Davey said. 'You were good. I liked that one where you danced with all the witches and we got to use black lights and fog machines.'

Sam stopped again. 'That was *Dark of the Moon*. I played the Witch Boy.' Sam paused. 'That was Grade Twelve.'

'Yeah, that was cool. I designed the lights for that. Ran the board, too.'

Sam stared at the white-haired man, recognition slowly sinking in. 'David O'Donnell?'

Davey flinched. 'Yeah, that's me, but I don't use the name any more. Just Davey or Davey O, OK?'

'Christ, I didn't recognize you. We used to hang together.'

'Sure, sure.' Davey grinned and pulled at his hair. 'I had a few misadventures. Human body can only take so much, you know?'

Sam looked off the path, spotted the warehouse, and began moving through a patch of long grass towards it. Davey followed, the overgrown weeds brushing at his knees.

'You ever see any of the old gang?' Davey asked.

'Nah. I left town right after graduation. Only came back a few months ago.'

'I heard from someone, can't remember who,

but they said you were on *Magnum P.I.* That hadda be cool.'

Sam smiled. 'Yeah. Just two episodes though.'

'Still . . . fuck, eh?'

Sam reached the chain-link fence separating the warehouse from the riverbank. 'Let's get out of this grass. The bugs will eat us alive.'

Davey pointed downstream. 'There's a break down that way. There's no bugs, though. Too cold for 'em.'

Sam began walking again. Davey kept pace beside him.

'So how did you end up here?' Sam asked.

Davey's voice was pained and hollow. 'Drunk killed a little kid. Driver only nineteen. That was the end of the road, man. Broke something that can't be fixed. Not ever.'

'You were the driver,' Sam said.

Davey dropped his chin to his chest as though hiding, not wanting to put voice to it.

Sam found the break in the fence and climbed through. He crossed a gravel yard and stopped beside four large, industrial garbage containers. There, he swung the knapsack off his back and laid it on the ground. As Davey approached, Sam reached inside the pack and retrieved one of the large bottles.

Davey's eyes lit up as Sam handed it over.

'Rum.' Davey licked his lips as he unscrewed the top. 'Bottle this big could kill a man.'

Davey took a long swallow and handed the

bottle back. Sam joined him, feeling the alcohol burn down his throat.

Davey retrieved the bottle and took another deep swallow. Grinning, he dropped his backpack on the ground and began to rummage inside.

'Gotta show you somethin',' he said excitedly.

After a few moments, Davey stood up with a large, half-inch-thick hardbound book in his hand. The cover featured a silver ink etching of an Indian Warrior and the numbers '1984' embossed in faded gold.

'Recognize it?'

'It's our high school yearbook.'

'Fuckin' right.' Davey's eyes filled with glee as he took another long swallow of rum. 'They changed the mascot the year after cause somebody thought it was racist. I carry it everywhere.'

'Why?'

'*WHY?*' Davey screeched. 'Why?' Davey tipped the bottle again, his mouth filling so fast, alcohol squirted from the corners. 'This was my life, man. Everything good that ever happened to me happened in that school. Everything since has been shit.' He began to yell. 'You understand what I'm saying. Shit! Shit! And more shit!'

Tears erupted from his eyes as he placed his hand on the yearbook as though swearing on the Bible. 'It was like walking among gods, man. And I was there, and I was pure, and I was . . . I was good.'

Davey sunk to the ground and crossed his legs,

bottle beside him, the dog-eared book on his lap.

'Let me show you.' He opened the glossy pages and began to point at the photographs.

Unsure of what else to do, Sam sat on the ground beside the man he had known as a boy and listened to his stories as they shared the bottle.

44

The watcher looked down from his perch on the rooftop to study the scene playing out on the lot below.

The moon was barely a sliver low in the sky and the darkness was so deep the figures were un-recognizable to the naked eye. The voices, however, carried through the night without hindrance, every word as clear as if he was sitting beside them.

Intimate.

Cozy.

The watcher removed a pair of night goggles from a small pack and slipped them over his head. He powered them up with the flip of a switch and immediately the scene below was bathed in a phosphorous green light. He saw the distinct shapes of the two men now, huddled close together, looking at the book.

They had been friends once, but how flimsy the bonds to be so easily broken. Sam White was like that. So focused on himself, he didn't stay in touch with one of the most loyal friends he ever had.

When Davey went through the trial, the attempted suicide and the years in prison, Sam hadn't even known – hadn't cared to know. What did the pain of others really matter to him? People were drawn to the actor like moths to a flame, never understanding the flame didn't care who or what it burned in an effort to stay bright.

Yet, even after being abandoned in his time of greatest need, Davey was laughing with him like nothing had happened.

The watcher shook his head. Davey should have been so angry at the betrayal, the uncaring selfishness, of the man he called a friend. The sight of him should have incited a riot of fists and feet, teeth and nails. Not laughter.

Sam White should be begging for his life as the truth of his own narcissism was pounded home.

The watcher clutched the disposable lighter tight in his hand, his thumb rubbing the side so hard it began to burn his flesh.

He didn't flinch.

Sometimes he wished he was more like Davey and capable of feeling all the vibrant shades of pain. Still, he and Davey were alike in other ways. They both tried to hide the scars that made them the men they were. Survivors.

Switch

Yet to see Davey laughing now sent a bolt of confusion through his brain. Perhaps Davey needed a gentle reminder of what his old pal really was.

45

When the cellphone rang, Sam jumped, his insides fluttering with dread.

'All caught up, Sam?' asked the distorted voice.

'Why are you doing this?'

'Do you want your family back?'

'Yes.'

'That's all you need to concentrate on.'

'I've done what you asked.'

The voice laughed, an electronic cackle and hiss.

'You haven't even begun.'

Sam stared at Davey who was so lost in another era, a time before cellphones even existed, that he didn't seem to notice that Sam had been yanked away to the present.

'What do you need me to do?' Sam asked coldly.

'I want him to burn,' said the voice.

'Christ!'

'You have shared the first bottle, now spill the second. Make him burn.'

'Jesus, I don't—'

'It's either him or your daughter. You choose.'

'You sick fuck.'

'I want to hear,' said the voice. 'Keep this line open. Let me hear him scream.'

Keeping the phone pressed to his ear, Sam searched the surrounding area for any sign of his tormentor. The only clear line of sight would be from the roof of the warehouse, and that would require some form of night-vision. Although Sam couldn't see any movement, or telltale shimmers of reflected glass, he could sense the voice's presence.

Sam crouched to place the phone at his feet and became acutely aware that the garbage containers blocked his view of the roof as he dropped.

With the phone on the ground, Sam tensed his muscles and concentrated on MaryAnn and Hannah. He dug deep within himself, blanking his mind, channelling anger and rage, and clearing all thoughts of Davey as a friend . . . or even a human being.

With a snarl, Sam sprang to his feet and moved quickly in a blind, unforgiving fury. Davey yelped as he was yanked to his feet by the scruff of his coat, his prized yearbook tumbling from his grasp.

'Wha—'

The protest abruptly became a whoosh of

expelled air as Sam's fist slammed into Davey's mid-section.

Sam threw the wounded body to the ground between two of the large metal containers. Davey weighed so little that he skidded on the ground and rolled until he hit the side of a container with a hollow bang. As Davey floundered, Sam grabbed the open bottle of rum and sent it crashing at his feet.

Davey held up his hands against the shards of flying glass, eyes bulging, his mouth opening and closing silently like a dying fish.

In a red frenzy of rage, Sam reached into the dumpsters and began throwing chunks of broken pallets and hunks of flattened cardboard down upon the helpless, quivering man.

Davey began to babble, saliva bubbling on trembling lips.

'IS THIS WHAT YOU WANTED?' Sam grabbed the second bottle from his knapsack and smashed it on top of the piled rubble.

'Please,' Davey croaked, gaining his voice. 'Don't do this, Sam.'

Sam ignored his friend's pleas and reached down to pick up the yearbook.

He held it over the lighter –

'NOooo!'

– until the pages caught fire, and then tossed it on top of the alcohol-soaked pyre.

Davey's ear-shattering screams echoed around the yard as the alcohol burst into white-hot flame with a whoosh that ignited everything. Thick black smoke billowed into the night sky as the dry wood crackled and snapped and cardboard began to dance in the rising currents of furnace-hot air.

Sam turned his back on the raging fire and strangled screams. He snatched the cellphone off the ground. His blackened cheeks were streaked with tears.

'Did you hear all that?' Anger seethed into every word.

'Who's the sick fuck now, Mr White?'

46

The watcher removed his night goggles and observed the flames, listening as Davey's screams died into silence.

The screams never lasted long enough.

Never.

The watcher gently placed his hand over his heart, feeling the tight, hairless skin underneath soft, black cotton. He knew well the dangers of fire in the hands of someone who thought they controlled it. From the age of three, he had tasted its vengeful tongue against his skin. There was no part of him that hadn't been tested.

The devil don't burn, boy.

His father's voice whispered in his ear, the speaker so close he could feel warm spittle upon his neck. He closed his eyes, remembering the lessons that shaped his life.

Why does he live in hell, boy?

'Cause the devil don't burn.'

That's, right. We test ourselves; test our flesh.

Switch

If we burn, we're pure. And if we scream?
'We're pure?'
That's right. You've got to scream to the Lord, boy. Scream to your Maker. Scream for Him to take away your sin and scorch the demon's caress from your flesh.
'I don't feel the pain, Pa. I try to. I really do.'
Satan's trying to trick you, boy. The pain is in there. Maybe buried deep, but fire brings it out.

The watcher concentrated, wishing the long-dead ghost away.

When he opened his eyes again, he was alone on the roof, the fire still burning below. As he watched, Sam began to walk away, then stopped. His whole body shook and he sank to the ground.

The sound of torment carried on the breeze. The watcher smiled.

'A lesson learned,' he said. 'A lesson to open your eyes, to see who you really are.'

The watcher packed away his night goggles and stood. Dressed completely in black, he remained invisible to prying eyes.

He hummed softly to himself as he walked away, words joining the tune of their own volition, but the voice that escaped his lips was not his own.

'The devil don't burn, boy. The devil don't burn.'

47

Sam sat on the cold, lumpy ground with his back to the smoldering embers of the fire. His entire body shuddered as the rush of adrenalin slowly retreated from his veins.

Thirty minutes earlier, he thought he'd heard the sound of a vehicle crunching over gravel as it retreated from the other side of the warehouse, but he couldn't be sure.

A low groan drifted from the darkest corner where the two oversized garbage containers met. Sam hugged himself to control the shaking.

The groan grew louder, and then erupted in a series of hacking, wheezing coughs before abruptly stopping. The night was perfectly silent for the briefest of moments.

'Why did you do that, Sam?' asked a small, trembling voice.

'Somebody wanted you dead?' Sam kept his voice barely above a whisper. 'And they wanted me to do it.'

'Why?'

'I don't know yet.'

'You burned my book.'

'It was either that or you.'

'You did burn me. My legs are blistered. My shoes are melted.'

'I needed you to scream.'

Davey snorted. 'Mission accomplished . . . fuck, it hurts. My skin is raw.'

'Don't move.' Sam's voice was tight.

'Why?' Davey snapped. 'You not done yet?'

'He might still be watching.'

'Who?'

'I don't know.'

'You're fuckin' useless.'

'I saved your life.'

'You set me on fire,' Davey squawked.

'Stay where you are until morning, then get it treated. I assume there are places you can go that don't ask for I.D.'

'Yeah, so?'

'You need to keep a low profile.'

'You don't get much fuckin' lower than livin' under a bridge, Sam.'

'He found you this time.'

'You found me.'

'No. He told me *where* to find you.'

'Great. So I need to crawl under a rock, but not the same rock I usually do, and I need to watch out for someone I don't know.'

'But you're alive.'

Davey snorted again. 'You call this livin'?'

Sam stood and brushed dirt off his pants. The shaking had subsided. He kept his back to the warehouse, his face, mouth, hidden from view.

'Davey,' he said, his voice barely carrying, 'back in high school, did you know a black kid named Parker? He would have been one of the nerds.'

'Don't ring a bell,' Davey said huffily. 'If you hadn't burned my book, we could've looked him up.'

'I'll get you another book, Davey.'

'Yeah?' Davey's voice brightened. 'For sure?'

'Yeah,' Sam promised. 'For sure.'

48

At the Jeep, Sam tossed his dying flashlight into the hidden storage area as he retrieved his gun and make-up kit. With heavy footsteps, he walked to the driver's side and slipped the key into the ignition.

After grabbing the bag that contained his soiled uniform, he turned away. In this neighbourhood, the Jeep would be stripped, stolen or burned to the ground before morning.

Walking through the night, he thought of Davey, wondering why he had been chosen as a victim. They hadn't seen each other since high school. That was nearly a quarter century ago. Sam didn't know anyone – apart from the old friend he had just set alight – from that long ago. So how could they possibly share an enemy?

A disturbing thought caught him by surprise. The owner of the liquor store had said he recognized him. What if it wasn't from TV? Could he have attended the same high school, too?

Sam rubbed at his eyes, his skin oily with soot. He thought of Davey's screams and his own unmasked brutality. Davey could just as easily have died as not. He thought of Zack and how he had not only destroyed his career, but also the way others would always remember him.

If Sam was going to continue down this path, a path so completely out of his control, he needed to know for certain the end could be justified. And that was the monster's best trick of all, leaving Sam to wonder if his family was even alive.

Sam pulled out the cellphone and dug his hand into the front pocket of his jeans. He returned with a white business card that had a private number pencilled on its back.

He hesitated, his finger tracing a line under the numbers. He took a deep breath and keyed them in.

The phone was answered on the third ring.

'If this is you, Preston,' grumbled a groggy voice, 'I'm going to goddamn-well shit in your hat.'

'Detective Hogan?'

The voice became instantly alert. 'Who's this?'

'It's Sam White.'

'Liquor-store-robbin' Sam White?'

Sam was caught off guard. 'Yeah,' he said finally.

'Interesting,' Hogan mused.

'Is he all right? The owner.'

'He's alive, but mighty pissed. I would shop elsewhere from now on.'

'Good,' Sam said quietly. 'I mean, it's good he's alive.'

'Well, he certainly thinks so.'

Sam hesitated again. 'I need to ask you something.'

'Go on.'

'What did the coroner say about the bodies?'

Hogan inhaled sharply. 'I'm told it takes a while for this work to be done, but we know the younger victim, the child, isn't your daughter.'

Tears leaked from Sam's eyes. The official word made it more real that what he was doing was right. His family was still alive.

'Are you going to tell me who she is?' Hogan asked.

Sam's voice trembled. 'I don't think that's my place.'

'Well, that's an odd way to put it. She was found in the remains of your house.'

'Is she a black child?'

'Yes.'

Sam felt a sharp pain deep in his chest that radiated out to the tips of his toes and the strands of his hair. He thought of Zack and what he had said about wanting to die, but not having the courage to pull the trigger. Was there still hope there? Did Zack believe that like Sam's family, a resurrection was possible? Sam needed Zack to remain strong, but this news, this confirmation, could shatter him into a billion pieces.

189

After a moment of hesitation, Sam said, 'Her father will call when he's ready.'

'Oh, so her dad is alive?'

'Yes.'

'And the mom?'

'She's the other body.'

Hogan sighed. 'Did you kill these people, Mr White?'

'No! Christ, no! How could you—'

'What? You think that's a tough assumption to make?'

'It's not what it seems. My family has been kidnapped. He's making me do things . . .'

'*He's making me do things?* Do you know how that sounds, Mr White?'

'Yes,' Sam conceded.

'You should turn yourself in, Sam. I can come get you right now. We can work it out. Get you a good lawyer.'

'I can't do that.'

'What are you going to do?'

'I need to find out who's behind this,' Sam said. 'And stop them.'

'We can help, Sam. Just turn yourself in.'

Sam snorted. 'You think I'm psycho.'

'Hey, prove me wrong.'

'I'm trying.'

'Yeah?' Hogan sighed again. 'Well, the liquor robbery was a good first step.'

49

'Shit!'

Hogan had played it too tough. He was supposed to be acting as good cop, being a friend, gaining his trust.

He replaced the handset in its cradle and checked the caller ID. The call was listed as *Private* and the number blocked.

Hogan dialled the station and asked to be patched through to the tech desk. Once connected with the lone, late-shift techie, he requested a trace on the call he had just received.

'I don't need any triangulation hocus-pocus,' he told the techie to circumvent any grumbling about cops who watched too much TV and thought everybody had *C.S.I.* and *C.T.U.* resources. 'I just need owner ID on the phone and a billing address.'

After being assured the information would be on his desk by morning, Hogan rolled over and spooned the sleeping form of his wife. Her body was warm and her nightgown soft. She stirred slightly as he cupped one breast in his hand and gently kissed the nape of her neck. She murmured something unintelligible and a hand rose to squeeze his fingers before she resumed a gentle snore.

Hogan smiled and closed his eyes. As he tried to get back to sleep, a quote from *Alice in Wonderland* played in his head: 'Curiouser and curiouser.'

50

Sam exited a yellow cab two blocks from the motel and walked the rest of the way. The door to the room was locked, but Zack had given him the extra key.

Inside, Sam was surprised to find the room empty and Zack's bed unused. The clock on the nightstand said it was 2 a.m. Sam turned to the window and looked out. The Mercedes wasn't parked in its usual spot.

The absence of the vehicle, and the contents of its trunk, made his heart unexpectedly race faster.

Sam didn't have a clue how he could possibly get his hands on the quarter million he still needed, so what did the absence of the rest really matter? If Zack's idea couldn't raise the full amount . . . He didn't want to finish the thought.

Sam paced the room like a caged animal, stopping to stare out of the window at every turn. He felt himself growing angry . . . desperate.

He sat on the edge of the bed and switched on

the TV, but none of the talking heads made sense. He couldn't concentrate on the words.

He hit the shower, scrubbing the smell of stale smoke, rum and sweat from his pores. After towelling off, he returned to the window. Neon flames licked the pane, flickering reflections of the motel sign outside.

He waited.

51

Detective Hogan snatched a sheet of blue paper off his desk and grinned at its contents.

'You know why the paper's blue, right?' said Preston.

Hogan glanced up at his partner, waiting.

'Our late-night techie's gay.' Preston touched the side of his nose with one extended finger. 'But he's still in denial. He thinks blue paper makes him look more hetero.'

Hogan grinned a little wider. 'That's what makes you such a good detective. You're so full of horseshit, you can grow a tale taller than anyone.'

Preston pretended shock. 'You wait and see. Once our boy comes out, all your tech sheets will be pink and proud.'

Hogan laughed as he reached for the desk phone and dialled the cell number on the paper.

The phone rang once, and then a recorded message said: 'We're sorry, but this phone cannot receive unauthorized calls.'

Hogan hung up and waved the blue paper in front of his partner's nose.

'Feel like busting down a door and picking up our elusive Mr White? It's about time you made yourself useful.'

Preston grinned, showing two rows of healthy teeth. 'You're just jealous cause I cracked the blue paper case.'

52

Sam woke with a start, his hand reaching to his hip and feeling nothing but denim. He opened his eyes, the nightmare fading as the weight of reality suffocated all other thought.

He looked to his left and saw Zack sitting on the edge of his bed, still dressed in his soiled suit. His skeletal face looked impossibly thinner, his dark eyes sunk even deeper into their sockets than the night before.

'I didn't hear you come in,' Sam rasped.

'It was late.'

'You don't look too hot.'

'I'm fine.' Zack attempted a small, reassuring smile. 'Nights are the hardest.'

These last words were spoken so quietly, Sam wasn't sure if Zack meant to say them aloud.

'I work nights, but I know what you mean,' Sam agreed. 'The quiet times when the outside doors are closed and it's just the three of you.'

'I lived for those,' Zack said. 'Stretch out on the

couch with a new book; Kalli watching a silly movie with her headphones on; Jasmine curled up beside me, smacking her lips as she flips through one of her cookbooks.'

He paused, a cloud drifting over his face.

Sam broke the silence, his need for the words to be aired outweighing their possible impact. 'I called one of the detectives last night.'

Zack's face fell. 'Oh, fuck. How could—'

'I had to know,' Sam blurted.

'Know? He warned you—'

'I had to know if what I was doing . . . if the violence . . . if there was a reason for hope. And . . .' Sam paused, thinking of his connection to Davey.

'And?' Zack pressed.

'And if I could really trust you.'

Zack shook his head violently and dropped his gaze to his hands, the fingers of his right twisting the gold wedding band on his left.

'Trust?' Zack leapt to his feet and began to pace the room. 'Trust?' He moved in close again, his face looming over Sam's, his voice angry. 'You can't trust anyone, Sam. Not me, not the cops, nobody. We all have our own agendas. You want your family. I want revenge. The cops want someone to lock up. What good can the cops do except piss *him* off?'

'The detective confirmed the child wasn't MaryAnn,' Sam said in the hope of defusing the situation. 'You told me the truth. She was black.'

Zack staggered backwards as if he had been struck. Tears overflowed and began to pour down his cheeks in a waterfall of grief. He didn't try to hide it, but as the news sank in, grief was once again replaced with anger.

He rose up straight with clenched fists and gritted teeth, his whole body shaking and his breathing shallow and fast.

'What gave you the right?' he seethed. 'You selfish son of a—'

Zack lashed out, his right fist rising from the floor to catch Sam under the chin.

Sam spun across the bed, blood spraying from his mouth.

'What gave you the bloody right?' Zack staggered like a drunk as his voice crumbled into a blubbering mess of disjointed words. His hands moved to his head, fingers lacing into his hair before curling back into fists. He pulled his flesh tight until panic stopped him cold and he ran for the bathroom.

Zack heaved his guts into the toilet, but the bile in his stomach was nothing compared to the churning in his mind.

Sam had crossed a line. How could he have been so stupid? The watcher had warned them. He had been clear about that. If he found out that Sam had called the police, he might decide to cut his losses and kill his hostages . . . kill Jasmine.

Zack crossed to the sink and splashed cold water on his face.

Without knowing it, Sam had forced him to choose a side. He could never tell the watcher what Sam had done, but in choosing to go against him, Zack knew he could lose everything – again.

53

When Zack returned, Sam was standing at the window with his back to the room. He had a towel pressed against his mouth and his body language spoke volumes.

Zack moved behind the bed and cleared his throat. 'We didn't meet by accident, Sam.'

Sam turned, his eyes burning.

Zack held up one hand. 'You were right not to trust me, but let me say my piece before you react.'

Sam glanced down at the bed. The handgun he had left on top of the covers was missing.

'My wife is alive,' said Zack.

Sam was taken aback. 'How?'

'I don't know. I thought she was killed in the explosion, with . . .' his voice faltered '. . . with Kalli. But like you, I received a phone call.'

'You talked to her?'

'Yes.'

'He said you could save her?'

Zack nodded.

'By betraying me?' The towel fell as Sam's hand formed a fist.

'What would you do?' said Zack quickly. 'He asked me to spy on you, to make sure you kept your end of the bargain. I haven't told him any—'

'Fuck!' Sam screamed.

'I haven't told him anything he didn't already know, Sam.'

'Then what good are you?'

'I know how to get the money. I can help you get the full million.'

'And then what? Then you and him—'

Zack snapped, 'I still plan to kill him, Sam. I wouldn't be telling you this if I was going to keep lying.'

Sam turned and drove his fist into the wall. The plaster buckled and cracked under the blow. He was lucky he missed the studs. He spun back around, his face red, his knuckles raw. 'And I'm supposed to trust you?'

'YES!'

'Why?'

'Because we both have something precious to lose if you don't. For the first time we're both in the same spot. I won't tell him about you calling the cops. I just want my wife back.'

A troubling thought cut Sam to the bone. 'Hannah. Is the other body Hannah?'

Zack winced. 'I don't know. Who can tell with

202

this sick fuck? But you have to have hope, Sam.'

Sam bristled. 'How can I be sure that you don't know who he is? Where he's holding them?'

Zack's eyes narrowed into slits. 'Because if I did, he would already be dead.'

Sam exhaled heavily, his heart thundering in his chest. He turned back to the window. Rage and anger weren't helping him, he needed facts.

'Why did he pick you?'

'To spy?'

'No. To torment. Why you? Why me? He sent me to torture an old friend from high school last night. Why? I hadn't seen or spoken to Davey since grad, but the caller wanted me to burn him alive.'

'Jesus!' Zack gasped. 'Did you?'

Sam turned and locked eyes. 'I followed your example with the actress. He screamed enough to make it convincing, but he'll be OK.'

A heavy silence filled the room, and then Zack took a deep, staggered breath that made his whole body shake.

'There's another connection,' he said hesitantly. 'Do you remember Rick Ironwood?'

Sam thought back, faces he hadn't thought of in years flickering in front of his eyes. 'Ironman. Football player. Running back or something. Egotistical meat puppet with a scholarship all sewn up.'

'I killed him.'

'What! When?'

'It was my last assignment before driving to your house to collect my family.' Zack's voice was distant. 'When I first saw him, I barely recognized—'

'Recognized?'

'I went to Brookside High, too. Graduated the year before you did, but I didn't put it together until . . . high school was a long time ago.'

'You knew Ironwood?'

'He was the golden boy who terrorized every nerd in the hallways.' Zack's voice drifted. 'He used to grunt like a pig when he caught me: "*Piggy Parker. Piggy Parker.*" That's how he made all the girls laugh.'

'Sounds like a reason for revenge.'

'True,' Zack agreed. 'And even though I hadn't thought about him in years, I must admit the first punch felt good. But that's all I needed. He wasn't the young bully who tormented me in the hallways. He was just another overweight, middle-aged guy trying to make ends meet. My revenge was my life – my family, my career – until this bastard took that away from me.'

'How did you kill him?'

'I shot him. In his garage. It was quick.'

Sam couldn't keep the flash of horror off his face.

'It's not as though you wouldn't have done the same,' Zack said defensively. 'After all, you thought you killed that guy in the liquor store.'

'You couldn't fake it?'

Zack shook his head. 'He was filming me. I had no choice.'

Sam's eyes were stone. 'Why Ironwood?'

'I don't know. Maybe he thought it would be easier for me to kill him if it was someone I hated.'

'Or did the kidnapper hate him, too?'

'Yeah,' Zack sighed. 'That thought crossed my mind when he chose you next.'

'So what now?' Sam asked.

Zack reached into his pocket and pulled out Sam's gun. He tossed it on the bed. 'That's up to you, I guess.'

Sam picked up the gun. It felt cold in his hand.

'I promised to kill you if you ever lied to me.'

'You weren't the first.'

'How can I believe you now?'

Zack shrugged. 'Cause I'm all out of secrets. Cause my daughter is dead and my wife is missing. Cause we want the same thing and we're both out of other options.'

Sam weighed the gun in his hand before slowly slipping it into his waistband.

'You know how to get the money?'

Zack nodded. 'I met with an old acquaintance last night and explained what we needed. He's agreed to meet you.'

'This friend can deliver a quarter million?'

'He definitely has the money,' Zack said carefully. 'I just don't know what he'll ask for in exchange.'

54

Preston's breathing was laboured as he bent over in the passenger seat and shoved his back-up piece, a snub-nosed .38, into the top of his cowboy boot.

'Remember when they used to give cops decent cars with lots of elbow room and a trunk that could hold three bodies?' Preston smoothed his pant leg over his boot. 'Hell, I had a Caddy in Texas once that could fit four if you folded them just right. These new compact models make it difficult to get ready for a good door kickin'. And just try and get forty winks in that back seat.' He snorted. 'Do your bleepin' back in, let me tell you.'

Hogan ignored his partner as he studied the grey house with primer trim that matched the address on his blue piece of paper. He remembered the neighbourhood from his days in uniform.

It had been a good family community at one

time, tossed up in a hurry during the last building boom in the early eighties. But the years hadn't been kind and most of the houses looked in bad need of repair.

'Think we need back-up?' Hogan asked.

'For a bleepin' actor?'

'For an armed security guard,' Hogan clarified.

Preston grinned menacingly. 'With the training those guys get, I could give him the first two shots free and he still wouldn't be able to hit me.'

'Let's wear vests,' Hogan said. 'We don't know who might be in there.'

The two detectives approached the suburban house and Preston tested the first rule he ever learned about house invasion: *Try the damn handle.*

It was locked.

He waited.

His radio squawked.

'I'm at the back door,' Hogan said. 'It's locked, but there's no fancy security. Any sign of movement?'

'Negative. You?'

'Negative.'

'On three,' Preston said. 'One, two—'

Both detectives kicked in their respective doors at the same instant and rushed into the house with guns drawn. At a quick, but meticulous pace, they swept through the three-bedroom split-level.

They met in the living room, a barren rectangle

of carpet holding a single loveseat and a sad-looking pair of analog TVs.

'Anything?' Preston asked.

'Half-eaten plate of cold spaghetti on the kitchen table and an open bottle of beer.'

'For breakfast?'

Hogan shrugged. 'Man after your own heart.'

A scratching noise made both men turn to a shallow hallway off the living room that led to a narrow doorway.

'Garage?' Preston muttered.

Both men made their way to the door. It was slightly ajar and the scratching sounds were coming from within.

Preston held up three fingers, folded one into his palm, then the second. He yanked open the door as Hogan dropped low—

A black cat with a lightning bolt of orange running between its ears wrestled with the broken windshield wiper of an old Trans Am. The faded screaming eagle logo on the hood was covered in tiny paw prints. The prints glistened red in the cold light of a lone bulb hung from the rafters.

The detectives rounded the car to see the stark white body of a big-bellied man sprawled on the garage floor. Dressed in baby blue boxers and an old Kiss T-shirt, he was face up in a congealed pool of blood and surrounded by oilcans. The man's destroyed face, especially the mangled lips, appeared to have been partially eaten.

'Death by bored house cat?' Preston asked.

'Apart from the bullet hole in his skull,' Hogan said drily. 'I would say you were on to something, Detective.'

The forensics services squad swarmed the dead man's house with cameras, tweezers, powder and tape, while Hogan and Preston waited outside with nothing to do until the crime scene was recorded, tagged, dusted and bagged in minute detail.

'Detectives!'

Hogan and Preston turned as the garage door slid open. A lanky officer in a baggy white jump-suit approached and handed Hogan a clear plastic bag containing a worn, leather wallet.

'It's already been dusted,' the officer said. 'We found it on the victim.'

Hogan reached in to retrieve the wallet. Inside was a driver's licence that matched the name on his blue piece of paper. He showed it to his partner.

'So, Mr Ironwood,' Preston said, 'what's the bleepin' actor doing with your cellphone?'

55

Zack parked the Mercedes at a kerbside meter outside the aptly named Old Towne Fish House. The historic Old Town district was located just north of Burnside and within easy walking distance of the popular Waterfront Park.

Sam looked at Zack suspiciously as the smell of garlic, grease and seafood was sucked through the air vents into the Mercedes' interior.

'Your friend runs this place?'

'I wouldn't exactly call him a friend, but, yeah, he manages it,' Zack said. 'The outfit he works for owns this one, plus a few other choice spots in the neighbourhood.'

'Nice neighbourhood,' Sam said, 'but what can I offer a restaurateur in return for a quarter million?'

'Let's find out.' Zack's face was unreadable as he opened the car door and stepped out.

Sam resettled the gun deeper in his waistband and pulled the tail of his vest over the top before following behind. A menu posted on the front door showed the restaurant wouldn't open to customers for another three hours. Despite that, the door was unlocked.

Zack led Sam through the deserted dining area to a large industrial kitchen strung with a garland of glistening steel pots in every shape and size imaginable.

Two men in immaculate white aprons, their hair flattened against their skulls by elastic hairnets, sat on bar stools, chopping a mound of white and yellow onions into a large bowl.

One of the men nodded at Zack and wiped his burning eyes on the back of his hand before standing up and leading the way to a walk-in freezer.

Inside the large freezer, the cook reached down to the floor, hooked his hand into a steel ring and yanked. An insulated trapdoor swung open noiselessly on a pair of shiny red pistons. Zack walked to the dark opening, nodded his thanks to the cook, and descended a wooden staircase. Sam followed, but glanced nervously over his shoulder as the cook slowly lowered the door to seal them in.

When the trapdoor closed, there was a second of complete darkness before twin rows of electric lights flickered to reveal a large passage carved into the earth. The packed-dirt and red-brick walls had been smoothed into a wide opening that curved to a height of nearly eight feet and a width that allowed both men to stand side by side with a little extra elbow room on either side.

Where parts of the tunnel walls had crumbled, they were patched with fresh brick, new timber and modern concrete pilings. The dirt roof, however, still looked original and was supported by ancient, fourteen-inch wooden beams and incredibly intricate stone archways. The archways were made from hand-cut grey stones, at least twelve inches square that climbed in perfect vertical columns until gently curving at the top to form an inverted U.

Near the bottom of the stairs and set directly into the right-hand wall, a small wooden door, six inches thick but barely three feet tall, sat ajar. Cut into the door was a single, square opening lined with three jagged iron bars flecked with rust.

Sam glanced inside. It was a dirt and brick cavity, barely six feet wide by eight feet deep, with crumbling walls braced by thick cedar planks. The wood was scratched and chipped as if it had held back a tiger.

'That's where the crimpers kept their men until the boats were ready to sail,' Zack said. 'I did a history paper on it in university.'

'Crimpers?'

'The original corporate head-hunters. Portland was infamous for it back in the 1800s. Get a drink in the wrong bar on the wrong night, and you woke up on a ship bound for China. Sold for the going rate of fifty dollars per head. They say thousands of men were kidnapped and sold over the years.'

Sam touched the tender bruise under his chin. 'I guess if you were going to kill me. This would be the perfect spot.'

Zack stopped. 'I only want one thing, Sam.' His voice was barely controlled. 'And that's Jasmine. I don't know how to prove it to you, but we need each other. No more secrets, no more lies.'

Zack headed further down the passage, which quickly narrowed as it left the restaurant's small cavern behind.

'These tunnels run everywhere,' Zack continued in a voice that strived for normality. 'It was a good way to transport men and goods to the river without being seen. At the turn of the last century this whole area was full of bars, flops and whorehouses. Perfect fodder for a crewless captain heading out on a long voyage.'

'Charming.'

Sam ducked beneath another elaborate stone archway and entered a second cavern, much larger than the first. A thick, blood-red carpet covered the dirt floor, and in the middle of the ceiling, a large trapdoor had been sealed with a heavy steel lock.

Zack pointed at the trap. 'That was set in the floor of one of the original bars or whorehouses. Drink too much or drop your pants in the wrong room and the owner pulls a lever. They'd usually leave an old mattress on the ground to make sure you didn't break a leg, since no one would buy a lame sailor. When you hit the mattress, one of the bullyboys would crack you over the head with a sap. Then you're off to a cell to await the next ship. It could take three to six years before you ever saw home again.'

'Why have I never heard about this before?' Sam asked. 'It sounds horrible.'

'After prohibition – since the tunnels were busy then, too – the city tried to bury its sordid history and focus people's attention on bridges and rose gardens. People forgot about the tunnels and the smugglers. It wasn't until the 1970s, when the city had to do some serious roadwork in these old neighbourhoods, that local historians re-discovered them.'

'And your friend reopened them?' Sam asked.

Zack shrugged. 'This is the only one I've seen.'

'You came here last night?'

Zack nodded. 'Wish I could have seen it when I was writing the paper. Most of my details came from dusty old records and historical diaries.'

Sam studied the large cavern with the red carpet, wondering what the hardened crimpers would think if they could see it now. In one corner stood a large, semi-circular couch in a matching shade of red that was so fabulously plush it inspired visions of a *Playboy* photo shoot. It faced a large plasma TV similar to the one Sam had coveted in the window of the Sony store.

'This place is impressive.' Sam's gaze swept the other walls, taking in two more imposingly constructed archways. The tunnel beyond the first

215

doorway on his right remained ominously dark, while the second was sealed by a wooden door. It was medieval thick and studded with rusted iron dimples.

The archway above the door was inscribed with mysterious symbols.

'I haven't been able to figure those out,' Zack said. 'You'll find them all over the tunnels. The language of the day was English with a few bits of Chinese thrown in from the imported labourers who built the railroads and docks. But these symbols are neither. Closest I can guess is some kind of Masonic code left behind by the builders.'

Zack rapped knuckles on the heavy door. The ancient wood absorbed the sound as though he had pelted it with cotton wool.

'I think you're supposed to hit it with a studded mace,' Sam said. 'Your knock didn't even echo.'

Before Zack could respond, the door was opened by a large Asian man with muscled shoulders almost wider than the archway, his shiny black T-shirt moulded perfectly over carved pectorals.

The man's shaved head glistened in the cold artificial light and the sneer on his face was enough to turn lesser beings into pillars of salt.

'He's expecting us.' Zack's voice was surprisingly firm.

56

The guard opened the door wider and stepped aside to let them pass, but he left one of his trunk-thick arms locked on the doorframe, forcing both Zack and Sam to duck under.

Inside the third cavern, Sam was stunned by yet more opulence. Rich curtains draped the cavern walls, and Persian rugs blanketed the floor. On several walls, the curtains had been pulled back to expose vibrant oil paintings by artists rarely exhibited outside of museums.

Sam gawped at a small seascape, which looked identical to one he had read was recently stolen from a gallery in Amsterdam.

'Are you an art lover, Mr White?' asked a raspy male voice.

A thickset man in a tailored black suit had appeared from behind one of the curtains. The suit did little to disguise his bulky figure. Built from the ground up for manual labour on the Siberian Steppes, the man had thick legs, a barrel chest and the largest hands Sam had ever seen on someone so short. Although standing at least four inches shorter than Sam, the man radiated muscle and power.

'Is that really a Van Gogh?' Sam asked.

The man shrugged. 'Probably. I don't know much about it myself, but the boss likes his luxuries.'

Zack stepped in to make the introductions. 'Sam, this is Vadik. He and his daughter were sent to my clinic by a mutual acquaintance.'

'So modest,' said Vadik. 'Dr Parker saved my daughter's life. She was badly burned and the scars were . . .' He shivered. 'The scars were devastating.'

'But Tasya is well,' Zack said.

'She is beautiful,' Vadik said proudly. 'Thanks to you. So come, let me help.'

Vadik led them to the far corner of the cavern where a solid horseshoe-shaped desk glowed from the light of four large computer monitors. Each monitor pulsed with an abstract screen saver that reminded Sam of the movie, *Matrix*.

Zack and Sam seated themselves on a pair of leather armchairs while Vadik settled into a swivelling office chair. The imposing guard stayed by the door, his eyes never leaving the visitors.

'Dr Parker has told me of your plight,' Vadik began. 'And I want to say how sorry I am. If you find you need guns or muscle, just let me know and they're yours. No upfront fees. Fair enough?'

Sam nodded.

'Good.' Vadik slapped his hands together. 'Now I'm also told you want $250,000.'

Sam tried not to look guilty.

'As Dr Parker explained it,' Vadik continued, 'you have no means, nor intention of paying it back, and we won't see any interest. This is an unusual request.'

'Please can you help me?' Sam blurted.

Vadik smiled darkly.

'Dr Parker also informs me that by the time your ordeal is over, there is a very good chance you will be either in prison or in a grave. Is that not correct?'

Sam glanced over at Zack. He was sitting rigid, his eyes locked unflinchingly on Vadik. Sam was on his own. *No more secrets*, he said to himself, recalling Zack's words, *no more lies*.

Sam nodded, deflated.

'Not to worry, Sam,' Vadik assured. 'Dr Parker and I go back a long way. If I didn't believe I could help, you wouldn't be here. I've already spoken to my boss and he has given me free licence.'

Sam stared into the man's dark brown eyes. 'I'll do anything,' he said, and meant it.

'Good. Now I understand you can acquire access to your place of employment.'

'The mall?'

'Precisely. In exchange for the money, we require full access to the mall.'

Sam looked puzzled. 'You're going to rob a store?'

Vadik chuckled. 'Nothing so common as that, Sam. We're going to rob the entire mall. Every store on every floor, and you're going to make sure we're not disturbed until we're done.'

57

The men hadn't returned.

The woman worried when she opened her eyes that they had taken away their meager supplies as punishment, but they had retreated without thought for the food. They obviously preferred physical punishment. From the pain that coursed through her ribcage when she breathed, the woman was sure she had suffered broken ribs from a sharp-toed boot while she lay defenseless.

Her strategy of trying to engage the larger one in conversation had had little effect. She had read in a psychology book that kidnap victims should repeat their names in order to get the kidnapper to see them as flesh-and-blood human beings. If he could recognize them as woman and child, rather than disposable cargo, it might spark some memories of a mother, a sister, of someone he must have loved. But the man was unmoved, showing not the slightest glimmer that he heard her pleading words.

The woman had used some of their precious water to clean the blood off the child's face and to examine her bones for any breaks. Her nose was badly swollen and her eyes were puffy, but the woman was fairly sure everything was where it was supposed to be.

It had taken her a long time to soothe the child after she had been returned. Although physical wounds could always be mended, the woman worried for MaryAnn's spirit. Once that was broken, there would be nothing to stoke her will to survive.

The woman had thought her own spirit was lost, but the child had given her the strength she needed to stay alive long enough to make someone pay for everything that had been done to them.

58

Zack pulled into the parking lot of a Wal-Mart superstore and turned off the ignition. Neither of them had spoken since leaving the tunnels, although Sam had twice opened his mouth as if to start, but then closed it without a word.

Finally, Zack said, 'What is it?'

Sam sighed. 'I wanted to ask if you think we can trust him, but what the fuck good does that do? I mean, what good is your word to me now?'

'I got you the money, didn't I?'

'No, you introduced me to a gangster who wants to use me to rob a mall.'

'And pay you a quarter million to do it. Did you have a better idea?'

'Fuck!' Sam punched the ceiling.

Zack bristled. 'If you don't trust me, Sam, I'll leave and find Jasmine on my own.'

Sam met Zack's icy glare.

'I don't think I'll be successful,' he continued. 'But I don't think you will either. So we have to put this behind us and work together or we go our separate ways and our loved ones die. What's it to be?'

'That's a bit harsh.'

'No,' said Zack, 'that's the God's honest truth.' He stuck out his hand.

It trembled until, finally, Sam took it in his and squeezed.

'Now we need new licence plates,' Zack said to change the subject. 'If the police connect us, these California plates will stand out like a beacon.'

Sam scanned the parking lot. 'Look for a car that doesn't get washed too often and they shouldn't notice the switch.'

Zack opened his door.

'And then we need to find a high school yearbook,' Sam continued. 'The fucker who has my family must be in there somewhere. Name, photo, the works.'

59

'So what do you think?' Hogan asked.

The two detectives sat at a picnic table in Waterfront Park while a stream of joggers clogged the river path in front of them.

Preston squeezed some hot mustard on his first steamed hotdog and licked the excess off his fingers.

'It's like I said before,' he began, 'the actor's gone off the deep end and is in a full-blown killing spree.'

Hogan took a long sip of root beer.

'I don't buy it,' he said. 'People don't just wake up one morning and decide to a) kill their family, b) kill somebody else's, c) blow up their house, d) rob a liquor store for two lousy bottles of booze, and e) kill some down-on-his-luck schmuck for his cellphone.'

'That's very impressive.' Preston stuffed half the hotdog in his mouth and reached for his own can of root beer.

'What is?' Hogan asked.

'The way you keep the alphabet in order like that.'

Hogan ignored the jab. 'Your theory suggests that Mr White, a reasonably normal man by all accounts—'

'An actor,' Preston injected as he stuffed the second half of the hotdog into his mouth.

'Woke up one morning and decided to become a – what? – mass murderer? . . . Serial killer?'

'If he had stuck with killing the two families, his own and the mystery pair in the morgue, then he might be a serial.' Preston wiped mustard stains off his lips with a fresh paper napkin. 'But he messed that up with the cellphone and liquor jobs. So I think we're left with whack-job, which definitely makes for a trickier, although often wittier, morning headline.'

'But why?' Hogan asked. 'We don't have a motive and so far we can't even connect the victims. There's no logic.'

'That's the trouble with you.' Preston loaded his second hotdog with mustard.

'What?'

'You love to poke holes in a nice, simple theory.'

Preston took a large bite of his hotdog, and Hogan looked away. He had lost his appetite.

60

Zack drove the Mercedes into the teachers' lot of Brookside High and parked in an empty spot marked for visitors.

'It's smaller than I remember,' he said.

The building was spread over two floors of industrial grey stone that engulfed nearly an entire city block. Designed for capacity rather than aesthetics, the only break to its boring box dimensions came in the form of an M-shaped canopy roof across the main entrance.

Sam noticed that several of the windows were boarded over, and there was more graffiti than he remembered. The school looked tired, past retirement and finding itself slumping, but too old to give a damn.

A group of teenagers hung out by the front doors, all attitude and hair, with logos emblazoned on everything from skateboards to underwear.

'Did we ever look that young?' Sam asked. 'I

remember feeling so . . . *cocky* back then, like I had the world by the tail and everything would just magically fall into place.'

'Yeah,' Zack agreed, 'we thought we knew everything there was to know.'

'Davey said it was like walking among gods.'

'A bit extreme, but I can see his point. We were so sheltered, so cocooned in our own shells, that minor celebrities stuck out like fireflies. The football player, the cheerleader . . .' Zack turned to Sam. 'The actor.'

Sam returned Zack's stare. 'The science nerd?'

Zack paused and inclined his head. 'The general population didn't notice us, except as targets of ridicule. But a younger geek may have looked to us as role models.'

'And somehow you . . . what? Shunned him so badly he became a psychopath?'

'As did you, apparently,' Zack added defensively.

'That's tough logic to follow. We're looking for someone who felt betrayed by both of us to such a level that he seeks revenge decades later when – what? – he has a mid-life crisis.'

'And not just us,' Zack interjected. 'The targets he sent us after. Your friend last night, Iron—' Zack faltered, his voice breaking at the memory. 'Shit. What could we have done to cause this much pain?'

'Maybe we didn't do anything,' Sam reasoned. 'That's why we can't solve the riddle. Whatever it is we're being blamed for, it's been twisted to such a degree inside this freak's mind that there's no logic left. He's been stewing about something so insignificant to us that it doesn't even register in our memories, yet it scarred him so deeply he's become a monster.'

'So how do we find him?' Zack asked.

Sam nodded towards the school. 'We walk down memory lane.'

61

Hogan's cellphone rang as Preston drained the last of his root beer.

'Detective Hogan?' asked a gruff voice.

'Speaking. Who's this?'

'Walt Toler. Toler's Tonics. I got smacked in the head for two lousy bottles of booze.'

'Right, Mr Toler. What can I do for you?'

'One of the officers gave me your card, said if I remembered anything to call.'

'Which you have.'

'Yeah. Listen, I thought I recognized the guy, but wasn't sure. Then I was watching some TV here, and there he is.'

'On TV?'

'Yeah, in a fuckin' commercial for the Beavers.'

'We know the suspect is an actor.' Hogan prepared to hang up.

'But that's not where I know him from,' Walt continued.

'Oh?'

'No. It took a moment to click, it's been a few fuckin' years, but I went to high school with him.'

'Really?'

'Yeah. We didn't hang out or nothin', which is why it didn't click. But I saw a couple plays he was in cause there was some hot chicks in drama who didn't mind shakin' it a bit, you know?'

Hogan thought for a moment. 'Did he recognize you?'

'Nah,' Walt said dismissively. 'But then I don't look nothin' like I did back then. The Viking they called me. My hair was down past my shoulders and the colour of Tropicana orange juice.'

Hogan smiled into the phone as he tried to picture the balding man with the walrus moustache sporting long red hair.

'That must have been something to see.'

Walt laughed. 'Yeah, The Viking and Ironman ruled the fuckin' roost. Chicks, booze . . . crazy, crazy times.'

'Ironman?' Hogan's brain twitched from the possibility. 'Not Rick Ironwood, by any chance?'

Walt laughed again. 'Sure. You know the Ironman?'

'I was just at his house.'

'No shit! I haven't seen him in ages. How's the old bastard doing?'

'He's dead. Murdered,' Hogan said flatly. 'I was there on official business.'

'Oh, crap.' Walt released his breath in an audible wheeze. 'I always meant to give him a call, get together for a beer. Shit. Time slips through your fingers, don't it?' A pause. 'Any idea who did it?'

'Do you?'

Walt sucked in another deep breath. 'I don't like to speak ill of old friends, but Ironman had trouble keeping his shit together, you know? He owed some money. He liked his dope. Could be a hundred people who hated his guts. He was an all right guy, though. It was just . . . he never really got over not making it in college.'

'What happened in college?' Hogan asked.

'Ahh, shit, you know? They expected him to make grades. Ironman was great on the gridiron, but none too bright in the classroom. Lost his scholarship and that was that.'

'What about Sam White?'

'Huh?' Walt was stumped.

'The man who attacked you,' explained Hogan.

'Oh, right. That was his name. That's been bugging me. I paid more attention to the chicks. What about him?'

'Could he have a reason to hate Ironwood?'

'Not from high school. The jocks and drama freaks didn't hang at all. Sometimes there was crossover, one of the jocks who thought he could act. But there was no way Ironman was interested. Why? You think the actor took him out?'

'We're following all leads,' Hogan said, revealing nothing.

Switch

'Fuckin' high school,' Walt mused. 'Those were the days, huh?'

'Personally,' Hogan said drily, 'I hated everything about it.'

62

Zack and Sam walked through the front door of the high school to a ten-stare salute from the droopy-pants crowd chillin' on the concrete steps. Two of the teenagers held skateboards that were almost as tall and wide as themselves.

'You see the skateboards?' Sam asked.

Zack shrugged.

'When the craze was big in the seventies,' Sam continued, despite Zack's disinterest, 'if you showed up at school with a skateboard that size, you would have been laughed outta town. Skateboards were short and narrow. You needed the balance of an Olympian just to go in a straight line. I preferred the Roller Rink. At least there, you had four wheels on each foot and girls who loved to help a new guy keep his balance.' Sam winked. 'Especially on the slow songs.'

'I never tried either,' Zack said dismissively. 'The only time I was part of a craze was when Rubik's Cube became the hottest thing.'

Sam scoffed, caught up in the moment. 'What about the frisbee and ghetto-blaster years? Down at the beach, blasting Pink Floyd and Sabbath, smoking a little pot and making that frisbee bend, curve, dip and soar to your will.'

Zack stopped walking and his eyes turned hard. 'We need to focus, Sam, OK? Leave the past where it belongs. Not everyone enjoyed it.'

Sam shrugged, knowing Zack had a point, but damned if he was going to admit it.

He stopped to get his bearings. The lobby divided the school into quadrants. The wide double doors to the gymnasium loomed on the right, lunch room on the left. Further up on the right was the auditorium, split from the gym by a long, narrow hallway – a no man's land that sustained a truce between jocks and drama.

'It was easier then,' Sam said, remembering back.

Zack flashed him a look of exasperation.

'No, hear me out,' he continued. 'Jocks had the gym; Heads took the east doors beside the garbage bins; Nerds and Brains had the library; Misfits and Wallflowers, the lunch room; Preppies took the rear doors to show off dad's car; Grease Monkeys and Builders took the west doors by the shops; Drama freaks had the stage.'

'Are you saying we all knew our place?' Zack asked.

'We all knew where we felt most comfortable,' Sam said. 'The only time trouble happened was when the cliques were forced together in the hall-ways, then Ironman and his ilk descended upon the nerds or whoever else caught their eye. But in our own parts of the school, everything was cool.'

'Sounds like segregation,' Zack said, his tone disapproving.

'You're right,' Sam said, 'and maybe that's wrong, but I know that I never feel as accepted as when I'm surrounded by other actors and people who love making movies. It doesn't matter what sex, religion or skin colour, it's their mindset. And you can't tell me that jocks and nerds don't feel the same way.'

Zack's brow knitted into a furrow. 'So you're saying that's what's wrong with our kidnapper?'

'Exactly. He doesn't fit in.'

Zack nodded in understanding and took the theory one step further. 'He doesn't fit in *any-where*,' he said. 'Maybe he tried *all* the groups: the nerds, the actors, the jocks.'

'And none of us accepted him,' Sam jumped in.

'We didn't do it on a conscious level,' Zack continued. 'We were just being ourselves and he would have been on the outskirts, never able to blend in.'

'And he blames us for his life.'

'Yes. It took him nearly twenty-five years, but somehow he's arrived at the idea that everything that's gone wrong in his life started back here. Back with us.'

'Christ! My family is paying the price for what?

A moment of selfishness when I was seventeen. Who isn't selfish at that age?'

'We were the leaders,' Zack said. 'We were the gods.'

Sam processed the theory as he crossed the lobby towards the administration office, but it didn't sit well.

'That's crap,' he said finally. 'The more I think about it, the more absurd it sounds. How could anyone think we were gods?'

'You said Davey did?' Zack reminded.

'Davey is fucked up. He's been living in prison or on the streets since he was nineteen. He hasn't been able to move on.'

'I'm not saying it makes total sense, Sam. But in this little self-contained universe, people like you and Ironman stood taller than the rest. People looked up to you. Heck, they *idolized* you. Can you imagine how that must have looked to someone nobody even knew existed?'

'But it was so damn long ago,' Sam said quietly.

'Maybe not for everyone.'

63

Sam and Zack approached the battle-scarred, waist-high counter that acted as a barricade between students and administration.

A woman in a flowery wallpaper-pattern dress stood up from her desk and approached. Her hair was pulled into a bun so tight it stretched her face until it looked ready to snap.

'The principal's not in,' she said sourly. 'Not expecting her back for hours, either.'

Sam softened his voice to TV-commercial smooth. 'That's OK, I'm sure you can help. We're looking for information.'

'What kind of information?'

'We need to look through some yearbooks from the early eighties.'

She studied the two men for a moment, as if judging their characters. 'Library might have some, but they've probably been scooped into the clutches of Nancy B.'

'Nancy B?' Sam asked.

'She's a volunteer who runs all the reunions. She talked Principal De Gama into giving her an office in the library, which is something Principal Pierce would never have allowed if *he* was still on the job.'

'Would we find her there?' Sam enquired.

'Should do. You know the way?'

'We're former students.'

'No kiddin'.' The woman frowned. 'That must have been a *long* time ago.'

Sam's smile faltered slightly as he departed.

64

In the library, Zack and Sam were directed to a corner office that overflowed with books. Waist-high stacks of them littered the floor and spilled out the doorway.

Behind the precarious piles, they found a mass of coiffed blonde hair piled atop a short, plump woman in a body-hugging lime-green dress.

Sam cleared his throat to attract the woman's attention, and when she looked up she positively beamed. The extra weight she carried had smoothed out any wrinkles, and her face shone with good humour.

'Well, hello, there,' she gushed. 'Two handsome gentlemen on my doorstep. To what do I owe this pleasure?'

'We're looking for information,' Sam said. 'Old yearbooks.'

'That's my specialty. What years?'

'Eighty-three and eighty-four.'

The woman clapped her soft hands together

excitedly. 'Those are my years, too. I graduated in eighty-five.'

'Class of eighty-four,' Sam said.

The woman gasped and swept one hand up to cover her mouth. 'Wait a minute . . .' She stood up and stared into Sam's eyes. 'I thought you looked familiar. Don't tell me . . . Sam White. The actor. You played the Witch Boy in that play and wore those cute hairy chaps. All bare chest and tight buns. I remember you.'

Sam could feel himself unexpectedly blush. Twenty-five years in Hollywood and his name meant nothing; yet here in Portland, people still remembered a cocky wannabe who dared to reach for the stars.

'I was in drama, too,' Nancy continued. 'Well, for half a term. It took away from my dancing.' She wagged her finger at him and squealed. 'You were sooo cute.'

'Thanks,' Sam muttered.

'And who's your friend?'

'Parker,' said Zack. 'Class of 'eighty-three.'

'Hmmm,' Nancy pondered. 'Nope, don't remember you.'

Zack shrugged. 'I wasn't the memorable sort.'

'We're looking for someone,' Sam said, 'and thought we might spot him in the yearbooks.'

'Oh, sure. I have them all here somewhere.' Nancy turned to her stacks and began to run her finger down the gold and silver spines.

She pulled two yearbooks from the pile and

handed them to Sam. 'These are the years you're looking for. But they can't leave the library, OK?'

'We'll be careful.' Sam looked around to find an empty table. Most of them were unoccupied. Sam indicated one with his chin. 'We'll be just over there.'

'OK, but don't go looking up my picture,' she warned. 'I was just a little ol' plain Jane back then.' She grabbed her breasts with both hands. 'No va-va-voom!'

She laughed, her eyes bright with daring, and the two men smiled uncomfortably in return.

'If you need anything else, Witch Boy,' she continued, 'you know who to ask.'

Sam winked. 'We certainly do.'

Nancy blushed and returned to her computer.

65

They had only been looking through the books for a few minutes when Zack tapped a photo of three cheerleaders in uniform.

He pointed to the girl in the middle. 'Remember her?'

Sam looked at the photo and smiled. Susan Millar was a stunning beauty with an oval face framed by long, raven-black hair. Any softness of youth was disguised by dramatically sharp eyebrows atop piercingly dark eyes the colour of wet slate. Her two companions were bubbly blondes with generous curves and wide grins.

'Yeah, I knew Susan,' he said. 'We worked the stage together. She played the female lead opposite me in *Dark of the Moon*.' Sam stared hard at the photo, becoming lost in thought. 'We had a kissing scene in that play, and for a joke on opening night, the guys fed me a ton of garlic – garlic sausage, garlic dip, you name it. She didn't even bat an eye. She could have been kissing a snowman.'

He paused before adding, 'She warmed up to me unexpectedly though.'

Zack tensed. 'Grad night, right?'

'How do you know that?'

'I was there,' Zack said. 'Susan was my date.'

Sam rocked back in his seat. 'What? I thought you'd already graduated.'

'It was my sister's idea,' Zack explained. 'Susan wanted to stir things up and my sister hooked us up. I knew I was being used – a black college kid on the arm of a white cheerleader – but I found myself enjoying the jealous looks. Every guy wanted her, but for a short while, she was with me. The evening was going well until we arrived at the after party and she saw you.'

'Oh, Christ. You said we never met.'

Zack shrugged. 'It was a long time ago. It's not connected.'

'How do you know?'

'Because if anyone feels guilty about that night it's me.'

'You?'

'I was a prick. Susan disappeared with you, I got pissed and left her there without a ride or even an explanation. When the cops talked to me after—'

'The cops?' Sam asked.

Zack frowned. 'You didn't hear?'

'What?'

'Susan was raped at the party. It was a scandal at the time, but . . .' Zack sighed. 'If I hadn't left her alone . . .'

'I remember now,' Sam said. 'My parents mentioned it one time when I called, but I didn't realize it was the same night that we . . .' He paused. 'Who raped her?'

Zack looked away in embarrassment. 'I never followed the trial. I was in college and, truth be told, I was ashamed.'

Sam chewed the lining of his cheek. 'Is this the connection?'

'Susan and you?' Zack asked.

'And you.'

Zack shook his head. 'I was angry at you both for one night, Sam. Your tryst hurt my feelings and made me feel like a dope, but I got over it. Susan and I mended our fences a long time ago, too. She's doing OK. Last I heard she was married with two kids. Besides, the trial was a long time ago and we had no involvement in it. This stems from something else. Something *we* did.'

Twenty minutes later, Sam slammed the yearbook closed in frustration.

'I don't know what I'm looking for,' he said. 'It wasn't like we were in a gang with some weird initiation rite. I was in drama. Kids came and went, some got parts and some didn't. The lucky ones fell in love with it, but others hated every second.'

Zack closed his own book. 'What did Davey do?'

'Set lights and ran the board.'

'Ran the board?'

'The lighting board,' Sam explained. 'It's all computers now, but everything was manual then. Davey controlled the banks of dimmer switches used to light the stage. Change day to night, bring up a spot, that kind of stuff.'

'How many people would have worked with him on that?'

'Less than a half-dozen; sometimes just himself.'

'Why was he chosen as a target, then?' Zack asked. 'He doesn't consider himself one of the gods like Ironwood.'

'No, he was always behind the scenes,' Sam agreed. 'He never took the spotlight.'

'You were good friends?'

'We hung out together and had a lot of laughs.' He paused. 'I never stayed in touch.'

'This isn't about what happened after,' Zack reminded. 'During high school, you were close?'

A pang of guilt made Sam lower his gaze. 'Yeah, I guess we were close. He was my friend.'

'So,' Zack concluded, 'if you're the focus, a good way for someone to get close to you without looking like a groupie would be to first get close to Davey.'

Sam saw the reasoning. 'By joining Davey's lighting crew.'

Zack nodded. 'If we can get the printed programmes from your plays, will they list all the people who worked behind the scenes?'

'You bet. Signing everyone's programme was

always a highlight of the cast parties. We made sure everybody had their name in there no matter how small a role.'

Zack tilted his chin at the office in the corner. 'Time for you to turn the charm back on.'

Sam rolled his eyes. 'OK, but first I need you to do me a favour.'

66

Nancy spun in her chair, her eyes twinkling with mischief, as Sam leaned over the mini-towers of books that guarded her small office.

'I have another question for you,' Sam said.

'Anything,' Nancy breathed.

'Do you have copies of programmes from any of the school plays I was in?'

Nancy's face dropped. 'No, sorry. Those would have been nice to see, wouldn't they?' She tutted. 'Nobody thinks at the time that they'll want to look back and remember. People just don't realize how special the moment is.'

Sam didn't hide his disappointment.

'I'm sorry,' Nancy sighed. 'Maybe one of your classmates held on to them. They must have been very special.'

Sam turned to leave and collided with Zack, who was knocked off balance and sent crashing into a wall of books. A dozen stacks toppled to the floor, sending yearbooks everywhere. Nancy screamed in horror and dropped to all fours to guard several other teetering stacks.

'I'm very sorry,' Zack said. 'Let me help you.'

'Get out!' Nancy's face flushed a deep crimson. 'I'll fix it.'

'I was just—' Zack stopped as if his tongue was suddenly frozen to the roof of his mouth by Nancy's icy stare.

Sam grabbed hold of his elbow and steered him away.

Zack and Sam hurried out of the school and across the parking lot to the Mercedes with its mud-encrusted Oregon licence plates.

'That was cruel,' Zack said.

'True.' Sam pulled the 1984 yearbook out from under his T-shirt. 'But I promised this to a friend,' he grinned, 'a friend who kept everything.'

67

Sam directed Zack across the Burnside Bridge and into the empty lot where he had parked the night before. What remained of his Jeep lay in a blackened ruin. It had been stripped of its wheels, hood and front windshield before being torched.

Sam walked over to it and rested his hand on the dented rear fender. The blackened metal was still warm. His last possession gone.

Zack joined him. 'Is that—'

'Not even worth stealing.'

Sam turned his back on the smouldering heap and headed for the bridge.

Zack walked alongside. 'You'll want company down there. Your friend might not be as friendly after you set him on fire.'

Sam accepted the offer, and the two men walked to the bridge in silence.

At the top of the stairs, Sam stopped and looked across the river. The sky was beginning to turn a vibrant orange as the sun slid behind a thin cloud on its slow journey to the ocean.

'We used to come here as kids,' Sam said. 'Smoke pot, drink beer, cause trouble. The cops didn't care so long as we kept it on this side of the bridge.' He looked down into the darkness beneath the concrete and ironwork spans. 'I wonder if it's the same with them? So long as the tourists on the west shore aren't bothered, the cops leave them be.'

Zack shrugged. 'Probably. They have to live somewhere.'

'Segregation again? We go where we're comfortable, where we fit in.'

'Or ghettoization,' Zack retorted. 'We go to the only place the cops won't harass us.'

Sam accepted the opinion and looked over the water again. 'Did you know what you wanted to be? In high school, I mean.'

'Mostly,' Zack said. 'I knew I wanted to go into medicine, specifically surgery, but I was also fascinated by the new era of computers. In university, I studied both for a while. Specializing in cosmetic work came later. You?'

'It never crossed my mind that I could be anything other than an actor,' Sam said. 'I was so determined, so focused on that goal, I just assumed everyone felt the same way. The idea of not knowing where you belonged never entered my head.'

'You're talking about the kidnapper,' Zack said.

'Yeah, and about people like Davey. It's like

251

graduation takes them by surprise and suddenly their entire support network is gone. One day you're part of this cool club, and the next you're on your own. As soon as graduation was over, I was off to Hollywood to become a star. But what did Davey do? He's still here, smokin' dope, drinkin' beer and causing trouble.'

'And now we're back here, too.'

Sam raised one eyebrow as if to protest, but then let it drop and began descending the stairs.

At the bottom, he turned and walked under the bridge. The makeshift village looked deserted and the burning barrels were unlit. A few cold eyes peered from the darkness of the bridge's iron-works, fearful faces hidden beneath masks of soot.

Sam called out, 'I'm looking for Davey O. It's important.'

A pile of rags beside a large wooden spool rustled and shifted, then rose up to form a familiar shape. The hobbit strode forward, his western slicker dragging behind him. His beard was matted with egg yolk and tiny fragments of bright blue shell.

He strode to within a foot of Sam and placed his hands on his hips. 'Davey don't want to see you. You hurt him last time.'

'That was unavoidable,' Sam said. 'But I have something for him. Something I promised I would bring.'

The hobbit's eyes narrowed. 'He said you burned his book.'

'I want to make it up to him.'

The hobbit cleared his throat of phlegm and spat a thick glob on the ground. 'Why should he trust you again?'

'I made a promise,' said Sam.

The hobbit snorted. 'Promises are like shit round here. Plentiful supply, but it can't buy bread.'

'I have his book,' Sam explained. 'A new one. I want to give it to him.'

'I can deliver it.'

Sam shook off the suggestion. 'It needs to be me.'

The hobbit showed his teeth. They were the colour of wet coffee grounds. 'Cause you need somethin' else, right? Never nothin' for free round here. Not even on a promise.'

Sam bristled, but held his tongue, knowing the man was right. 'Can you get the message to him? I'll be back later tonight.'

The hobbit didn't nod or shake. 'If he wants to see you, he'll be here.'

68

At the motel, Sam held up his arm to stop Zack in his tracks. The door to their room was ajar.

Sam motioned for Zack to stand back before he crouched and nudged the door with his foot. The door creaked open, but nothing moved within.

Sam peered around the doorway. The room looked undisturbed.

He stood and entered. There was nowhere for anyone to hide, so he walked quickly to the bathroom and kicked open the door. Empty.

When he turned to give the all-clear, Zack was standing in front of the TV.

Scrawled across the screen in white grease pencil was a simple message:

Mall
Midnight

The cellphone rang as Sam leaned over the sink,

scraping the stubble off his face with a disposable razor.

He answered on the second ring.

'Have you thought about the money, Sam?'

The electronic voice sent a chill across Sam's skin, raising goose bumps despite the steamy warmth rising from the sink.

'Yes.' Sam thought of the message left on the TV. 'I'll be getting the last of it tonight.'

'Very good. I had faith in you even when you doubted yourself.'

'Can I talk to my family?'

'They are scared, Sam. They don't like the dark.'

Sam fought back his anger. 'I need to know they're alive?'

'Soon, I would think. Very soon. You are almost finished.'

'Please don't hurt them,' he pleaded.

'That's not up to me,' said the voice. 'Their fate is entirely in your hands.'

69

The watcher looked down upon the frightened woman huddled in the darkness with nothing but a moth-eaten blanket to keep her warm.

The army surplus cot had become fragile with mould, the bottom third of its canvas length already split with rot and preventing her from stretching out. At least she should be grateful that its steel frame kept her off the damp ground, which would leech every bit of heat from her shivering body.

He surmised that if he cared anything about her survival, his choice of prisons didn't reflect it. But he also knew the harshest environments produced the fastest results.

The woman didn't look so beautiful now. Some of the bruises on her face and arms had turned ugly colours and her hair was an unkempt mass. If she looked in a mirror, she would probably scream. But there were no mirrors here, just him. He would become her world; her saviour; her prince on a charging white stallion.

Fortunately, he still had his imagination and the secret photos that he stuck to the wall as a reminder that he never stopped watching. Once she was completely his, he could make her exactly the way he desired.

Her body and face were simple to repair; a little food to bring back the curves, a long bath to make her skin glisten, and, of course, time to heal. Her mind, on the other hand, was more delicate to control, but it was almost there.

He closed the cell door behind him and walked closer. Her eyes lifted to his and he greeted them warmly. Within those red-rimmed orbs he still saw the pulsating fear of the man who had ripped her from her comfortable world. But it was only a matter of time before that terror was replaced with utter devotion.

She was already willing to do most of the things he asked of her. All he needed was to make her *want* to do them.

The watcher stroked the woman's hair and cradled her head against his thigh. She started to cry again, but he made her stop with gentle shushing sounds and a tightening of the grip on her neck.

'Now tell me again,' he whispered soothingly, 'why you love me so.'

70

The dark-haired woman cooed to the sleeping child, rocking her gently upon her lap. She felt so weary. The pain in her ribs combined with the lack of food, water and light drained her energy with every movement. Time was immeasurable in the dark, the passing of days or hours no longer relevant to their existence.

When MaryAnn awakened, the woman planned to teach her how to stretch her muscles and control her breathing, using yoga to keep up her strength without too much exertion.

She found she no longer cared about herself. Death wasn't something she feared. If she had been alone, she may have found a way to end it, but now she needed to keep the child strong.

A flame of anger still burned within her and whispered fiercely that an escape would present itself, a small crack, a mistake. The child would have to be able to run. She could tackle the man again, surprise him, hurt him – she had proven that – and hold him back for at least a short time.

The woman talked to herself, repeating the plan inside her head, a silent monologue of affirmations.

With every fibre of her being she swore she would allow no one to harm the child.

71

Sam stopped the Mercedes in the empty parking lot at the rear of the mall and retrieved his gun from the glovebox. He took his time reloading the ammunition and making sure the chamber under the hammer was empty. Once satisfied, he slipped it into the pocket of his vest and waited.

At midnight, a sleek black Cadillac Escalade SUV with tinted windows cruised by his window and stopped a short distance away. Sam climbed out and crossed the gap as the SUV's rear passenger window rolled down in whisper silence.

Vadik's wide face peered out from the inner darkness. Another figure sat beside him, but he sat deeper in the shadows, face turned away.

'You got my message?'

'Hard to miss.' Sam focused on his breathing as he struggled to keep the nervousness out of his voice.

'You up for this?' Vadik asked.

Sam nodded, his eyes hard, stance solid, showing confidence.

'Just like the movies, huh?' Vadik's smile narrowed. 'Only in this case, we want all cameras off.'

'It won't be a problem.'

'Good.' Vadik glanced down at his watch. 'My crew will be here in twenty minutes. Make sure the cargo doors are open and they have full access to every store.'

'What about my money?'

Vadik grinned and Sam saw a brief flash of white teeth from the stranger beside him.

'A man after my own heart.'

With a nod from Vadik, the driver's door opened and the hulking guard stepped out with a briefcase. He walked around the large vehicle and handed it to Sam. A short steel chain dangled from the black handle, ending in a single handcuff.

Sam accepted the case, noticing its heft. Paper isn't heavy, but a quarter million dollars' worth has real weight. The guard handed him two small silver keys on a single metal loop and returned to the vehicle.

'Once my men are inside and we're sure you've done your job, you're free to go,' Vadik said. 'Any questions?'

Sam shook his head, steeling himself for the job ahead.

Vadik stared at him a moment longer, the

silence uneasy. Sam could feel himself being measured, judged. He didn't flinch.

Vadik flicked his eyes to the side and the stranger gave a short nod. The window slid back into place, its dark tint obscuring the interior.

The SUV drove away as Sam approached the mall.

72

Sam rapped on the large metal doors at the rear of the mall, knowing that if Ken had stuck to his regular patrol schedule he would be in the immediate area.

He waited a few minutes and rapped again.

'Who's there?' asked a small voice from behind the door.

'Ken, it's Sam. Open up.'

There was a rattling of keys before the door opened a crack and Ken peered out.

'Hi, Sam,' he said guardedly. 'I thought you were taking a few days off.'

Sam beamed him a friendly smile. 'I am, Ken.' He held up the briefcase. 'Just need to pick up a few things.'

'At this time?'

Sam chuckled. 'Well, I wanted to see you, too, didn't I?'

Ken grinned and opened the door wider to let

him enter. 'It's not as good, patrolling without you, Sam.'

'Who did they partner you with?'

Ken rolled his eyes. 'Harry. He volunteered to do a double, but I haven't seen him all shift.'

'He in the locker room?'

Ken nodded. 'I had to switch off the radio. He started to bloody sing.'

Sam laughed and clapped a hand on Ken's shoulder. 'Let's go find him and make sure he's still conscious.'

Sam's smile faded as he led the way down the dark corridor.

When Sam opened the locker-room door, Harry was slumped on the floor, his chin on his chest, snoring loudly. An empty bottle of bourbon rested beside his hand. The sleeping giant wore only a white undershirt, blue boxers and an unusual pair of elastic garters. His uniform pants, dress shirt, holster and jacket were draped over the wooden bench.

Ken peered over Sam's shoulder. 'Th-th-that's not allowed,' he stammered. 'He could be fired.'

Sam bent to the bench and retrieved Harry's holster and his ring of keys. Then, with a heavy sigh, he turned to his partner. 'I'll need your gun and keys, too, Ken.'

'W-what? Why?'

'It's too difficult to explain. Just hand them over.'

Ken stiffened and pulled back his shoulders. 'I

won't. You taught me never to turn over my gun.'

'I also taught you not to do anything foolish. Now trust me and hand them over.'

Ken's eyes flicked left and right and his lower lip trembled. 'I can't, Sam. It's my job to—'

Sam casually pulled his gun out of his pocket and placed it against Ken's forehead. The young guard flinched as steel kissed flesh.

'I'm sorry, Ken, but I need to do this.'

'G-geez, Sam,' Ken stuttered. 'We . . . we're friends.'

'That's why I'm asking nicely, Ken. I want to make sure you survive this.'

Ken gulped. 'Survive?'

'I need you to stay here with Harry and not move or try to raise the alarm until the morning shift arrives. Do you understand?'

Ken shook his head.

'Yes, you do, Ken. Just relax and take a few deep breaths. Find something to read or have a snooze. It may not look like it right now, but I am being your friend.'

Ken sniffled. 'I trusted you, Sam.'

'Keep trusting and you'll walk out of here alive.'

Ken's shoulders slumped as he unbuckled his holster and handed it over along with his ring of keys and magnetic security card.

'They'll fire me for this.'

'That might not be a bad thing,' Sam said. 'It'll give you a chance to find something you love.'

'That doesn't always work out though, does it?' Ken muttered meaningfully.

Sam didn't hear him as he exited the room and locked the door.

73

Sam quickly made his way up the rear stairs to the second-floor security booth. During the day shift, three guards patrolled the bustling mall on foot and a rotating fourth guard monitored the close-circuit TVs from the booth. At night, with all the stores closed, it stood empty.

Sam opened the booth with Ken's keys and quickly shut down all external and internal cameras and alarms. It took five minutes to make sure he had covered everything before he left the booth and headed back downstairs.

When he swung open the doors to the loading dock, two semi-trailers had already backed into place with their rear doors open. A muscular black man approached.

'You Sam?' His voice was like gravel falling onto tin.

Sam nodded.

'We tha' first crew,' he said. 'You got keys?'

Sam held up an electronic pass card. 'This

will open every store. It's a master security card.'

The man plucked it out of Sam's hand. 'Tha's cool. Everyt'ing else set?'

'All cameras are off, the alarms have been disabled and the guards dealt with. You've got six hours before the day shift arrives.'

The man grinned. 'Plenty o' time. Anyt'ing you want as souvenir, help you'self. Nice TV, maybe? Decent suit?'

Sam patted his briefcase. 'I got what I came for.'

The man turned to the trucks and waved his arm. Ten behemoths in muscle shirts and loose pants walked from the shadows and vanished into the mall.

74

Sam entered the motel room quietly. Zack had fallen asleep on top of the covers, arms folded on his stomach. He was still dressed, his breathing so shallow that his chest barely moved, and in sleep he looked as fragile as a sparrow.

Sam moved to wake him, but Zack's eyes were already opening. He stared at Sam and blinked as if not recognizing him.

'Every time I close my eyes,' he said, his voice eerily distant, 'I see Jasmine and Kalli.'

Sam didn't know what to say.

Zack rubbed his face with the palms of his hands as he sat up and swung his feet to the floor. He cleared his throat. 'How did it go at the mall?'

Sam held up the briefcase. 'I got the money. They got the mall.'

'And your partner?'

'Ken should be fine if he does what I told him.'

'That's good. See. You're still a good man.' He

patted Sam's arm and stood up. 'Where we off to?'

'Back to the bridge. Davey should be waiting.'

In the motel parking lot, Zack popped the trunk to the Mercedes. Inside were two large red duffel bags.

'Have a look if you want,' Zack said.

Sam unzipped one of the bags and stared down at close to half a million dollars in US currency.

'It doesn't seem real,' he said. 'It's too perfect.'

Zack nodded. 'I'm used to having bills stuffed in my pockets, or a few crisp ones in my wallet, but when I see them like this, fresh from the printer, I realize it's just paper and ink.' He paused. 'All this pain for something so ... worthless.'

Sam closed the first duffel and unzipped the second, which had more room. He unlocked the briefcase and added its stacks of bills to the duffel. He didn't see the point in counting it. If Vadik had shorted him, what could he do?

75

The underbelly of Burnside Bridge was noisier than usual when Zack and Sam approached. Groups of people were huddled in large, protective circles: others wandered aimlessly from burning barrel to burning barrel.

Sam was disturbed to see several people wailing and babbling nonsensically as they pounded fists into the dirt until their hands were raw. A baby's cry cut through the din like a siren. It was joined by the frantic humming of a lullaby on speed.

The gatekeeper approached, his face tense.

'What's going on?' Sam asked.

'Jus' a bit busy,' the hobbit growled. 'Cops busted a few west-side camps tonight, so we have overflow. Regulars return to find their spot taken an' it don't go over well.'

'Is Davey here?'

Just as the hobbit nodded, a fight erupted behind him. Two snarling men, all teeth and claws, tore at each other's clothes and skin. Sam stepped back, stunned by their volcanic rage. One of the men fell onto his back and the other pounced. His fingers were curled into hooks. He landed on the fallen man's chest, digging fingers into his hair and slamming his head against the ground until he stopped moving.

The victor spat into the unconscious man's face and retreated to a corner where the tattered remains of a blue sleeping bag lay. No one else challenged him as he curled up on the bag and closed his eyes.

Sam glanced at Zack. His shoulders were stiff, but there was no sign of fear. Sam remembered how he had felt when he was sure his family was dead, how he was so certain there was nothing in this world that could scare him because he had nothing left to lose. Kalli's death had sent Zack to that place, and Sam sensed he could be even more dangerous than the desperate people around them.

The hobbit shrugged as he turned away from the unconscious man.

'It's the same out there.' He pointed indiscriminately across the river. 'Only in that world, you don't see it coming.'

Davey stood by the burning barrel, his upper body trembling as he muttered to himself. When Sam stepped into the circle of light, Davey glanced up and then quickly away.

'Did he send you back?' Davey asked.

'Who?'

'The one who wanted me to burn?'

Sam shook his head. 'He thinks you're dead. You're safe.'

'Never safe. Never.' Davey's eyes suddenly went wide with fear. 'Was it the father?'

'The father?'

Davey nodded rapidly. 'The father of the boy. He cried all the time. I could hear him behind me. Crying. They asked him to leave once, but he came back. I could feel his eyes on me, burning into me. I still have the marks.'

Davey spun around and lifted his hair to show Sam his neck. Apart from a layer of dirt, it was unscarred.

'He wants me to burn,' Davey continued, 'burn in hell.'

'I don't know who wanted to hurt you, Davey,' Sam said. 'That's why I need your help.'

Davey shook his head vigorously and spittle flew from his mouth. 'You're a liar! You were a god, but now you're a goddamn liar.'

'I was never a god, Davey,' Sam snapped. 'I was a punk kid with a big ego that hadn't been crushed to fucking pulp yet. High school is a launch pad for dreamers, but in the real world, most of us crash and burn before we get off the ground. That's not worth worshipping.'

Sam bit back his anger and reached under his vest to produce the yearbook. He held it out, the silver and gold foil letters catching the firelight.

Davey licked his lips nervously before striding

forward and grabbing the book. He retreated to his place beside the blazing barrel and carefully turned the pages. His fingers caressed the photos inside.

'My signatures are gone,' Davey said.

'Sorry, do you have others?'

'Yeah. Lots.'

Sam stepped closer. 'Are the other signatures on programmes, Davey?'

'Sure.' Davey's voice lifted. 'You remember those cast parties? Man, did they get wild. Everybody singing *Rocky Horror Picture Show* and doing the Worm at the end of "Time Warp"? I felt up my first boob at one of those. Had a boner for a week.'

Sam's own memories flickered through his brain: a legion of long-forgotten faces.

Zack stepped into the circle of light. 'Do you still have them? The programmes.'

Davey's smile faded. 'Who's this?'

'A friend,' Sam said. 'He's helping me find my family.'

'Your family?'

'The man who wanted to burn you has kidnapped them. We think he's someone we knew.'

'From school?'

'Someone in your lighting crew, maybe,' Zack interjected.

Davey narrowed his eyes.

'We just need to see the programmes, Davey?'

Sam pressed. 'Can you help us?'

'Not tonight,' Davey said. 'I put them in a safe place after . . .' He flicked his eyes at Sam.

'Could we go there?' Zack asked. 'To your safe place.'

Davey shook his head. 'Nobody goes there, man. Nobody but me. It's protected.'

'We can wait here for you,' Sam said. 'It's important.'

Davey shook his head again. 'Come back tomorrow. I'll have them then.' He returned to his yearbook.

Sam sighed and held up his hands in surrender. 'OK, Davey, we'll do that, but don't let me down.'

'I never did, Sam,' Davey said quietly. 'I never ever did.'

76

Detective Preston looked around the ransacked mall, tipped back his hat with the rim of a paper coffee cup, and whistled.

'They hit every store.' Hogan stretched out his arms and walked to the middle of the deserted concourse. 'Every single one.'

'It must have taken some crew to pull it off.'

'An organized crew *and* one familiar security guard.'

'Not the actor?'

Hogan nodded. 'We have an eye witness. White locked the night guards in a room, disabled the alarms and cameras, and let the crew inside.'

'That crazy son of a bitch,' Preston muttered. 'Did he hurt the guards?'

'Nope. In fact, he made sure they were tucked out of harm's way. Our witness is White's regular partner. He said White was very calm about it, very reassuring that everything would be OK if he just stayed quiet.'

Preston scratched his nose. 'This guy doesn't make sense. He's starting to piss me off. How do you kill one guy for a bleepin' cellphone, but then be all Mr Friendly when you're robbing an entire mall? How many stores are in here? Eighty? A hundred? The haul's worth millions.'

'If you know how to fence it,' Hogan interjected. 'And how would a security guard know that? I talked to robbery and they're saying this stuff was probably loaded directly on to a ship to Russia. There's a good market for American goods over there.'

'And the only face we have—'

'Is Mr White.'

Preston narrowed his eyes. 'So what are you thinking, partner?'

'Maybe there really is something to his story about his family being kidnapped.'

'And somebody is making him do this crazy shit?'

'It makes more sense than the alternative,' Hogan said. 'I can't buy that White woke up one morning and decided to go on a random killing spree, and then become a criminal mastermind.'

Preston sighed. 'Yeah, actors aren't that clever.'

Hogan grinned. 'Exactly. And if he wanted to get away with it, he wouldn't be leaving all these witnesses.'

'Which means whoever is really behind it—'

'Can't leave White alive,' Hogan finished.

77

Sam sat on the bed, eyes dry and sore, while Zack kept watch out of the window on the one thing he had failed to deliver to the kidnapper: $1,000,000.

They had both stripped to their boxers in contemplation of sleep, but it hadn't come. Zack had paced the room before taking up his station at the window, while Sam continued to replay his conversation with Davey, wondering if he should have pushed harder for the programmes.

Their only lead rested in Davey's hands and every minute till daybreak seemed like an eternity.

Sam glanced over at Zack. He looked like a burned scarecrow, his boxers barely clinging to narrow, bony hips. For the first time, Sam noticed several misshapen patches of skin around his lower back. They were smooth like burn scars but ghostly white against his black skin, as though he had tried to wash himself in bleach.

Zack released a heavy sigh and turned to stretch

his limbs. His back cracked audibly as he reached for the ceiling before bending at the waist to touch his toes. His movements exposed more splashes of white skin across his stomach and running down his legs.

'It's a condition called vitiligo,' Zack explained. 'It destroys the pigment of the skin.'

'Sorry,' Sam said quickly. 'I didn't mean to stare.'

Zack stroked his stomach. 'I used to fret over it: applying body make-up every day and praying that it wouldn't spread to a more visible area.' He sighed again. 'In India they call it white leprosy – charming, huh?' Zack paused for effect. 'Don't worry, it's not catching. Besides, you're so damn pale, you wouldn't know you had it.'

Sam attempted a smile, but it fell flat. His mind was preoccupied with other, more troubling, thoughts.

'I stopped using the make-up,' Zack continued softly. 'Jasmine always told me it wasn't important, that skin was skin. It took this . . .' his voice broke '. . . this fucking tragedy to make me see how right she was.'

An uncomfortable silence filled the room before Sam changed the subject. 'Do you trust Davey?'

Zack wiped at his eyes. 'I don't know him well enough. Why?'

'I've been sitting here thinking that he has no good reason to trust me any more. He has his year-book back, so why let me near his programmes?'

'You're right. If something was that precious to me and you set it alight, I wouldn't let you near it again.'

Sam leapt to his feet. 'Get dressed. We have to find him before he disappears.'

78

In the car, Detective Preston finished his coffee and crushed the paper cup in his hand before dropping it at his feet.

Hogan made a disapproving clucking noise with his tongue.

Preston ignored him. 'Did you hear anything back on that camera we recovered?'

'Not much,' Hogan said. 'Like I suspected, there wasn't a hard drive inside to store images. It was just a drone sending its data to either a relay station or a nearby computer. Some of the components were unusual, though, so our guys are searching to see where it was manufactured. They tell me it's definitely not American.'

'Is anything electronic made in America these days?' Preston asked.

Hogan shrugged. 'I doubt it. I hear those darn Texans hate anything small, and it's tough to be competitive when your MP3 players are the size of toasters.'

'We don't have the hands for it.' Preston held up a pair of massive hands, each finger the size of a plump ballpark frank.

Before Hogan could make a quip, the radio squawked. 'Hey, cowboy. Got a message for you.'

Preston snapped up the handset. 'Let me guess, darlin'. You've made buttermilk pancakes for breakfast and you need to know if I'm on my way.'

Darlene's cackle scared the static off the airwaves. 'You wish, cowboy. No, I've got a big, strong, pretty-as-chocolate-silk-pie officer here who has info on your BOLO.'

'Jeep?' Hogan asked.

'On the Jeep, Darlene?' Preston asked into the handset.

'Uh-uh. Mercedes. He talked to the driver.'

Hogan pressed his foot on the accelerator and made a sharp left-hand turn.

'Keep him there, darlin'. We're comin' in for a chat.'

79

When Zack and Sam arrived under the Burnside Bridge, the place looked deserted except for two skinny dogs fighting over a yellow bone. The bone didn't look worth the fight, but maybe, Sam thought, he had just never been that desperate.

In the light of day, the village was nothing more than a dirt path littered with empty cardboard boxes and discarded scraps of wood. A damp wind fuelled by dark clouds blew across the river.

Sam peered into the ironworks, scanning for any stragglers.

'Over there.' Zack pointed to a lump on the ground near a smouldering trash barrel.

Sam turned to see the wind had lifted the edge of a black trash bag to expose a pair of brown leather shoes. The legs sticking out of the shoes were wrapped in newspaper socks beneath a pair of baggy, mud-coloured suit pants.

Sam approached and lightly kicked the sole of one shoe. 'Hey! You awake?'

An indecipherable grumble was the reply.

Sam kicked the shoe again, and then sprang backwards as the owner spun with unexpected speed, his hand clutching a broken bottle. The ragged edge of glass missed Sam's legs by less than an inch.

Sam backed away. 'We don't want any trouble. We just need to know where everybody went.'

The man rose to his feet, his face forming a fierce scowl. His visage was made even more menacing by a ragged scar that ran from forehead to chin, crossing one eye. The empty socket locked on to Sam's face, daring him to look away.

'What time?' The man's voice was the snap of a rabid dog.

'Just gone eight,' Sam said.

'Breakfast.'

The man began to walk away, dropping the broken bottle as he went. He didn't seem to care that it shattered on the same ground where he might find himself sleeping that night.

Sam called after him, 'Where's breakfast?'

The man reached the stairs that led to the bridge deck. He turned slowly, spat on the ground and jabbed his thumb at the river. 'Westside,' he growled.

Sam looked over at Zack. 'You get the car. I'll follow Grumpy on foot.'

*   *   *

Sam followed Grumpy across the bridge. Pedestrians and cyclists gave the homeless man a wide berth as he snarled at every passer-by.

On the west side of the river, he continued up Burnside Street until he came to Third Avenue, and then turned north. Sam glanced behind him, saw the Mercedes crossing the bridge a block behind, and waved to get Zack's attention before continuing on to Third.

The border between Chinatown and Old Town was packed with over a hundred homeless waiting in line for a free pancake breakfast on one side of the street and a sack lunch prepared by the Union Gospel Mission on the other.

As he waited for Zack, Sam watched Grumpy growl his way to the front of the line and get served a plate of pancakes.

When Zack pulled up, Sam slid into the passenger seat.

'You spot him?' Zack asked.

Sam shook his head. 'He's not in the line-up for pancakes, but there's a huge crowd filtering through the Mission. Let's wait.'

It only took ten minutes before Davey appeared at the Mission door. The prized yearbook was under his arm and he was so busy digging through the contents of his brown-bag lunch he didn't look at the street.

Zack glanced at Sam. 'Now what?'

'He doesn't have his backpack,' Sam noted. 'He wouldn't leave it alone for long.' He glanced around at the jostling mob. 'We'll follow in the car until we can park. Then continue on foot.'

Zack drove slowly out of the congestion of desperate, unwashed bodies.

80

Davey led them further north before cutting back towards the river. This forced Sam and Zack to leave the car on the edge of Chinatown. Davey turned north again as he passed Steel Bridge and headed for Broadway.

Zack wrapped his suit jacket around himself to cut the chilly, morning breeze. 'He seems to be enjoying himself.'

'I guess for him this is a good day,' Sam said. 'He's got food in his belly, his yearbook back and it's not rain—' Sam stopped as the first drops of rain began to fall.

'It's just a sprinkle,' Zack said hopefully.

The clouds thundered and split open at Zack's words and large droplets began to fall.

Sam picked up the pace. 'We can't lose him. Come on.'

Davey sloshed through the rain at a half jog, oblivious to the company on his tail. Just before Broadway Bridge, he turned west across the park and headed in the direction of the rail yard. Zack and Sam kept close behind, the rain masking their footsteps.

Just before Davey reached an imposing concrete wall that marked the rear boundary of the Amtrak yards, Sam pulled Zack behind a small hillock and crouched down.

'What are you doing?' Zack's teeth began to chatter.

'It's fenced on either side,' Sam pointed out. 'There's nowhere to go.'

Davey stopped at the wall, bent over to catch his breath, and looked around. Sam kept perfectly still, letting the rain dissolve his silhouette.

After a moment, Davey moved to the edge of the wall and pushed against the wire fence. The fence folded under his touch, revealing a slim gap.

Davey checked behind him once more, and then slipped through.

'Let's go.' Sam darted across the last few yards of open ground.

81

Detective Preston stood with his back to the room and watched the sudden downpour. From the thirteenth floor of the Justice Center, 2,314 miles from the wide-open spaces where he grew up, the city before him was drained of all colour.

Behind him, Officer Colin Portsmith nervously drew condensation circles on the Formica table-top with his paper coffee cup.

'You saw the Merc yesterday morning?' Preston repeated slowly.

'Yes, sir.'

'And didn't report it?'

'I . . . I didn't realize at the time it could be the same vehicle you were looking for. The BOLO didn't list a licence plate and there are a ton of Mercs out there. But my partner read the reissued alert this morning and remembered the damage on the car. She thought . . . you know, that maybe . . . I, um—'

'You talked to the driver?' Hogan interrupted.

He sat in a chair directly across from the young officer.

Colin nodded sheepishly. 'He looked like a businessman who'd received some bad news and went on a bender. I thought he was harmless and could use a break. I want to make it clear that my partner didn't agree with my call.'

Preston laughed aloud and turned from the window. He looked down at the officer fondly, appreciating his loyalty. The good-looking ones were usually the worst, he had found. They were so used to receiving special treatment that they lacked an essential core of humility. This one's parents had raised him right.

'You don't need to cover your partner's ass, kid. The description we had was so generic we knew it was a long shot.'

Hogan nodded in agreement. 'It might've made our job easier if you had taken a few notes, but how were you to know? Just tell us what you can.'

The officer let out a deep sigh of relief and began to describe the dishevelled black man who had vanished over breakfast.

82

After squeezing through the gap in the fence, Zack and Sam found themselves at the mouth of a musty, concrete maintenance tunnel. A second chain-link fence topped with barbed wire separated it from a complicated grid of interlocking train tracks and, in the distance, Union Station.

The entrance to the tunnel was barred by an iron gate, but the lock was broken and the gate wedged open just enough to allow an adult to get through.

Despite wishing he had brought his flashlight, Sam plunged ahead with Zack following behind.

Inside the tunnel, Sam focused on the far end, seeing the shadowy outline of another iron gate. There was no silhouette of Davey blocking the way.

'There must be a side tunnel,' Sam whispered. 'Keep your eyes peeled. We don't want to spook him.'

Sam moved forward quickly, his arms out-stretched to skim either side for an opening.

Halfway along, his left foot brushed over the edge of a pit, finding nothing but air. Instinctively, Sam slammed his hands against the tunnel walls to stop his fall, but the stone was too slick with mould.

With a yelp, he fell into the darkness. His feet hit solid ground almost instantly.

'You OK?' Zack whispered.

'Yeah.' Sam stood in a chest-high hole. 'Watch your step.'

Sam crouched down to peer along another dark tunnel. This one smelled older. Up ahead, he heard a gentle humming and saw the glow of a Coleman lamp. In front of the lamp, blocking most of its light, was a human silhouette.

Sam moved forward cautiously until he was just a short distance outside the circle of light. But then his foot caught the edge of an empty soup can, making tiny pebbles inside rattle loudly.

Davey spun and snapped up a homemade knife that was stuck in the ground at his feet. His eyes caught the light. They were wide and afraid.

'Davey, it's Sam!'

Davey bared his teeth and a growl escaped his throat.

'I just want to talk.' Sam moved forward into the light and held up his hands to show he was unarmed.

Davey's lips slipped back over his teeth as

recognition dawned, and his body began to relax.

'Scared the shit out of me,' he complained.

Sam looked at the knife – a lethal shard of scrap metal, honed to a point and wrapped in black electrical tape. 'You took a few years off me, too.'

Davey slipped the knife into his pocket. 'What you doing down here?'

Zack arrived and peered over Sam's shoulder.

'We really need to look at some of your old programmes,' Sam said. 'We won't take them, I promise. We just need to find a name.'

Davey shuffled to one side, allowing the lantern to reveal more of the tunnel. An impressive stone archway was suddenly bathed in light above them. It bore the same strange markings that had adorned Vadik's lair.

Zack gasped. 'This must be another arm of the Shanghai Tunnels. I told you they went everywhere.'

Sitting in a circle, with Zack attempting to draw warmth from the lantern, the three men looked through Davey's prized programmes: *Arsenic and Old Lace*, *The Mouse That Roared*, *Inherit the Wind*, the yearly variety shows and others.

The signatures and witty comments – *See you and Sam in Hollywood. You can take my lunch order. Davey, you* Light *up my life* – from cast and crew made Sam smile as he remembered a simpler time when he had no doubts he was destined for stardom.

In the programme for *Dark of the Moon*, they found the name they had been searching for.

83

Detectives Hogan and Preston stood around a white table, its surface littered with dozens of plastic bags and trays that contained melted, scorched, blackened and twisted objects.

Preston crossed his arms, his face showing boredom, as Rico 'Fire Bug' Fernandez spoke rapidly in English and the occasional spurt of Spanish to confirm everything that was already in his preliminary report.

When Preston finally sighed with irritation and pointed at his wristwatch, Rico produced a tiny metal object, not much larger than a gentleman's cufflink, attached to a hunk of melted plastic. His eyes glistened with delight.

'Clever, huh?' He made his eyebrows dance.

'What is it?' Preston asked.

'This little beauty make house go boom.'

'It's a bomb?'

'Nah. A bomb? Come on. Look at it. It's a punch.'

Hogan placed a hand on his partner's arm to stop an explosive reaction. 'Explain.'

Rico grinned. 'This attached to gas line inside house. Using wireless transmitter, your arsonist hits button and this punches small hole in line.'

'That's it?'

'*Si.* Once gas begins to leak, all you need is a flame source and boom.'

'Any idea on manufacturer?'

He squeezed the hunk of melted plastic. 'This puppy is handmade, but steel punch is special machined part, very precise, but still not perfect. I'd say Eastern Europe. Perhaps Russian or Czech.'

Hogan squinted in thought. 'What kind of distance are we looking at to set it off?'

Rico shrugged. 'Receiver melted to shit, but from size I would say he had to be close. No more than quarter mile.'

Hogan glanced at his partner. 'The actor's alibi still holds. The mall's twenty, twenty-five miles away.'

'Yeah,' Preston agreed. 'But the Bug here is just guessing.'

'Hey!' Rico protested. 'I don't guess, I calculate.'

'Yeah?' Preston stepped close until he loomed over the shorter man. 'Can you calculate what I'm thinking right now?'

Rico grinned wide. 'I'm sorry, Detective, but I only like you as a friend.'

Switch

*   *   *

Hogan's cellphone rang as the two detectives rode the elevator down to the basement parking lot.

'Ah, Detective Hogan,' said a familiar voice. 'Chief Medical Examiner Randy Hogg, here. I have an ID on the young victim involved in that house explosion.'

'Who is it?'

'Well, I had the idea to post her information on the nationwide bulletin board, and there was a recent case of a black woman and child missing in San Diego that seemed similar in age.'

'San Diego?'

'Yes, I know, not what we were expecting. But I asked for the dental records and they're a perfect match.'

'So who is she?'

'Kalli Kayesha Parker. She was fourteen. There are several warrants out on her father, Dr Zack Parker, for gross bodily assault and attempted rape of a patient. He's a plastic surgeon and by all accounts a very good one.'

'Christ.' The elevator doors opened and Hogan stepped out. 'How did the body end up in White's house?'

'I can't help you there, Detective.'

'What about the other body?'

'Inconclusive, I'm afraid. Her jaw was shattered in the explosion, but my assistant is working on its reassembly. It is time-consuming work as I'm sure—'

'Yeah, thanks, Doc,' Hogan interrupted. 'Keep me informed.'

He hung up and turned to his partner. 'You drive. Head for that liquor store on Tenth.'

Preston smirked. 'You need a drink already? I'm the one doing all the work.'

Hogan scowled, his brow knit in concentration. 'I need to see a Viking about a doctor.'

84

The guard entered the cell with a plastic tray in his hands. The woman and child followed him with their eyes, not daring to make any sudden moves.

The woman had learned that he reacted with explosive fury to any physical challenge. A swollen eye and deep aches in her cheek, jaw and ribs were a painful reminder of his violence.

'Have you brought us food?' Her words were slightly slurred as she tried to limit the movement of her mouth against the pain of her last assault.

The guard ignored her.

'We could really use extra water,' she continued. 'You only brought one bottle last time and both MaryAnn and myself are very thirsty.'

The guard placed the tray on the ground near the door. He didn't make eye contact.

'Do you have children?' she asked.

The guard began to back out of the room as the woman swung her legs off the side of the bed. Her fleece shorts rode up her toned thighs. In the dim light, they still looked good, despite cuts and bruises, smears of dirt and days without shaving.

He stopped and his tongue darted across his lips.

'Why do you need us both?' she asked softly. 'You could let MaryAnn go. I'll stay here and won't cause any trouble, if you just let her go. It could be . . . more intimate . . . with just the two of us.'

A soft whine of protest rose from MaryAnn's throat. The woman clutched her hand on top of the blanket and squeezed tight.

The guard shook his head and left the room.

At the sound of the heavy bolt hitting home, the woman dropped her face into her hands while MaryAnn leapt off the bed to investigate the contents of the tray.

It carried barely enough to satisfy either one of them.

85

'Who the hell is Alan Robertson?' Sam asked as
Zack pointed at the only name in the programme
he recognized.

'He was part of the computer club,' Zack said.
'The brains behind it, really. Alan could think in
code.'

Sam turned to Davey. 'You remember him?'

'Yeah, yeah.' Davey scratched his head
excitedly, flakes of dandruff twinkling in the light.
'He didn't show up till Grade Twelve.'

'That was after I graduated,' Zack interjected.
'Alan and a couple others in the club were
younger than me. He never mentioned an interest
in drama.'

Davey flashed Zack an annoyed look.

'He was nice and all,' Davey continued, taking
back centre stage. 'A little too . . . uptight, maybe,
for the stage. He was all precise, measuring angles
and shit. I preferred to just point the damn things
where they looked good. I remember he recruited

a couple of geeks to help out when we wanted to position a mini-spot. Remember that scene, Sam, where you held up the ring as Barbara Allen dies?'

Sam nodded. 'You made it glow purple.'

'Right, right,' Davey gushed. 'The geeks helped me plot the positioning of that. It was tricky, but damn did it look cool, especially when we added the dry-ice fog.'

'Any idea where Alan is now?'

'I do,' Zack said. 'He owns a small software company here in Portland.'

'Could he be the kidnapper?'

Zack shrugged. 'He has a connection to both of us, plus he knew Davey. All the nerds were picked on by Ironman, so Alan would have hated him. He's obviously a genius, which may make him a bit odd, but I never saw him as mentally unstable or possessing any kind of grudge.'

Sam reached into the pocket of his vest to feel the cold metal of his gun. He looked at Davey.

'What's your take?'

'Fuck, man, I see people change every day. One minute they're watching your back, and the next they want to slit your throat for half a J or a decent pair of socks.'

Sam clenched his jaw. 'I'm tired of being led by the nose. If this is our best lead, let's pay the prick a visit.'

'Is that wise?' Zack asked. 'Maybe we should—'

'He'll talk to us,' Sam snapped. 'I'll make fucking sure of it.'

86

'Parker?' Walt Toler leaned on the store counter, his walrus-thick moustache twitching under a bulbous nose.

'Zack Parker,' Hogan said.

Preston picked up a clear bottle of pear brandy, a whole yellow pear floating inside the sweet liquor. 'How do they do that?'

Hogan glared at him.

'They grow the pears inside the bottle, and then add the liquor,' Walt explained.

'No shit.'

Hogan cleared his throat noisily. 'Parker?' he said again.

Walt snapped his fingers. 'Piggy Parker, Piggy Parker.' He grinned at the memory flash. 'A skinny black kid. King of the nerds. Ironman used to tease the snot out of him.'

'This was in high school?' Hogan clarified.

'Fuck, yeah.' Walt grinned. 'We roamed the hallways like fuckin' kings back then. Ironman used to love catching ol' Piggy Parker and his pals between classes.' He laughed aloud. 'We used to make their lives hell.'

'Parker became a surgeon,' Hogan said coldly.

Walt shrugged. 'Good for him.'

Preston placed the bottle of pear brandy on the counter. 'Did Parker know Sam White?'

'Might've knew *of* him, but they wouldn't hang together or nothin'. Nerds and freaks, man. Not much in common.' Walt rung in the brandy, took 20 per cent off, and plucked two twenties out of the three Preston held in his hand.

'It's a present for the wife,' Preston told Hogan as they exited the store. 'She'll get a kick out of the pear.'

87

At the mouth of the concrete tunnel, Zack caught up with Sam. The rain was hammering down in a noisy torrent, drowning the city in a wash of depressing grey.

Zack grabbed hold of his arm. 'We need a plan.'

'I have one.' Sam pulled free of Zack's grip before stepping out of the tunnel and squeezing through the gap in the fence to the park beyond.

Zack followed, the unforgiving rain striking his chilled skin like blunt needles.

'We can't just walk in there,' he said.

'Why not? We're old friends from high school.'

'But we don't know for sure it's him,' Zack protested.

Sam stopped and spun around, every muscle tensed, every bone rigid. Before Zack could react, Sam grabbed him by the lapels and pulled him so close their noses practically touched.

'I'm not playing games any more, Zack,' he hissed through clenched teeth. 'He's the only name connected to both of us. Now, this fucker is going to tell me where my family is or he's going out the fucking window. Are you with me or do I leave you behind?'

The hard rain poured down, reducing the world to just two men, locked together by Sam's anger.

'I'm with you.'

Sam released him, part of his anger washing away as he did so. Sam patted Zack's chest, taking a moment to straighten the suit's ruined lapels.

'You're a mess,' he said quietly.

'We both are,' Zack agreed.

'Let's make someone pay.'

88

Detective Preston removed the clear plastic cover from his Stetson and gave it a shake. An arc of water droplets flew across the squad room, splashing three robbery investigators at the next desk.

They all shouted 'Hey!' in unison.

'Sorry, ladies,' Preston apologized with a smirk. 'Some of us can't spend all day keeping dry inside a giant, empty mall.'

Hogan rolled his eyes.

'What are you doing now?' Preston asked.

'Running a check on the Parkers to see . . . here it is . . . nice.'

'What?'

'Dr Parker owns a silver Mercedes E320 Diesel sedan.'

'Our mysterious Merc?'

'I'll add the registration to our BOLO.' Hogan paused as he called up the San Diego police report on the rape and assault charges. 'Hmmm, this is strange.'

Preston lifted his eyebrows quizzically, but Hogan was already dialling the phone.

'Detective McNamara,' Hogan said into the handset. He glanced over at his partner. 'San Diego.'

Preston lifted his own handset and patched into the call.

'McNamara,' said a sandpaper-rough voice.

Hogan explained who he was and his suspicion that Dr Zack Parker was in Portland.

'Makes sense,' said McNamara. 'That's his home town.'

'In your report, you said you suspected the rape had been staged,' Hogan said.

'Yeah, really odd. We did a rape kit on the victim, but she hadn't been touched. One theory is that he was interrupted before he could get to penetration, but everything was too clean, too . . . calculated. As you know, rape is a violent act. But Parker showed none of that rage. In fact, it was practically the opposite. He didn't *want* to hurt her.'

'But the disfigurement of her face,' Hogan added.

'Yeah, sick stuff, I agree,' said McNamara. 'But I talked to the surgeon at the hospital, and he said the cuts were so precise it was like following a bloody blueprint. She'll be in bandages for a while, but there'll be no permanent damage. Again, no rage.'

'But to an outsider?' Hogan queried.

'Yeah,' McNamara agreed. 'She looked like she had been brutally raped and disfigured.' He paused. 'But that's not the strangest part.'

'It's not?'

'Nope. Parker had been looked at for rape before.'

'When was this?' Hogan asked.

'Nineteen eighty-four.'

'Fuck me. Twenty-five years ago?'

'Yeah. High school. Grad night. You should have the original case files. It happened in Portland.'

'Did Parker do it?' Hogan asked.

'Nope. He was cleared before it went to trial. Turned out he was the victim's date for the prom, but left the party before the rape occurred and had a solid alibi. Poor girl was passed-out drunk and there were a half-dozen suspects. Prosecution was originally looking at a gang-bang scenario, but they ended up going after just one guy.'

'You remember the other names?' Preston asked.

'Not off the top of my head. I only glanced at the report when I saw Parker had been cleared, but I remember one of them was some big football prospect at the time.'

'Ironwood?'

'Hmmm, that rings a bell. Could be.'

'Thanks,' Hogan said. 'You've been a help.'

'Hey, no problem, it's a strange case. If you

catch Parker up there, give me a holler. He's certainly got me puzzled.'

Hogan thanked the detective again and hung up. He turned to Preston, but his partner was already on his feet.

'I'll get the case files,' Preston said.

While Preston was gone, Hogan crossed to the robbery crew and leaned his hip against the desk of Detective Freyja Flosadottir.

Freyja was a raven-haired Icelandic beauty with a sharp face and smooth white skin. Her nickname, and one that she seemed to embrace, was Calico.

'Your partner has been riding us all day about the friggin' mall,' Calico said.

'Just thank the roster you don't have to work with him,' Hogan replied with an easy smile.

'So what's on your mind?'

'The mall.'

'Christ, not you, too.'

'I just want to know what you think.'

'As in who could have done it? Not that we can prove a damn thing.'

Hogan nodded.

Calico sighed. 'There are only three people in town who could pull something this big. Out of the three, only two enjoy working with foreign interests. One deals mostly with the Russian mafia, so he's a definite maybe. The other isn't so limited. He plays with the Chinese, Russians and the Europeans. This heist was ballsy, but I wouldn't like to guess whose are bigger.'

'You got names?' Hogan asked.

'Mmmm,' Calico teased. 'What's your interest?'

'We're looking at the security guard on an unrelated matter.'

'Unrelated?'

Hogan shrugged. 'For now. The connection's muddy.'

'But if you clear it up?'

'I'll be sure to call.'

'You know I stay up late.'

Hogan broke eye contact, his throat suddenly dry. 'The names?'

Calico laughed. 'I'll dig up the e-files and send them over.'

89

Preston returned with a large brown envelope containing the original police reports of the 1984 rape.

Hogan joined him at the desk. 'Ironwood?'

'Ironwood *and* your Viking friend.'

'Christ.'

'It gets better.'

'Go on.'

'The actor is mentioned, too.'

Hogan blinked in surprise. 'He was a suspect?'

'He might not have been aware of it,' cautioned Preston. 'The report says they couldn't contact him, and he was eventually cleared. The victim admitted they had consensual sex before she got shit-faced and passed out. White was never called for trial.'

'But Ironwood and Toler?'

'DNA was recovered that linked both of them, but this was 'eighty-four, three years before our first DNA-based conviction. That evidence was never brought to trial and they ended up taking the stand for the prosecution.'

Hogan scratched his chin. 'So out of three suspects, one is murdered at home, one has his skull cracked open during a robbery, and one is on the run after his house explodes.'

'You're forgetting the fourth,' said Preston.

'The fourth?'

'The one who went to jail.'

90

Zack and Sam walked into the lobby of The R Project looking bedraggled. The short ride in the car had done little to dry out their clothes and Zack's silk suit clung to him like wet tissue paper.

The receptionist, a husky woman in her mid-fifties, studied them with an ungenerous smile beneath hard, suspicious eyes.

Sam swept his fingers through his dark hair and switched on a movie-star smile.

'We're here to see Alan,' he said. 'Tell him it's Zack and Sam.'

'Is Mr Robertson expecting you?'

Sam laughed, friendly. 'No, we wanted to surprise him. We're old friends.' Sam jabbed his thumb over his shoulder at Zack who was pathetically trying to wring some of the water from his suit. 'Zack just popped up from San Diego. They started the high school computer club together, which is kinda where this whole company sprang from. He'll want to see us.'

The woman eyed Zack distrustfully.

'We got caught in the rain,' Sam added, keeping the laughter in his voice. 'He looks more like a drowned rat than a top surgeon now, doesn't he?'

'Indeed,' said the woman. 'Let me see if Mr Robertson is available.'

'Thank you. We sure appreciate it.' He flashed the woman another Hollywood smile, but she was invulnerable to its charm.

The lobby shouted cutting-edge with a hi-tech nautical design in sweeping glass and mirrored steel. The floor glistened in black marble, seamless and smooth, yet to Sam's amazement, green Zeros and Ones swam just beneath its reflective surface.

Sam pointed it out to Zack who immediately grinned.

'It's binary,' Zack said. 'Knowing Alan, if you had time to recognize the pattern, it spells out a message.'

'Huh,' Sam grunted. 'I thought they were little green fish.'

Sam's eyes were drawn to a glass office overlooking the lobby. Inside, a trim businessman, his sleeves rolled up and his tie slightly askew, sat behind an eight-inch-thick glass desk. He was talking on the phone. His face looked tight and drawn.

'That's Alan,' Zack said.

The receptionist cleared her throat. 'I'm sorry, but Mr Robertson is still on the phone.'

'Yeah, we can see that,' Sam said absently.

315

The receptionist flashed a genuine smile. 'Mr Robertson likes to be in plain view. He believes that as president of the company, people should see that he works just as hard, if not harder, than what he expects from his employees.'

'Very admirable,' Sam said dismissively. He felt his pent-up anger escaping as he wondered if this was the monster who had kidnapped his wife and daughter.

The receptionist crinkled her forehead at his tone. 'Mr Robertson is a very admirable man.'

Sam studied the man on the phone, the details of his narrow face: pinched nostrils, large ears, eyes spaced too close together. His hair was limp and so blond it was practically transparent.

'Did he used to wear glasses?' Sam asked.

'Yeah,' Zack replied. 'Elvis Costello frames.'

Sam mentally attached a pair of thick, round-framed glasses, but it didn't make any difference. The face meant nothing to him. Alan Robertson was a complete stranger.

As Sam watched, Alan placed the handset on his desk, lifted a black briefcase off the floor on to his lap, and opened it. He reached inside and pulled out a letter-sized memo pad and a gold pen. The pen flashed in the light as he jotted a quick note and placed the memo on top of his desk.

He took an extra moment to align the pad in the exact centre of his workspace and then placed the pen beside it. Once he was satisfied with its placement, he lifted his head and glanced down at the lobby.

Sam saw recognition bloom as Alan met Zack's eye and the tiniest flicker of a sad smile crossed his lips. He nodded as though they were friends passing in a hallway. Then he returned to his briefcase where—

He pulled out a small, chrome-plated revolver with a two-inch barrel.

The receptionist screamed as Sam rushed past her and tore up the stairs, taking them two at a time.

Zack remained where he was, unable to move, his eyes locked on Alan – brightest member of the high school computer club, the one who always rode shotgun in the Mustang, top down, still nerds, but uncaring – as he pressed the gun against the side of his head.

On the landing above, he heard Sam bellow in frustration as he yanked open the office door and charged inside.

Too late.

Alan Robertson lay on the floor beside his desk, dead eyes locked open in shock. A thin billow of smoke curled from a tiny charred hole, no larger than the diameter of a pencil, which dotted his right temple.

The left side of his head was flat, and Sam knew the exit wound would be the size of his fist. The glass wall that should have been splashed by blood and brain had shattered outwards as the bullet continued its destructive path, leaving the death scene virtually pristine.

Sam crossed to the body and touched two fingers to its neck, but it was the hopeless gesture of a desperate man.

As Zack entered the room, his breathing ragged, Sam stepped around the body and moved to the desk. Written on the perfectly aligned memo pad were three words: *For my family.*

Sam's heart hammered in his chest. He closed his eyes and tried to regulate it, but his ears became plugged as if he had suddenly plunged from a great height.

After a second, he felt his ears pop and then he heard an anguished voice, small and distant. For a moment, he thought it was Hannah, calling out for him, but then he realized that the voice was calling, 'Alan . . . Alan.'

Sam snapped open his eyes. On the base of the phone, one of the buttons was glowing. He picked up the discarded handset and held it to his ear.

'Alan,' said a woman's panicked voice. 'They let us go. The kids are OK. Are you there? Alan?'

'Who let you go?'

The woman gasped. 'Who is this? Where is my husband?'

'Who let you go?' Sam repeated.

The woman's breath caught, and then she broke into a sob. 'The men who came to our house.

They wore masks. I never saw their faces. I swear. Where's my husband?'

'I need to see you,' Sam said urgently. 'Right away.'

'What about my husband?'

'I can tell you when we meet,' Sam pressed. 'It's important that I get the details while they're fresh in your mind. We have to catch these bastards.'

'I just want my husband. They're gone now. I didn't . . . I didn't see anything.'

'Are you at home?'

'Yes, but—'

'Stay there. I'm on my way.'

'Are you the police?'

'Yes,' Sam lied. 'Don't leave the house and don't call anyone until I get there.'

Sam pushed the off button and placed the handset back in its base. As he did, his arm brushed the cordless computer mouse and Alan's monitor powered out of sleep mode.

Sam gawped at the screen and then turned to Zack who was still rooted in the middle of the office, his attention arrested by Alan's unblinking stare.

Sam snapped his fingers, breaking Zack's trance, and motioned him over.

Displayed on the screen were three news stories. One from the *Oregonian* detailed the explosion and recovery of two unidentified bodies from Sam's suburban home. The second, published in the *San Diego Union-Tribune*, was headlined

319

DR RAPE ON THE RUN and featured a smiling mugshot of a prosperous, less-skeletal Zack scanned from one of his office brochures.

A third story, set over one column and much shorter than the other two, was headlined LOCAL SURGEON TO BE HONOURED FOR CHILD AID. It featured a blurrier thumbnail of a smiling Zack. It was dated seven days before the 'Dr Rape' story broke.

'Alan's not our guy,' Sam said bitterly. 'He's just another bloody pawn like us.'

A noticeable shiver ran down Zack's spine and the blood drained from his face. He sank to his knees as Sam quickly handed him a metal waste-basket and grabbed his shoulders. Zack groaned and bent double.

'I'm sorry,' Sam said. 'He didn't deserve this.'

Zack raised his face from the bucket. 'Christ, Sam,' he gasped. 'This has got to stop. I can't hate this much.'

'When we first met . . .' Sam struggled to keep his voice calm. 'You told me this was a game, remember?'

Zack nodded. 'A sick, sick game.'

'Well, this is just another play. Only this time, we may have forced it.'

Zack's eyes widened in horror.

Sam continued, 'How did he know we would be here to witness this? It can't be a coincidence that Alan received that call just as we're about to talk to him.'

'We're being followed,' Zack reasoned.

Sam walked to the window and looked outside. Even in the pouring rain, he spotted a half-dozen bicycle messengers darting in and out of traffic. 'But this also means we're getting closer to the truth. We're not just chasing our tails, we're hunting.'

'But Alan—'

'We didn't make him pull the trigger,' Sam said forcefully. 'We're not to blame. This bastard is playing us. We have to focus on the next step. Alan is dead. Your daughter is dead. My family could be next. Someone has to pay.'

'Where do we look?' he croaked.

'Do you know where Alan lives?'

'Jasmine and I went for dinner about four years back. I think I remember it.'

'Alan's wife is waiting for us.'

Zack glanced down at the body. 'Does she know?'

Sam looked away. 'Not yet.'

A security guard in a pristine dark blue uniform, complete with razor-sharp creases and starched collar, pushed through the stunned crowd gathered outside the office door.

'Who the hell are you two?' he demanded. His eyes wavered between the men behind the desk and the body of his employer. He reached for his gun.

'We're just leaving.' Sam came around the desk

with his hands held high to show they were empty, and started to advance.

'The police are on their way.' The guard fumbled nervously with his brand-new holster, but couldn't get it unsnapped. 'You better wait.'

'Can't do that, bud. Come on, Zack.'

As Sam quickly closed the gap, the guard abandoned his holster and reached out to grab him by the shoulder. But Sam was prepared. Without breaking stride, he snared the man's wrist, bent it to the breaking point, and twisted – hard. The guard yelped in surprise as his body spun to avoid a dislocation. Then his feet were suddenly swept away and he was thrown to the floor.

'Stay down,' Sam hissed.

Embarrassed, the guard ignored the warning and reached for his holster again. Sam didn't hesitate. He spun on one foot and kicked the guard in the face with such force he loosened teeth. This time, the guard stayed down.

'Move it, Zack.' Sam pushed aside the shocked crowd and headed for the stairs.

In the lobby, the floor was littered with tiny squares of broken glass that glistened red upon the undulating green ripples of binary code.

91

After a rolling stop at the motel to grab Sam's guard uniform, the Mercedes headed north-east to Alameda Ridge.

Alameda was a turn-of-the-century neighbourhood, which boasted wide roads lined with mature trees, stunning views of the Willamette River and downtown skyline, trendy restaurants and ubiquitous, over-priced coffee shops.

Sam settled back into his seat as he finished changing out of his jeans and into his badly wrinkled uniform.

'What do you think?' He tucked in his shirt and straightened his tie. 'Do I look like a cop?'

'A sloppy cop, maybe,' Zack said testily. 'What's all that yellow crap on your shirt?'

'Paint,' said Sam. 'There was an incident at the mall before . . . well, before all this began.'

'At least it's not red,' Zack snapped.

'Look, I know you don't like this,' Sam snapped back, 'but we need to talk to her. She might have an idea about who's been setting us up. They must have done the same to Alan.'

'Or he was only ever given one assignment,' Zack said. His eyes never drifted from the road. 'And we watched him do it.'

'I thought you said this guy wants more than our lives. He wants to destroy us first.'

'That's us,' Zack said through tight lips. 'Maybe he decided to let Alan off easy.'

'Why?' Sam asked.

'Hell if I know.'

As the road climbed towards Alameda Ridge, the homes became grander. When Zack turned on to Klickitat Street, Sam watched the enormous Barnes mansion flash by his window.

Further down the block, they parked in front of a pretty Victorian home in green and white with carved gingerbread in the peaks.

'This is it.'

Sam looked over. 'You coming in?'

Zack shook his head. 'I'm tired of delivering bad news.'

'It might help to hear it from a friend.'

Zack shook his head again. 'Nothing helps that kind of news.'

Sam knocked on the front door and self-consciously tried to cover the paintball stains on his shirt by crossing his arms.

'Who's there?' asked a metallic voice to his left.

Sam turned to see a small two-way intercom

affixed to the wall. Someone had tried to make it look more Victorian by surrounding it with a wooden frame.

'It's Officer White, Mrs Robertson. We talked on the phone. I was at your husband's office.'

'You hung up on me.'

'Yes, I did, Mrs Robertson, but only so I could get here as soon as possible.'

'I didn't see a police car.'

'No, I used an unmarked car. I thought it best not to alert your neighbours. I know how quickly gossip spreads.'

There was an audible click.

'Come in.'

Sam opened the door and walked into the entrance hall. Directly in front of him, a short hallway led to the kitchen, which had patio windows and a large deck that overlooked the ridge and the city skyline below. On days when it wasn't grey with rain, Sam guessed the view would be spectacular.

To his right, he glimpsed a small library behind elegant French doors. Alan's widow waited in the room to his left.

Although it might once have been stiff and elegant, now the room had a casual, lived-in feel with toys scattered on the floor and an air of relaxed contentment. But that bliss had recently been shattered, the evidence plain on the face of the woman who sat rigid on the sofa.

Sam moved to sit in a chair facing her.

The woman lifted her gaze, tears overflowing red rims. 'The children are at my mother's. Just around the corner. They . . . they needed to be out of the house.'

'I'm sorry to intrude,' Sam said. 'It's just so important that we talk.'

'I don't know who they were.'

'What did they want?' Sam asked carefully.

'Nothing from us. It was Alan they wanted to talk to.'

'They threatened him?'

'Yes. They said they would do things . . . to me . . . to my children.' She turned to look out of the front window at the quiet street beyond. Her voice became unnervingly calm. 'If they had tried to harm my children, I would have killed them. They were large men, but I still would have—' She inhaled sharply. 'I never knew I had that in me.'

'How many men?'

'Three. One stayed with me. Another watched Dorrie and Clay. They had guns, but they kept them in their belts.'

'Who called your husband?'

'The third one. I never saw him. He entered behind the other two and went straight into my husband's library. He made the call from there. We were kept in here.'

'You heard his voice?'

'Yes, but not clearly. He was very calm, soft spoken. I only heard the occasional word when he was telling Alan what he planned to do to us. At one point, he called for the guard to make me scream. I . . . I found it harder to stop than to begin. A few moments later, there was a loud pop and the sound of breaking glass. The men left us, and I ran to the phone. It had been set to speaker mode. He wanted me to hear those sounds. That's when I talked to you.'

'Did you recognize the man's voice? Was it familiar in any way?'

She shook her head. 'It was just a voice. It could have been anyone's.'

'No accent, no familiar cadence?'

'Just a voice,' she repeated.

'Do you know of anyone who would want to harm your husband?'

Mrs Robertson's eyes were focused miles away. 'Everyone loves Alan. It even makes me jealous sometimes.' She smiled. 'People light up around him. He inspires them. He doesn't have a mean bone in his entire body.'

Sam huffed in frustration. 'What about the two men who watched over you? Did you recognize anything about them?'

'They were just large men with big muscles. They wore those clear plastic masks over their faces that always give you the creeps at Halloween. The masks frightened the children. Only one of them spoke.'

'What did he say?'

'Just what you would expect. Stay calm. His boss needed to speak to Alan. Just the essentials.'

'Was there anything about his voice?'

'Not really. He didn't have an accent or any-thing distinctive, but I had the feeling he wasn't very intelligent. All brawn and no brain.'

'Is there nothing that stands out?' Sam pleaded, desperation suddenly flooding his voice. 'Anything? Anything at all?'

The woman locked eyes with Sam and tilted her head, her focus shifting to take in his worn face and stained clothes.

'You're not the police.' Panic began to rise. 'Who are you?'

'They have my family,' Sam said quickly. 'My wife and daughter. I need to find them.'

'You're friends with Alan?'

'We went to the same high school, but we didn't know each other. Whoever did this to you has an agenda that we can't figure out.'

'We?'

'Zack Parker is with me. His daughter was killed.'

She gasped. 'What have you done?'

'We don't know. Just as we don't know what Alan did.'

'My husband is a saint,' she said angrily. 'He has done nothing wrong.'

Sam held up his hands. 'None of us deserve this, but we need to find out who believes we do. That's why I came here. To find something. Anything.'

The woman shook her head angrily, white

saliva beginning to pool at the corners of her mouth. 'Where is my husband? I want to see my husband.'

Sam looked down at his hands. 'I'm sorry.'

Mrs Robertson got to her feet. 'What for?'

Sam looked up. 'Your husband shot himself in his office. Those were the sounds you heard.'

The woman's face distorted before him like a funhouse mirror. Sadness and rage seemed unable to mix. And then she began to scream; a hysterical cacophony of noise that threatened to raise the roof and shatter the windows.

Sam lurched to his feet and tried to comfort her, but his closeness enraged her further and she lashed out at him with fists and nails. Sam stepped back and tripped over a rug, suddenly afraid for his own safety.

Zack burst through the front door, his eyes wide with panic. 'What did you do?'

The woman spun to face him, her lips curling in a snarl even as her face crumpled in grief and anger.

'GET OUT!' she screamed. 'GET OUT! GET OUT! GET OUT!'

Sam scrambled to his feet and dragged Zack outside to the car.

'Drive,' he commanded. 'The cops will be here any minute.'

'What about her?' Zack asked.

Sam looked back at the house, the woman's screams still echoing. 'She needs a doctor more than she needs us. The police will call for one. Now let's go.'

Zack took a deep breath and put the car into drive. Neighbours were already rushing towards the house as they drove away.

92

Detective Preston walked around the large office, fascinated by the massive windows that over-looked the lobby.

'Nice,' he said. 'If you don't mind people gawping at you every time you scratch your ass.'

Hogan walked behind the desk and glanced at the computer screen. The screensaver showed binary code falling like rain. He nudged the mouse to cancel the effect and called to his partner.

'This is why patrol called us.' He indicated the three news stories displayed on the monitor. 'The late Mr Robertson was looking into White and Parker.' He frowned. 'Is that receptionist still outside?'

'The plump one? Yeah.'

Preston stepped out in the hallway and returned with the receptionist. The woman had black mascara tracks running down her cheeks and her attempted clean-up had ruined her foundation, leaving odd-shaped blotches where her natural flesh showed through.

Hogan smiled encouragingly as he crossed in front of the transparent desk. 'Thanks for sticking around. I know it must be difficult. You probably want to be home with your family.'

The woman sniffled, her hand automatically dabbing a crumpled tissue below her nose.

'Had you known Mr Robertson long?' Hogan asked.

'We just had a company party celebrating twenty years. I was one of his first employees.' She sniffled again. 'Mr Robertson hired me right after he moved from his parents' garage to his first real office.'

'Wow!' Hogan said, impressed. 'He must have been a good boss for you to be here so long.'

'He was a very generous man. Every employee here is also a shareholder. He's made a lot of us very comfortable. I just hope—'

'He ever talk about high school?' Hogan interrupted.

'He went to Brookside, right here in the city. He was invited to speak there many times over the years at graduations. He was a very good speaker. Inspirational, you know?'

Hogan smiled receptively. 'Any old school friends ever show up? Apart from the two you mentioned who visited just before . . .' Hogan let it trail off, not wanting to invite another round of waterworks.

The receptionist shook her head. 'Not that I recall.'

After the woman left the room, Hogan crossed to the broken window and looked down at the lobby.

'Why does it tie to that?' he said after a moment. 'High school. Christ, some people can't let it go.'

Hogan's voice drifted and he suddenly pulled a file from his jacket pocket. He began to read.

Preston knelt down by the blood spot and scratched his nose. 'Forensics uncover anything at the wife's house?'

'It looks professional,' Hogan said mechanically, his attention diverted. 'Gloves and masks. No names used and no prints left behind.'

'At least that rules out White.' Preston stood up and his knees cracked. 'He hasn't been shy about showing his face. And I'm assuming this Zack fellow the receptionist mentioned is our elusive Dr Parker.'

Hogan turned, his face alight with an idea. 'I'm thinking Parker and White came here to warn Robertson that someone was holding a grudge. Maybe it's tied into the rape back in high school, but somehow they figured out he was next on the list. They just got here too late.'

'But Parker and White were cleared of any involvement in the rape,' said Preston. 'They weren't even called as witnesses at the trial.'

'No, but Robertson was?'

'What?'

Hogan tapped the file in his hand. 'He wasn't a suspect, but his name appears as a witness for the prosecution.'

93

Sam pushed open the motel door. 'You know what doesn't make sense.'

'Like any of this does?' Zack snapped. He kicked the door closed and stripped off his wet jacket.

Sam ignored the outburst. 'If the kidnapper wanted money, why did he come to me for it and not Robertson? He obviously had the dough.'

'Maybe that was the problem.' Zack began to shiver violently as he unzipped his pants. 'It would have been too easy for him. He–he's playing us . . . destroying us. He let Robertson off light.'

'But why?'

'I don't know.' Zack, his skin a sickly grey in the room's harsh light, headed for the shower. 'Maybe he disliked him the least.'

'Or he was just a loose end,' Sam said to Zack's back. 'Someone who could point a finger in his direction. Nothing personal, like with us, just business.'

'But if it is personal with us—' Zack stopped in mid-sentence, his hand on the door to the shower.

Sam picked up the thread. 'If it is personal, then the money means nothing. Even though we've raised the full amount, my family could still die.'

94

As they exited Robertson's office building, Preston turned to his partner. 'This actor really got to you, didn't he? You've been willing to accept his innocence from the start.'

Hogan shrugged. 'It's not him so much as the story.'

'About his family being kidnapped?'

'Yeah. Somebody also threatened Robertson's family, but instead of money they demanded he take his own life.'

'Pretty harsh.'

'Fucking brutal, more like.' Hogan exhaled noisily. 'What would you do?'

Preston didn't hesitate. 'I wouldn't trust them. If I'm dead, how do I know they don't kill my family anyway?'

'You wouldn't trust them if they were strangers,' Hogan proposed. 'But what if it was someone you knew, someone who sent you proof of how they were destroying the lives of other people you had a connection to?'

'Like Parker and White.'

'Exactly. So now your choice is to take your own life or have that life, and your family, destroyed.'

Preston bristled angrily. 'That's one sick fuck.'

Hogan looked at him in surprise. 'I thought you hated the F word.'

Preston snorted. 'If you're right, this bastard warrants an exception.'

95

Sam gathered up Zack's crumpled jacket and pants as the shower shut off.

'I saw a dry cleaner's just a block over,' Sam called through the closed door. 'I'll take your suit and get it dried.'

The bathroom door opened, releasing billows of warm, moist steam. Zack walked out of the fog, his face flush from the heat, a white towel wrapped around his waist. He was so skinny, Sam could see every rib and bone.

Zack wiped a knuckle across his eyes as he unashamedly dropped the towel, exposing more white patches on his upper thighs.

'We could buy new ones,' he said. 'You still have a credit card, right?'

Sam shrugged. 'I wouldn't mind the walk. Get my head clear, you know? I need to figure out our next step. After the scene at Robertson's, the cops will be looking for both of us.'

Zack crawled into bed. 'I just need to close my

eyes for a bit.' He paused. 'Seeing Alan today . . .
I swear I saw my daughter's face in his eyes.
Like he was already with her . . . holding my
place.'

'Take an hour. I'll drop your suit at the
cleaner's, but then we'll need to blow this place.
We should probably ditch the car, too.'

Zack was no longer listening.

Sam dropped Zack's suit at the dry cleaner's and
asked for a one-hour turnaround. The male clerk
rolled his eyes and Sam had a flash of anger so
violent he wanted to grab the snot by the hair and
smash his face into the counter until flesh turned
to bloody pulp.

Instead, he hissed, 'Is that going to be a
problem?'

The young clerk quickly shook his head.

Sam stormed back outside, not wanting his
frustration to be directed at someone who didn't
deserve it. He so desperately wanted to be in
control.

He stood in the rain, his vest soaking it up like
a sponge. Half a block down, two dancing martini
glasses in pink and green neon shone through the
wet afternoon: a lighthouse in a stormy sea. Its
promise of numbness called to him, but he shook
it off.

The last thing he needed was to drown in a
bottle while his family waited to be found.

A wave of hopelessness swept over him and he

felt the same fatigue that had driven Zack to bed. It wrapped around his shoulders like a coarse blanket, growing heavier by the second as the rain pounded down.

96

Detective Hogan hung his wet jacket beside his partner's slicker and sat down at his desk. Unlike Preston, Hogan liked to keep his desk neat and orderly, with everything from reports to memos having their own place or in-box.

Because of this, he immediately spotted the new sheet of blue paper that waited in his memo box. The same memo on Preston's desk could sprout leaves before he noticed.

Preston approached and handed him a cup of black coffee. 'Last of the pot. Be warned.'

Hogan took a tentative sip and shuddered. 'It tastes the same as a fresh pot.'

'Damn, I was hoping it would mellow with age.' Preston noticed the memo. 'That about our camera?'

Hogan nodded as he took another sip of coffee and read over the slim report.

'Components are mostly Taiwanese.' He flipped the page. 'But it was assembled and sold in Russia.'

342

'Boxy but good, comrade,' Preston said in a remarkably good Russian accent.

'Our techs also say this model was never available for export.'

'Which means?' Preston asked.

'Whoever owns it either bought it while visiting Russia or had Russian friends ship it over.'

'That narrows it down. How many Russians in Portland?'

'More to the point,' Hogan added, 'who has Russian friends and also needed some leverage on Mr White?'

'The mall robbery?'

'Calico suspects the contents of the mall were hauled directly to the docks and shipped to Russia. She's been checking the yards for details on outgoing vessels.'

'She have a local organizer in mind?'

Hogan nodded and turned to his computer. 'She had two candidates . . .'

The first set of records appeared on screen and as his eyes reached the name at the top, Hogan's mouth broke out in a grin.

'Got him.'

97

Sam returned to the dry cleaner's, his anger buried in a dumpster of self-pity, and slumped on a vinyl chair in the corner.

As he waited for Zack's suit, his cellphone rang. He snapped it open.

'I'm here.'

'You have the money, Sam?' asked the altered voice.

'Yes.'

'All one million?'

'Yes.' Sam paused. 'Do you still want it?'

'Of course I do. It's good to have friends, isn't it, Sam?'

Sam didn't know how to answer.

'We'll meet tonight,' continued the voice. 'I'll call later with instructions.'

'Will my family be there?' Sam knew the question was expected of him even if he could no longer trust the answer.

'Yes. You will see your family again. Very soon.'

'Can I talk to them?' Sam blurted. 'Can I talk to Hannah?'

'Don't push me, Sam.'

The sudden menace in the distorted voice lifted Sam out of the darkness and filled him with such burning rage that it forced its way out from between clenched teeth. 'Why are you doing this? What could I possibly have done that was so god-damn awful you had to involve my family?'

The store clerk looked up at Sam's tone and quickly vanished into the back room.

The caller's response was not immediate, but Sam could hear him breathing. Then the line hissed with static and, 'Everything was so fucking easy for you.'

'What are you talking about?' Sam sputtered. 'Have you seen my life?'

'You shouldn't have come back.'

'I came back because I failed.' Sam gripped the phone so tightly he could hear its plastic shell creak. 'I failed to make my mark. I blew it. To have a dream that can't be fulfilled is a fucking curse. Ask Hannah. She's had to live with my sorry ass when all I could get was rejection and crappy—'

The phone squawked sharply. 'You know nothing of rejection, of suffering, of—'

Sam snorted. 'Well, that's a crock—'

'Tonight,' interrupted the voice sternly. 'Bring Parker.'

The line went dead.

* * *

Sam shook Zack awake.

'We have to move. Time's run out.'

Zack opened his eyes. They were red and raw. 'He called?'

'We meet tonight. With the money. He wants you there.'

Zack sat up and rubbed his eyes. He inhaled deeply through his nose and released it slowly from his mouth. 'What's our plan?'

Sam held up the freshly pressed suit.

'They couldn't get all the stains out, but it's dry.'

'Where are we going? Supper at the Benson?'

Sam shook his head. 'Somewhere less elegant, I'm afraid.'

98

Zack and Sam descended the long wooden staircase, their torsos dry inside makeshift ponchos
made from knee-length plastic bags taken from
the dry cleaner's.

At the bottom of the stairs, they walked to the
underbelly of Burnside Bridge. The homeless
huddled in the centre of the span, away from the
rain. But even with dry ground beneath them,
the wind and damp trampled through the open
court with frigid abandon.

Davey, his upper body wrapped in a black
plastic trash bag, saw them approach and moved
to meet them.

'Did you find him?' he asked.

'He wasn't the one,' Sam said.

Davey blinked rapidly. 'You sure?'

Sam nodded. 'He's dead, Davey. He was one of
us. A pawn.'

'Oh!' Davey looked down at the ground, his left
toe digging into the dirt. 'He'll come back for me

now. Burn me again. Make my skin melt. Make me scream.'

'I don't think so,' Sam said. 'He believes you're dead, but we still need help.'

Davey's eyes narrowed. 'How?'

'We need you to look at the yearbook again. You said Alan brought friends to help out. We need to know who they were.'

Davey's excitement returned. 'OK. That's easy.'

Zack and Sam followed Davey to his makeshift lean-to and waited as he dug into his pack and retrieved the yearbook.

'I thought you were keeping this stuff in the tunnels,' Zack said.

Davey shrugged. 'Safer with me now.'

Davey opened the yearbook and turned to the mugshots of over 500 students. He placed his finger on the first face and began to move along the rows, mouthing each name as he did so.

He stopped at the first face he recognized as one of Alan's helpers. Zack looked down at it and shook his head.

'Don't know him,' he said. 'How many were there?'

'Three.' Davey tapped his temple.

'Find the next one,' Sam said impatiently.

Davey dragged his finger along the mugshots again. This time he stopped mid-way through the book.

Zack looked, sighed, and shook his head.

At the Qs, Davey stopped again, his finger

hovering over the face of a husky youth with round, black-rimmed sunglasses and lifeless chestnut hair that hung in greasy strands to his shoulders. Beneath the veil of hair, his face had an odd, plastic-like quality and his nose lay as flat as a retired boxer's. His eyes were hidden beneath the dark glasses and his thin mouth emoted nothing.

'You remember him, Sam?' Davey tapped the photo. 'He was real book smart, but clumsy as an ape. I had three Fresnals blow after he handled them.'

Sam looked at the photo, a dim memory coming into focus. 'What's up with his face?'

'He was burned,' said Zack, his voice trembling. 'He originally told me that he accidentally tipped a pot of boiling water over himself when he was a toddler. When my Kalli was born, I became paranoid about making sure the pot handles were always turned away from the edge of the stove.'

Sam snapped his fingers. 'That's right. We used to get him to score all the booze for us before the cast parties. When he pulled his hair back, the cashiers were too embarrassed by his face to ask for I.D. Came in real handy.'

Davey broke out in a grin. 'Yeah, that was cool.'

Sam continued. 'I drove him home one time after a party and met his old man. Now there was a scary dude. His arms were burned, too. Real serious stuff. Industrial accident, I think he said. What was the kid's name again?'

'Lucas,' said Zack.

'You knew him?'

'Remember I told you that Vadik and his daughter were sent to me by an acquaintance?'

'That's him?'

Zack blanched at Sam's accusing tone. 'We haven't spoken in years. He came to me about ten years back. He was broke and in a bad way. I guess I felt sorry for him. I did what I could, but his injuries were more extensive than he had said. He's burned everywhere but the injuries took place over a long period of time. I was able to do some decent work on his face, but there really wasn't enough good tissue left on his body to do much else. I thought we parted on good terms, especially when he sent Vadik's daughter to me.'

'Fuck!' Sam kicked the ground in frustration. 'He was in the car with Vadik, but his face didn't register. How can a twisted little fuck blame us for his life? Ironman was a real bastard, but what did we do?'

'Maybe he simply wanted to *be* us,' Zack said as he worked it through. 'But every time he tried to fill our shoes, he failed.'

'So destroying us will make everything better?' Sam asked bitterly.

'Or maybe he's just finally figured out exactly what he is.'

'A monster,' spat Sam.

Zack nodded. 'He's cleaning the slate. Ironwood, the football player with a future and a mean streak a mile long; you, the egotistical golden boy aiming for a Hollywood career. Even I was being recognized for my work as a surgeon. You saw the newspaper clipping on Robertson's computer. He wants to erase us.'

Sam ground his teeth. 'On the phone he said everything was easy for us, but he refuses to see what that led to. Ironwood was washed up at nineteen and my biggest role of late is a fuckin' commercial for the Beavers. I can see him being jealous of you and Alan, but why the rest of us?'

'Because,' Zack said, 'he isn't just looking at who we've become. He's also focused on who we were.'

Davey's eyes went wide as he followed the conversation.

Sam rubbed at his temples, the fingers working deep. 'You think Lucas is capable of this?'

Zack nodded again. 'He's been badly scarred and no matter what he claimed, his burns weren't an accident. They're too precise, too continuous. He has layers of scar tissue.'

'But is he unbalanced enough for this to make sense to *him*?' Sam pushed.

'Who can say?' Zack replied. 'In high school he was always a follower, never a leader. It's possible the only way he saw to fit in was to adopt other people's passions. At first, he followed me, but I was a year older and medical school was too much of a leap. Then he chose you, but couldn't make it on stage. He was then left with Alan, who must have carried him along some, but eventually he failed there, too. I also got the feeling from our sessions that he lost more than skin during those burnings. He might have no trouble with the morality of kidnap and murder.'

The air around them went silent as all three men stared down at the photo of the blank-faced boy.

'He fits,' Sam said, breaking the silence.

Zack agreed.

Sam rose to his feet, noticing the rain had slowed to a steady drizzle. Thick clouds still held the sun at bay, making the early evening feel more like night.

'How do we find him?' Sam asked.

'Vadik will know.'

Davey leapt to his feet. 'Can I help? I know my way around.'

Sam ground his teeth. 'We can use every friend we've got.'

99

Back in the Mercedes, with Davey stretched out in the back seat, Sam turned to Zack.

'So if Lucas is the kidnapper, and he's connected with Vadik, why did he help me raise the money?'

'You said yourself this isn't about money,' Zack answered. 'By using you to rob the mall, he made you an outlaw, and he got to keep playing the game.'

'Then what about you?'

Zack looked at him questioningly.

Sam continued. 'Why is he still torturing you? He's destroyed your career, killed your daughter and kidnapped your wife. Why not end it like he did with Ironman and Alan?'

'He still needed something.'

Sam frowned. 'We've already agreed it's not about the money?'

'But my share gave you the incentive to play his game, Sam. You said yourself that a million was

impossible, but once you had three-quarters . . .'
'I had hope,' Sam finished.
Zack nodded.
'But what did that leave you?'
Zack's voice was ice. 'I have hate.'

100

'So,' Detective Preston began as he drove Hogan to Old Town, 'this Lucas fellow spent fifteen years in jail for rape, and took over the Russians when he got out?'

Hogan nodded. 'He must have made contacts inside. According to Calico, Lucas appeared on the scene ten years ago, working as an underling for a Russian heavy, Georgy Malkin, who is said to have ruled his mini empire like the crimpers with good old-fashioned leg-breakers at his beck and call.'

'What happened to Malkin?'

Hogan smirked. 'I asked the same question. Calico says his car mysteriously burst into flames on his way to work one day. Numerous witnesses said they could hear him screaming as the car kept moving down the street at high speed and ended up in the river.'

'Fire, huh?'

'A rival gang was blamed, although Calico

claims there was no evidence to back it up. One week later, three of its members were found on the riverbank where Malkin's car left the road. Their eyes and tongues had been cut out before they were stripped naked and burned alive.'

'And Lucas moved up?'

'The Russians liked his communication skills.'

'He must have studied *The Secret* in the joint.'

Hogan laughed. 'There's also a juvenile record of petty crimes, including incidents of setting his neighbours' pets on fire. Two dogs, one cat and a basket of newborn bunnies.'

'Twisted little prick.'

'His record was clean for two years prior to the rape. He was seventeen at the time of that incident, but turned eighteen shortly after. The court tried him as an adult.'

'He had form,' said Preston. 'I would have thrown away the key.'

Hogan flipped through the copy of the police report he was reading. 'Lucas claimed he didn't do it. He admitted that he and Robertson found the girl naked and unconscious in the bedroom. The sight excited him and he confessed to touching her breasts. Robertson got squeamish and left, but Lucas was too pumped up. He masturbated over her.'

'Charming.'

'The girl woke up just as he was ejaculating.'

Preston winced. 'Bad timing.'

'There was evidence linking four of the suspects

– Toler, Ironwood, White and Lucas – but Lucas was the face the victim saw.'

'Pretty tough to claim innocence if you're caught waving your dick in the victim's face,' Preston said.

Hogan nodded. 'That's how the jury saw it, too.'

Detective Hogan parked the car outside the Olde Towne Fish House and inhaled the salty air.

'This is one of the legitimate businesses that Lucas owns. According to Calico, it's also our best bet for finding him.'

'I thought something smelled fishy,' Preston quipped.

The two detectives walked into the restaurant and flashed their badges at a college-age waitress standing by the reservation book. Her authentic 'wench-style' period costume squeezed her plump bosom until it resembled two baby-smooth grape-fruits, which were about to explode.

'We're looking for the owner.' Hogan's gaze was firmly fixed on the woman's face.

Preston's eyes weren't as disciplined.

'I haven't seen him,' said the woman. 'Try the cooks.'

She jabbed a tooth-gnawed thumbnail in the direction of a door with a round porthole at the rear of the restaurant.

Hogan pushed through the door to enter chaos. Six chefs were busy at their stations and the aroma was an exotic soup of herbs, garlic, salt and brine.

It was impossible to tell who was in charge, so Hogan held up his badge and said loudly, 'We're looking for the owner.'

'Good luck, mate,' called out an Australian accent. 'We only look for him on pay day.'

The other cooks laughed and continued to cook, cleave, steam and stew.

'Does he have an office?' Hogan asked.

'Stairs at the back, just past the pots,' called an Indian accent. 'Sometimes he there, but often not.'

Preston nudged his partner towards the small flight of wooden stairs beside a large, walk-in freezer.

They climbed a dozen stairs to a makeshift office with thin plywood walls built above the freezer. When Hogan knocked, the flimsy door rattled in its frame. In response to the silence that followed, Hogan turned the handle and entered.

The office was unoccupied, but from its layout it was obviously used for book-keeping. Shelves of box files were organized by date, going back at least four years. The lone desk held a standard Dell computer and a large calculator that printed off paper records.

'Maybe we should have called first,' said Preston.

'And missed the chance to see this?' Hogan retorted.

'We could always take the waitress in for

questioning. Who knows what she's hiding.'

'Whatever it is,' Hogan answered drily. 'I'm sure it's not a fancy for old lawmen. Besides, you need more than a good lasso trick to keep up with college girls these days. They all read the *Kama Sutra*.'

'What the hell's that? And can I rent the DVD instead?'

Hogan laughed. 'Lucas owns two other restaurants near by.'

'Any of them serve steak?'

'Well, number two on my list is a place called The Olde Steak House.'

'Being a detective, I would deduce we could find ourselves a bit of beef there.'

'Let's test your theory.'

101

A brown car was pulling away when Sam, Zack and Davey arrived outside the popular fish house. Inside the Mercedes, Zack was sweating despite a chill in the air, but Sam discovered he felt strangely calm.

He pulled out his revolver. 'I'm not leaving without answers,' he said. 'Consequences be damned. If you're not up for it—'

Zack leaned over to the glovebox and withdrew his tiny, stainless-steel pistol. Dried flecks of blood marred the gun's shiny finish.

'I'm in,' he said.

Sam turned to Davey. 'Keep low. We'll be back soon.'

Davey slipped down further in his seat. His eyes were as wide as a kid on a Ferris wheel.

The restaurant was busy with customers, but Sam didn't hesitate to walk briskly past the tables and through the swinging door at the rear. The young waitress at the reservation desk didn't even bat an eye.

Several cooks glanced up at the two men, but didn't seem particularly interested. Zack and Sam entered the walk-in freezer without hindrance or objection. After all, who would enter a lion's den without an invitation?

They descended into the tunnels with less confidence than they had entered the restaurant. The pitch darkness and heavy air crowded in on their resolve.

At the bottom of the stairs, Sam stopped and switched on a pocket flashlight. Its weak beam barely pierced the thick, stale darkness.

'Close the hatch,' he said. 'See what happens.'

Zack retreated up the stairs and pulled the hatch closed. Instantly, the row of electric lights overhead lit the tunnel. Sam switched off the flashlight and they moved forward.

In the cavern with the red sofa, Sam felt his stomach flutter with nervous anticipation. With every step his mind screamed that he was going in the wrong direction.

He crossed the room and knocked on the door that led to the inner sanctum. No reply. He knocked again, and then tried the door. Locked.

Frowning, Sam turned to Zack just as a distant scrape of metal on stone echoed from deeper in the tunnels. They both approached the second stone archway, but unlike the tunnel they had followed from the restaurant, this one remained in darkness.

Sam switched on his flashlight and plunged ahead. Zack trailed nervously behind.

Inside the unexplored tunnel, Sam moved cautiously, the flashlight focused on the ground. A few feet into the darkness, they came across another cell dug into the wall. This one was barely four feet deep and its door was one solid piece of wood without bars or window.

'That's probably a crimpers' punishment cell,' Zack whispered. 'If you caused them trouble, you were moved to one of these. The isolation and darkness drove a lot of captives mad, but the crimpers would knock them unconscious and sell them anyway. It became the captain's problem once they were at sea.'

'Charming,' Sam whispered back.

'There was one infamous case,' Zack continued, his nervousness making him chatter, 'where legendary crimper Bunco Kelly sold a crew of dead men for thirty-two dollars a head to the captain of *The Flying Prince*.'

'Dead men?'

'The story goes that a gang mistook the cellar of a mortuary for the saloon next door. Thinking they had scored big, the men cracked open a keg and had a party. Unfortunately, the keg was formaldehyde. When Bunco happened along, all the men were dead or dying. Thinking quickly, Bunco and his crew carted the bodies through the tunnels and out to the docks. Legend has it, he even told the captain that he should really charge him more since he had to get the men so drunk first.'

'Sounds like someone Lucas would admire,' said Sam, his voice taking on a nasty edge.

Zack took the hint and shut up.

After a few more feet, they came to a heavy steel door that sealed yet another stone archway. It definitely wasn't part of the original construction. Sam tried the handle and found it locked solid. As he bit back a curse, his flashlight shifted to the left and illuminated the entrance to a smaller, secondary tunnel. The dirt floor was well travelled.

Sam moved forward until the tunnel dead-ended at a narrow wooden door.

Instead of a handle, a thick piece of knotted rope dangled from a thumb-sized hole bored near its right edge. With hope in his heart, Sam tugged on the rope. The rope slid partway out of the hole until the knot on the other end hit home. The door swung open effortlessly to reveal a heavy red curtain.

102

'What the fuck! How did you get down here?'

Vadik stood up at his desk as Sam pushed through the curtain to find himself in the same office where he had betrayed his old partner for a briefcase full of cash. Vadik's overgrown bodyguard was nowhere in sight.

'We want Lucas,' said Sam.

Vadik stepped out from behind his glowing bank of computer monitors. Despite his short stature, he looked tough enough to rip the interlopers limb from limb without breaking a sweat.

'You got your money,' he said. 'We have no more business.'

'Lucas has my daughter.'

Zack stepped through the curtain. 'And he killed mine.'

Vadik twisted his head in surprise. 'Dr Parker, I did not know.'

'We don't care what you knew,' Sam said. 'We just want Lucas.'

Vadik curled his lip in distaste. 'I do not care for this venture you say that my boss is on. There is no profit, but what kind of a man would I be to betray him after all he's done for me?'

'Like we give a fuck what kind of man you are.' Sam raised his gun and pointed it at Vadik's face.

Vadik raised his hands and shrugged again. 'It is one thing to point a gun. Quite another to pull the trigger.'

Sam pulled the trigger and an explosion of rock blasted from the wall directly beside Vadik's head.

'See?' said Vadik, his voice perfectly calm. 'Professionals don't miss.'

'I didn't—'

Vadik roared as he lowered his head and ran directly at Sam. His broad shoulders slammed into Sam's chest and sent him flying backwards. Sam hit the floor with a loud clap, his gun firing by mistake, the bullet smacking harmlessly into the low ceiling.

Sam gasped with surprise and tried to recover, but Vadik was too fast. With a move Sam had only ever seen on TV wrestling, Vadik dived on top of him with a body slam. The air whooshed from Sam's lungs and he felt ribs crack, but he had too much rage to lose focus. Using the only weapon at hand, he drove the butt of the gun into the man's skull with such force he heard bone crunch.

Vadik grunted, but instead of rolling away from the pain, he bore down, his muscled arms encircling Sam's waist. He began to squeeze. Sam felt his spine twist and his kidneys scream as he continued to hammer away at the man's thick skull. Blood was pouring from a dozen cuts when Sam's strength began to ebb.

He gritted his teeth, willing himself not to black out, when suddenly a heavy metallic clunk snapped Vadik's head to one side. The unexpected blow made Vadik's eyes roll in his head and his grip finally released.

Sam inhaled sharply as Zack stood over them with a bronze Degas statue in his hand.

Sam rose up on his knees to match his stunned attacker. He stared into Vadik's cold eyes and instinctively knew that whatever secrets they held couldn't be pried out with force.

His body shook with adrenalin as he also realized they couldn't risk Lucas discovering how close they were getting, and Vadik had been very clear about whose side he was on.

Until these last few days, Sam had always considered himself a pacifist, but that resolve had never been truly tested. Now, with his family missing and in grave danger, that resolve was a distant memory.

There was only one choice.

Sam slammed all of his weight down on top of Vadik's skull until the light went out in the criminal's eyes and he crumpled unconscious to the floor.

And God help me, Sam thought, but the violence felt good.

103

Dragging himself to his feet, ignoring the pain that flared across his chest, Sam moved to the bank of computer monitors in the corner.

He beckoned Zack to follow. 'Come on. You're the genius.'

Zack pulled up a chair in front of the computer and hit the Enter key. Instantly, the four monitors came to life, each displaying a blank desktop. Zack tapped a few more keys and a series of large icons appeared.

From over Zack's shoulder, Sam pointed at the icon that represented a movie camera. 'Click that one.'

Zack grabbed the mouse and clicked the icon. Instantly, four windows opened on each of two monitors, simultaneously displaying eight different locations. Four of the locations were outside: one showed the loading dock of a warehouse, another an empty field of grass, a third showed the rear entrance to the Fish

House, and a fourth displayed an empty gravel lot.

The second series of windows were all interior and they glowed in hazy, night-vision green. Sam studied the four windows carefully, noticing a subtle movement of shadow in the lower right.

'Can you enlarge that one?' He tapped it with his finger.

Zack punched a few keys and the window enlarged to fill the screen. It was difficult to discern exactly what they were seeing, but it appeared to be a small cell. Sam could make out the shape of a bucket in one corner and what looked like the legs of a metal cot in the other. The movement was coming from a bundle wrapped in a blanket on the bed.

As if startled by their presence, the bundle moved again and the blanket slipped to expose a pale and frightened face.

'MaryAnn,' Sam groaned as his hand reached out to touch the screen.

Sam's daughter didn't look at the camera. Instead, she seemed to recoil from something out of sight.

'Where is she?' Sam asked, his voice tortured, pleading.

Zack punched a few more keys and a series of letters appeared in the corner of the screen. Zack pointed at them. 'Looks like Union Street?'

Sam shook his head. 'Never heard of it.' He looked at the letters. They didn't spell Street, just the abbreviation: ST. 'Union Station,' he said. 'They're under the station.'

They looked at each other and in unison said, 'Davey's tunnel.'

Sam touched the screen again. Whatever was frightening his daughter hadn't moved any closer and he wondered if it was something she was hearing, a noise approaching from beyond her cell.

'Hang on, MaryAnn,' he whispered urgently. 'Dad's on his way.'

Zack and Sam dashed back through the tunnels like the bulls of Pamplona, fear driving them blindly forward, rage strengthening their resolve to gore anyone who stood in their way.

104

MaryAnn recoiled in fright as the cell door opened and the large man with the shaved head entered. His boss followed behind, a wiry bleached ghost whose skull-like face and tiny nose reminded her of a barracuda.

'It's time to come with me, MaryAnn,' the ghost said. 'We'll be meeting your father soon.'

MaryAnn shook her head vigorously from side to side, not trusting a single word uttered from the man's thin colourless lips.

'Don't defy me now, MaryAnn,' he warned, his voice like ice. 'You've been a good girl and I've treated you as such.'

MaryAnn choked back a sob. Her skin crawled within filthy clothes; her body burned from lack of food, water and even the barest of essentials. Every part of her felt gross and her heart ached with longing for her parents to gather her up and take her home.

MaryAnn would have given anything to be

back in her own house now, her own bed, her own bathroom with shampoos and soaps, toothpaste and floss.

She felt a stirring beside her. Another flash of guilt as she knew she had eaten more than an equal share of what little food they had received. The woman protected her as her own mother would have – risked her own life to help her when she had tried to escape.

The ghost turned to his guard. 'Bring her.'

The massive man strode forward and snatched away the blue blanket. The girl shrieked and kicked her skinny legs as he reached for her.

Then MaryAnn heard a growl, and a blur of nails and teeth sprang from the bed. The guard released a high-pitched squeal as he tried desperately to fight off the demon.

MaryAnn looked on in horror, barely recognizing the woman within the beast that clawed and bit the massive guard. She was so entranced by the battle that she was taken by surprise when the ghost grabbed her by the hair and yanked her off the bed.

MaryAnn screamed, the pain in her scalp deeper than anything she had felt before, as the man dragged her, kicking and squirming across the dirt floor. At the cell door, he yanked her into the tunnel with a final tug.

MaryAnn rolled across the ground and slapped heavily into the wall. She gasped, her arm going numb as her shoulder collided with stone. She heard the cell door close, shutting out the sound of a fierce struggle still echoing inside. When she looked up, the ghost was grinning down at her, his small, sharp teeth the same pale white as his skin.

Taking to heart everything the woman in the cell had taught her, MaryAnn launched herself at her abductor.

But the ghost didn't even flinch, and as MaryAnn closed in, a hardened fist shot out to smash the side of her skull.

MaryAnn dropped to her knees, her eyes rolling back in her head, and she crumpled forward into blackness.

105

Sam had barely scrambled inside when the Mercedes leapt into traffic and headed for the park.

'Did you get him?' Davey asked.

Sam turned in his seat, wincing at the pain in his ribs. 'Lucas is holding my family under Union Station. Does your tunnel connect to his?'

Davey nodded. 'Yeah. Lucas is bad, man. He had people chase me out when I went in too deep. I got to be real careful now.'

'Is that why he wanted you dead?' Sam said, thinking aloud. 'Not because of high school, but because you were trespassing in his tunnels?'

Davey shrugged. 'What do I know?'

'You weren't one of the gods,' Sam said. 'Lucas simply saw an opportunity to get rid of a nuisance.'

Davey pouted. 'Great.'

'We have to stop him, Davey. You have to get us inside that tunnel. Do you remember how?'

Davey tapped the side of his head. 'Fuckin' right, I do.'

Zack pulled a tight right-hand turn, tyres sliding effortlessly across the slick asphalt. Then, as if channelling his teen years in the Mustang, he flattened his foot on the accelerator. The Mercedes roared as it chewed up Third Avenue.

The heavy rain had stopped falling, leaving the streets glistening. The Mercedes slashed through the puddles like a mechanical shark, all teeth and chrome.

Zack showed no sign of slowing as the road dead-ended at the park. Sam braced his hands against the dash as the Mercedes hit the concrete kerb with a sickening crunch. The steel-belted radials, however, took the punishment without blowing-out and the car leapt off the road. Its blunt nose hit the flimsy park fence and ripped through without hesitation.

On the wet grass, the car's rear-end fishtailed wildly, but Zack controlled the slide and pressed the accelerator even harder as they whipped past a stand of trees.

The park was practically empty except for a few brave pedestrians with wet rain slickers tied around their waists and dog leashes firmly in hand. But those who noticed looked on in disbelief as the large car soared over the lush, green lawn. Even the ever-present joggers put the digital soundtrack to their lives on pause to stare open-mouthed at the silver-grey beast as it glided past.

From the back seat, Davey waved at everyone, his face alight with the thrill of it, as if he was a teenager again.

106

The cell door opened and Lucas's guard staggered out, blood dripping from several long gashes across his face.

Two of the deepest wounds ran across his left eye – one had torn the eyelid – and ended in a chunk of broken nail that protruded from his gashed cheek. Other wounds covered his arms, the nastiest being a bite that had torn a ragged half-circle of flesh from his arm.

'Did you kill her?' Lucas asked casually.

The guard shrugged his over-developed shoulders. The muscles that had erased his neck barely able to rise.

'Bitch hurt me.'

He reached up to touch his cheek, his fingers brushing the broken piece of nail. He plucked it out with a spurt of blood and threw it to the ground in disgust.

Lucas smiled. 'We all have an animal inside us, Richard. As civilized human beings we attempt to contain it, but given the right circumstances, it is quickly unleashed.'

The guard stared at his boss with blank eyes, the speech obviously lost in translation.

Lucas was only slightly annoyed. He hadn't hired the man for his brains.

'Tie the girl up,' he ordered. 'I need to attend to a personal matter.'

The guard hesitated and glanced over his shoulder.

'Yes, yes.' Lucas sighed. 'Once I leave, you can finish with the woman.'

Lucas entered the cell and sat beside his other captive. His experiment had been a failure. The creature beneath the blanket was nothing more than a pitiless animal, a husk without meat.

He stroked the blanket, feeling the frail woman shiver beneath the tattered wool.

'I know you love me,' he said, 'but I need to hear it in your own words.'

A soft whimpering sound fluttered from beneath the cloth.

Lucas lowered his face and pulled back the corner. The woman's face was hollow and bruised, with two terrified red holes where her eyes should shine.

'Tell me,' he cooed softly, 'why you love me?'

The woman licked her misshapen lips, but no words escaped her throat.

Lucas had memorized all the correct answers to

his father's questions, but none of them helped him escape the burnings. His father believed that fire was the only enemy the devil knew. It was the one element that kept him deep beneath the soil and the only thing that could drive him back down when he surfaced in the body of a sinner.

'The devil don't burn,' his father would say as Lucas writhed, 'but he fears the flames.'

Lucas dropped the woman's blanket and stood up. If she loved him even a little, she would have known the right answers.

He looked at the armada of photos he had pasted to the wall. She wasn't the woman he had thought she was.

With an irritated sigh, he pulled out a tiny squeeze bottle of lighter fluid and poured its contents across the blanket. The woman didn't move, not even after he flicked a lit match in her direction.

Lucas exited the cell and locked the door as the blanket caught fire with a noisy whoomph.

Lucas returned to his temporary office. The windowless dirt cell was sparsely furnished with a simple rug on the floor, a desk and chair. On the desk sat a high-end Apple laptop computer with a wide seventeen-inch screen.

When the laptop had powered up, Lucas ran his fingers across the keyboard to tap into his main-frame and take control of all his systems.

He slid his finger across the trackpad as eight

windows opened on his desktop. Each window showed a live feed from one of his security cameras. He frowned at the sight of a familiar car speeding across the green lawn behind Union Station. He tapped the button to fill the monitor with that camera's view.

As the car stopped and three men exited, Lucas angrily reached for his phone.

107

Zack, Sam and Davey climbed out of the Mercedes and headed for the wire fence. They were alone: few visitors ever bothered with this empty corner of the park, especially on a damp afternoon.

Davey loped ahead, grinning like a kid at Disneyland. His face clearly showed the thrill he felt at once more being Sam White's sidekick just as he had been in the glory days of high school.

As Sam neared the fence, his cellphone rang. Both he and Zack stopped in their tracks, worry evident on their faces.

Sam lifted the phone from his pocket and pressed the Receive button.

'You lied to me, Sam,' said the scrambled voice.

'About what?'

'You didn't kill Davey.'

Sam's breath caught in his throat as he quickly scanned the area above the fence. He spotted the box-shaped security camera attached to a pole, eight feet above the entrance to the tunnel.

'You didn't tell me to kill him.' Sam kept his voice calm. 'You wanted him to burn and to scream. I delivered that.'

The line hissed. 'Don't fuck with me, Sam. Your deception will cost you.'

Sam swallowed hard, his strength of will crumbling.

'I have your daughter here with me, Sam.'

'Don't hurt her,' Sam blurted. 'Please. I'm begging you.'

'The choice is yours, Sam. Do you still have your gun?'

'Yes.'

'Show me.'

Sam quickly swapped the phone to his left hand and pulled the gun out of his vest pocket with his right. He held it up to the camera.

Beside him, Zack tensed as he realized that they stood right in the centre of the field of grass they had seen on the screen in Vadik's lair.

Davey stood by the fence, confused. He cocked his head to one side and scratched an itch on his scalp.

'Very good,' said the voice. 'Now you don't want me to harm your daughter, is that correct?'

'Yes.' Unwelcome tears began to blur Sam's vision.

'Then, in exchange, I need you to do something for me. A third task. Are you willing?'

'Yes,' Sam said quickly. 'Anything.'

'No tricks this time.'

'I have none.'

The line crackled with a burst of static. 'Remember I'm watching you.' A pause. 'Kill Zack.'

'What?' Sam gasped and spun to look at Zack with panicked eyes.

'I don't like repeating myself, Sam. But if you need incentive—'

'Daddy!' a girl's voice screamed over the airwaves.

'MaryAnn!' Sam shouted back.

'Touching,' said the voice. 'Now kill Zack before I lose my temper.'

Sam pointed the gun at his friend.

Zack stared at him, his eyes so large, the whites were the size of river stones.

'I'm so sorry.'

'Jesus Christ, Sam.' Zack held up his hands.

Sam hesitated. 'I don't have a choice.'

Zack's face sank and a resigned calmness came to his eyes as he slowly lowered his hands. 'Your daughter?'

'Your life for hers.'

Zack locked eyes with his friend. 'Do it, Sam. You'll be doing me a favour.'

'Christ, Zack. I . . . I—'

'DO IT!' Anger made Zack's face boil.

Sam's gun began to shake and tears ran down his cheeks. He still hesitated.

'Do it, Sam,' Zack pleaded, his voice quivering

as he reached into his pocket and produced his own gun. He pointed it at Sam. 'Do it now or I'll kill you where you stand, Sam. I'll take the money and run. Your family will die with—'

Sam pulled the trigger and a geyser of blood erupted from the side of Zack's head. His body collapsed noiselessly to the ground with barely a twitch or spasm.

Davey screamed in horror, his mouth opening so wide it looked as if his jaw had come unhinged.

Sam held the smoking gun at his side, his face a contorted mask of sorrow and fury. 'You bastard.'

'You had the choice, Sam. I always gave you the choice.'

Sam howled in frustration and jammed the gun barrel against his temple. His finger trembled on the trigger.

'DON'T!' screamed the voice. 'Do that and your daughter dies, too.'

Sam collapsed to his knees, the gun still aimed at his head.

'We're not done with you yet, Sam.'

'Fuck you!' Sam instantly brought the gun to bear on the camera and pulled the trigger. The camera lens shattered and the box sparked blue as the gunshot echoed across the park.

After a moment of silence, the voice said, 'Feel better now?'

'No.' Sam's voice was tight.

The voice chuckled. 'I'll add the cost of a new camera to your bill.'

Switch

'Where do I pay?'

'I'm glad you asked. It's time to deliver.'

'Where?'

'Bring the money to the station. I'll meet you on the platform by the first track.'

'When?'

'Now, Sam. I would hate for you to get arrested for murder before you see your daughter again.'

The line went dead.

108

The detectives in-car radio reported: *Shots fired in Waterfront Park*.

Detective Preston glanced over at his partner. 'Should we go?'

'If someone caught the bullet, we'll get the call,' Hogan said. 'For now, let's keep on Lucas. He's the connection. Everyone connected with that rape is being punished.'

'Because one of them got away with it?' Preston mused.

'And Lucas paid the price for a crime he doesn't feel he committed.'

Preston drove through an amber light and turned east. 'Twenty-five years is a long time to plot revenge.'

'For some people, high school still feels like yesterday.'

'True,' Preston agreed. 'That's why they invented Viagra, right?'

Hogan's laughter was cut short when the

broadcast updated to report a grey Mercedes sedan was seen leaving the scene of the park shooting.

Hogan lifted the transmitter and asked for more information on the Mercedes as Preston pulled a quick U-turn and headed for the park.

109

Sam fishtailed out of the park on to Hoyt and then pulled a sharp right on Sixth Avenue. The 150-foot-tall clock tower, the centrepiece of Portland's historic Union Station, served as a beacon as Sam rushed the few blocks to his final destination.

The Mercedes glided through the parking lot and came to rest against a yellow kerb.

Sam scrambled out of the car and popped the trunk. He looked down upon the two large duffel bags and felt the realization dawn of just how little the contents really mattered.

He had spent his life chasing a dream that included wealth as a reward for success, but now it was irrelevant. The only important thing was his family.

With feelings of dread, guilt and sorrow chewing at his gut, Sam lifted a heavy red bag on to each shoulder and walked under the clock tower to enter the station.

110

Detective Hogan slid out of the car and approached a uniformed sergeant who stood beside a series of skid marks that blemished the untamed green lawn.

'You investigating trampled weeds now, Detective?' the sergeant asked. 'Cause we ain't got a body.'

'We were interested in the car.'

'The Merc?'

Hogan nodded.

'Tied to something you working on?'

'Could be. Anybody see a plate?'

The sergeant casually snapped open his black leather notebook, making a show of flipping the pages. 'Oregon plate, but no number.' He pointed down at a page with his finger. 'The witnesses were all pretty far away.' The sergeant closed his notebook. 'Your guy camera shy?'

Hogan frowned. 'Why?'

The sergeant pointed above the fence to the

broken surveillance camera. 'We're pretty sure that's what he was shooting at.'

Hogan studied the camera, noticing its familiar box shape. 'Why's it pointing out here?'

The sergeant shrugged. 'I assumed it must have something to do with security at the station. With all these colour-coded terror alerts, cameras are popping up everywhere.'

'Can you check that for me?' Hogan asked. 'See if the station owns it?'

'Sure.'

As the sergeant reached for his radio, Hogan turned to find his partner kneeling on the ground a short distance away. He was poking a ballpoint pen at something in the grass.

Hogan walked over. 'What you got?'

'Blood,' Preston said. 'And something odd.'

Hogan stepped closer as Preston lifted a small black box, not much larger than a standard 9-volt battery, on the end of his pen. Protruding from the box were two lengths of thin wire. At the end of the wire was a melted glob of red plastic attached to a thin metal plate. The metal was scorched on top and several strands of curly black hair protruded from its underside.

'What is it?' Hogan asked.

In response, Preston dipped his finger in the blood coating the ground and brought it to his mouth. As Hogan watched in revulsion, Preston touched his finger to his tongue.

'It's fake. Strawberry, I think. Never was very

good with fruits.' He held out the device for his partner to get a closer look. 'This is a squib. Homemade Hollywood magic at its best.'

'Somebody faked a shooting?'

'Oh, the shots were real.' Preston indicated the shattered camera. He then turned to face the direction of the blood splatter and pointed at a tree. 'We'll probably find another slug in that trunk. They faked a killing.'

'For the camera?' Hogan surmised.

'That would be my guess.'

'Bleepin' actors, huh?'

Preston sighed. 'You can say that again.'

The sergeant approached across the grass. 'Detective?'

Hogan turned. 'Yes, Sergeant?'

'Just received a call on an illegally parked Mercedes. The plate doesn't match your BOLO, but—'

'Where?'

The sergeant jabbed a thumb over his shoulder. 'Union Station.'

111

Zack followed Davey's lantern through the dark tunnel, his eyes straining to avoid any loose rocks or sudden dips in the dirt floor that could trip his feet and break an ankle.

When a train rumbled overhead, the whole tunnel shook, making Zack quickly scramble to find shelter beneath one of the solid stone archways. As he grasped the stone, waiting for the train to pass, his fingers found the pillar's mysterious, undecipherable carvings, but he no longer cared what secrets they held.

His head pounded from the tiny explosive charge Sam had stuck to the side of his skull, along with a condom of fake blood hidden in his hair and disguised with a small patch of wig. The wig had blown off in the blast, which Zack guessed must have added to the realism of a bullet blasting through his skull.

Davey had been struck dumb, even though he had watched them attach the squib in the car before they drove to the restaurant. The realism must have erased Davey's short-term memory as his face showed horrid fascination when Zack later rose from the dead and pulled the depleted squib out of his hair.

He thought back to the tortured look on Sam's face and the agony that filled his voice before he pulled the trigger. The performance had made him forget Sam was an actor, and for a brief moment the unnerving thought had crossed his mind that the squib was just there to placate him, a placebo, so he wouldn't run if Sam was forced to shoot. They had both known that with Sam in possession of the full one million dollars, Lucas's need for Zack was over.

When Zack triggered the explosion and collapsed to the ground, he had even imagined he could feel Sam's bullet passing before his eyes, a whisper of warm, electrically charged air brushing against his brow.

Sam had driven off without a word, trusting that Zack would follow the original plan.

Even though he knew of the earlier betrayal, Sam had still entrusted him with all he held dear. Zack could only hope that, this time, he could honour that trust.

112

Sam entered the lobby of the train station.

Polished stone walls and elegant archways bordered a marble-lined floor, its grid pattern echoing the ornate ceiling two storeys above. Long mahogany benches filled the centre. They glistened with fresh polish under the dangling, chandelier-style lights.

It was the type of location a movie director would use to film happy endings of husbands coming home from war and rushing into their lovers' arms. It was not where one would imagine money being exchanged for the lives of a woman and child.

Sam scrutinized the sparsely populated benches for Lucas, but saw no one he recognized. He scanned the concourse, stopping in front of a large marble clock, its face scuffed by time. The tall, black letters beneath the clock indicated the trains lay just beyond its doors.

Switch

Sam gathered all his courage, and, with a bag over each shoulder, headed for the platform beyond.

113

The giant smoothed a dab of Vaseline across his face, feeling bloody welts rising from his flesh. The puckered skin burned from the alcohol swabs he had used to disinfect the cuts.

The damn tunnels were always damp and Richard wondered what century-old illnesses still thrived in the dark, cobwebbed corners. He knew the history of the tunnels, knew that dozens if not hundreds of people had died down here. Some were victims of violence, others of drink. But still others had succumbed to plagues and other skin-boiling, lung-eating maladies that modern medicine had thought long eradicated. And destroyed they may be, but that was on the surface, not down here in the dark and the dank.

Richard wiped an alcohol-soaked cotton swab across the bite on his arm and gritted his teeth against the pain. The bitch had bit deep into muscle, tearing out a good-sized chunk of bloody flesh with her flashing white teeth. He hoped the resulting scar wouldn't ruin the perfect shape of his bicep and destroy his chances at the upcoming National Bodybuilding Competition in Seattle.

He had placed third in his last two competitions, and was feeling confident in his chances of moving up a notch this time around. Last week at the gym, he spotted his main competition, a large Asian who worked for Vadik, and noticed his treatments for testicular cancer had begun to show on his body. The man was definitely shrinking, which meant second place was there for the taking. He just prayed the bitch's vicious attack hadn't fucked things up.

Women had long been his bane. And this one wasn't even supposed to be down here. He had put up with her mouth, her crying and her mind games for the first week, and as long as he didn't go near the child, she had been relatively easy to deal with.

The fuck-up – *his* fuck-up, according to Lucas – at the switch had changed all that. Richard didn't believe he deserved all the blame. After all, there were two women and two kids and he was all on his own. If Lucas had drugged the wine properly that white bitch wouldn't have woken up and turned into a screeching banshee when she saw . . .

The woman screamed when he appeared in the doorway with the chloroformed girl in his arms.

The drug should have knocked her out for

hours, but somehow the mother had woken up. She approached him on rubbery legs, a pair of No.4 knitting needles clutched in her hand.

MaryAnn tumbled from his grasp as the woman lunged at him with murderous intent. Before he could raise his arms in defence, one needle broke off in his chest and the other dug into his thick neck, just missing the bulging carotid artery. Richard howled as he instinctively backhanded the woman with enough force to snap bone.

Hannah flew to the side, blood spurting across her face from a broken nose as her head cracked loudly on the laminate floor. Richard expected her to stay down, and when she didn't, he felt genuine fear.

The woman before him was no longer a suburban housewife who read romance novels and knitted the occasional scarf. Instead, she was a demon with fireball eyes and razor claws.

The woman sprang forward, her fingers curled into ten deadly claws, her teeth watering for flesh. Richard let her come, trying to calm his mind and remember his training. The woman moved blindly and without skill, her entire focus bent on ripping out his throat.

As soon as her nails touched him, Richard trapped her throat between his forearms and performed a lethal scissor move. The woman's neck twisted so violently that her spine snapped.

The anger remained in her eyes as she slumped

lifelessly to the floor, and the hatred he saw reflected back filled Richard with a boiling rage.

'You bitch!' He lifted his foot and brought it crashing down on the dead woman's skull. More bones cracked as he repeated the action over and over until his rage ebbed.

When he was done, his breathing laboured under the effort, the woman's head was unrecognizable.

Frustrated, Richard rubbed both hands across his smooth skull and wondered what he should do. Lucas expected him to return with a woman and child, but now . . . fuck it. There was only one thing he could do.

He picked up the drugged child and returned to his van. The other woman was still unconscious in the back. She would have to do.

After the stinging in his arm stopped, Richard wrapped a clean bandage around it and knotted it tight. Satisfied with his handiwork, he flexed his muscles and rotated his head to work out any kinks.

When he was warmed up, he placed a scowl on his face, headed out of the cell and back into the tunnels.

It was time to finish that bitch once and for all.

114

Davey turned a corner and stopped beneath a stone archway, his chest heaving and eyes glistening. When Zack arrived a few moments later, Davey flashed a set of rotting teeth.

'This is as far as I've ever gone,' he said. 'There's a door here that leads to a whole series of tunnels.'

'Can we get through?'

Davey grinned again. 'They locked it, but the hinges are on this side. I took the pins out weeks ago, so we just need to pry it loose.'

Zack leaned forward and touched the rusted hinges before sliding down the seam, his fingers finding a slim gap between wood and stone.

'You don't have a crowbar handy, by any chance?'

'Just this.' Davey held up his homemade knife.

Zack slapped the man on the shoulder. 'Let's get to work.'

115

Detective Hogan parked beside the Mercedes and climbed out to quickly circle the car. When he arrived on the other side, his partner was peering into the open trunk.

'If your theory is correct, then this has all the earmarks of an exchange,' Preston said.

'Money for his family.' Hogan glanced at the station's clock tower. 'Strange place for it: public, open, few escape routes.'

Preston shrugged. 'Makes the delivery man feel comfortable, and if you're not expecting him to follow you out . . .'

'Because the delivery man is dead,' Hogan finished.

In the tunnels, Davey swore a blue streak as he strained against the thick, wooden door. His knife had proven useful for piercing flesh and keeping night thieves at bay, but it was awkward against the spongy, time-ravaged wood.

'You move to the top again,' Zack suggested as he squeezed in beside him. 'You've moved the bottom enough that I can jam my fingers in there.'

Davey did as he was told and jammed his blade deep into the upper part of the door, directly above the top hinge.

'On three,' Zack said. 'One, two—'

Both men strained, sweat popping on their brows as the door began to groan. Suddenly, it jerked in their hands with a popping of air and both men fell backwards into the dirt.

Zack bit his tongue, drawing blood, as his head slapped the ground. Davey fell on top of him, too, all sharp elbows and boney butt. When the dust settled, both men looked at the door. It didn't appear to have budged.

'Damn it.' Davey kicked the door with all the frustration he could muster. Upon impact, the door groaned and then fell, forcing Davey to scramble out of the way before his feet were crushed under its weight.

After the door struck the ground, Zack pushed Davey off and crawled to the opening. The tunnel beyond was dimly lit by a string of bare bulbs attached to the ceiling. It was also just as ancient and dangerous as the one they were in.

Zack looked left and right, swallowing blood from his injured tongue, as he tried to decide which way to go. Then he heard a scream – a woman's scream.

Switch

Zack scrambled to his feet and rushed headlong
down the tunnel in the direction of the sound, his
face a mask of determined rage.

116

Sam walked on to the main outdoor platform that served as the introductory conduit to a series of black iron stairs and high metal bridges. The iron-works funnelled passengers across the tracks to each of the numbered platforms beyond.

Sam stood like a rock in a stream as passengers flowed around him. He watched the crowds thin as passengers ascended the stairs, found their platform number and vanished. No one appeared to be waiting for him.

With a sinking heart, Sam turned to his left and froze. A thin man with skin so white it practically glowed stood on the northern edge of the platform. His face was skeletal and hairless except for a triangle-shaped patch of purple-black hair beneath his lower lip and a matching pair of thin, sculpted eyebrows. His eyes were a piercing glacial blue, but his nose was so perfectly tiny, it was barely visible.

He reminded Sam of an alabaster eel.

Lucas stood with a brick wall at his back and no easy exits within reach. It was a private spot, unused by passengers; a place someone would pick only if they were confident no one could stop them from leaving.

Beside him, MaryAnn trembled, her shoulders shaking as she stared unblinkingly at the platform floor. She was pale and frail, her face hidden beneath a mass of tangled, greasy hair. Her favourite nightgown was soiled and ripped.

To Sam, she had never looked more beautiful in her entire life.

'MaryAnn,' he called softly.

The girl lifted her head at the sound of her name, her eyes blinking into focus.

'Daddy!'

Sam gasped at the sight of her face: bruised, bloody and swollen. The bastard had beaten her. MaryAnn attempted to rush forward, but Lucas yanked her back by the nylon straps around her wrists. She cried out and every sob tore at Sam's heart. He wanted to snatch her away, but knew he couldn't take that risk.

'Let her go, Lucas. I have your money.'

'Bring it closer. But keep your hands where I can see them.'

Sam moved forward. 'Where's Hannah?'

'All in good time, Sam. I need some insurance.'

'Why? You don't care about the money. Hell, I still don't understand why you feel the need to hurt me.'

Lucas raised his eyebrows and hardened his eyes. 'You thought you were better than the rest of us, that nothing could touch you. I proved you're not. You're a thief and a cold-blooded killer, Zack was a murderer and rapist, and Alan was a coward. You're not worth following.'

Sam stopped a short distance in front of his enemy and dropped the bags. He stared into Lucas's eyes, searching for the madness, but finding a deep, aching hurt.

MaryAnn struggled against her bonds again, but Lucas's grip was iron.

'I never asked you to follow me, Lucas,' Sam said, searching for an opening, a weakness. 'High school ended twenty-five years ago.'

'And you moved on.'

'Yes!' Sam cried. 'That's what people do.'

'You abandoned me.'

'Abandon? What are you talking about? We went to a few parties together, it wasn't a fucking marriage. I had my own plans and got on with them.'

'You had responsibilities, Sam. You all did.'

'That's nuts, Lucas. The whole point of high school is the lack of responsibility. I didn't owe anyone a damn thing.'

Spittle flew from Lucas's mouth. 'I lost fifteen years and you don't owe me?'

Sam was taken aback. 'What do you mean?'

'Fifteen years, Sam. Do you know what they did to me inside? Do you think any of *my* plans even had a chance? I wanted to die, and where were you?'

Sam held up his hands. 'I don't know what you're talking about.'

'Prom night.'

'I left early. My car was packed and I was hell-bent on Hollywood. It wasn't a secret.'

'You made Susan lie.'

'Susan? Susan Millar? What are you—'

'You had sex with her.'

'Yes, but . . .' Sam shook his head angrily. 'I was a kid, Lucas, having a good time. I never took anything that wasn't freely given. Susan and I fooled around, so what?'

Lucas's eyes narrowed and he tugged on MaryAnn's bonds to elicit a squeal. 'She looked at me with such hatred.'

Sam tried to bite back his fury. 'Who? Susan?'

Lucas's voice broke as he attempted to laugh. 'You didn't even know. That's how important I was to you.'

'Didn't know what?' Sam's gaze darted down to his daughter. He desperately wanted to grab her and run.

'She accused me of rape,' Lucas said. 'But I never touched her. You touched her. Ironwood touched her. Even fucking Viking touched her. But I went to jail for it. You didn't even show up for the trial. You could have explained what a whore she was.'

'You were convicted of the rape?' Sam was

407

shocked. 'No one contacted me. Not Susan, not the police—'

'Everything came into alignment,' Lucas said, cutting him off. 'Your commercial on TV. Zack honoured for work he practised on me. Even that vicious prick Viking was being lauded as some kind of hero. Could the message have been any clearer?'

'What message?' Sam asked, exasperated. 'We're just living our lives.'

'Lives you don't deserve.'

'Why?'

'Because you stole them. From me.' Lucas bared his teeth. 'Now back away from the bags.'

117

Zack ran down the tunnel, drawn onward by the sounds of fighting: a woman screaming; a man yelling, cursing.

When he burst into the cell, a giant of a man was holding a woman against the wall by her throat. The woman was in deeper shadow, but Zack could see the man was in a rage. Blood poured down his cheek from a gash across his eye.

Then, as Zack's eyes adjusted to the dimmer light, he saw the woman was Jasmine. Her face was swollen and bruised and her eyes were bulging from exertion, but it was definitely his wife – *Alive!*

Zack screamed, 'Put her down. NOW!'

The giant turned his head and sneered, while his hand squeezed tighter. 'Where the fuck did you—'

A bullet tore through Richard's deltoid muscle at 2,600 feet per second, its cone-shaped nose widening into a flat dime as it ricocheted off a shoulder blade and hit the collarbone – shattering the bone into four pieces.

Jasmine fell to the ground as her attacker's arm went limp and he lurched sideways to collide with the cell wall.

'What have you done?' Richard hissed in disbelief as his knees buckled from the shock, and Zack rushed forward, the stainless-steel Pocket Nine in his hand.

Zack knelt by the woman he loved, her face nearly blue as she clutched her bruised throat and sucked in deep, shuddering breaths.

'Oh, Jesus—' Zack's voice broke with emotion. 'Jasmine.'

The woman locked eyes with him, a wave of love and understanding passing between them, and then she turned to face the wounded giant and croaked, 'Kill the bastard.'

Richard's eyes went wide as Zack unhesitatingly squeezed the trigger, sending twin bullets in perfect grouping into the bastard's heart.

118

Sam held up his hands and walked slowly backwards. MaryAnn began to whimper – louder and more desperate with each step he took.

'Give me my daughter, Lucas,' pleaded Sam. 'You don't need her any more. I've done everything you asked.'

Lucas's face softened into an expression of mirth. 'It'll be a short reunion, Sam. The robbery and murder charges should see you locked away for a long, long time.'

Lucas bent to MaryAnn's ear and whispered. The act was so intimate that Sam felt his insides churn with murderous rage. MaryAnn's eyes grew large and then she was suddenly free – running across the platform and into Sam's waiting arms.

Sam crushed her to his chest, his whole body shaking with relief as he kissed his daughter's face and the top of her head, his heart swelling with love and joy.

'How touching,' Lucas said menacingly.

Sam glanced up as Lucas aimed his gun.

'The devil don't burn, Sam . . . but you will.'

Lucas cocked the hammer—

Sam spun and closed his eyes, his body shielding MaryAnn, as—

'Freeze, fuckface!'

Sam opened his eyes to see the two detectives who had questioned him rushing on to the empty platform with guns drawn. The one in the cowboy hat was yelling at Lucas.

Sam quickly glanced over his shoulder, expecting the impact of a bullet, but instead saw Lucas leaping off the platform and on to the tracks – *escaping*.

Sam grabbed his daughter's face in his hands and locked her gaze.

'There are two detectives directly behind us,' he said quickly. 'Run to them. I need to find your mom.'

The girl's eyes widened in panic.

'I'll be back soon,' Sam added. 'Trust me. I love you so much.'

MaryAnn nodded bravely as Sam released her and leapt off the platform in pursuit.

119

Detective Hogan cursed as Sam leapt off the platform, leaving the girl behind. He rushed to her side and saw her hands were tied behind her back.

'Are you MaryAnn White?'

The girl nodded rapidly, tears streaming down her face.

Hogan turned to his partner. 'Take care of her.'

And then he, too, leapt off the platform in pursuit.

Detective Preston radioed for back-up before he reluctantly slid his gun back into its holster and knelt down beside the girl. He smiled and saw her eyes grow large.

'What can I say? You got stuck with the ugly one.'

The girl blinked in surprise. 'A–are you really a policeman?'

Preston grinned. 'I'm not only a policeman,' he said proudly, 'I'm also a Texan.' He lowered his voice to a whisper. 'Which means I will shoot any bad guy who even thinks of coming to hurt you.'

MaryAnn smiled and her body began to relax.

'Let's get these hands free, OK?' Preston pulled a small penknife out of his pocket and cut the plastic bonds around the girl's wrists. As soon as her hands were free, the girl wrapped her arms around the detective's neck and held on for dear life.

Preston rose to his full height, the girl wrapped tight in his arms. 'Everything will be OK,' he said soothingly. 'Your dad will be back soon.'

At that moment, a porter in a smart blue uniform rushed up. 'Can I be of assistance?'

Preston nodded at the ransom abandoned on the platform. 'Get a cart to carry those bags, and then show us where we can get a warm dressing gown for the young lady and a couple mugs of hot chocolate.'

The girl lifted her head. 'And a hamburger?'

'Definitely,' agreed Preston. 'A Texas burger with all the trimmings. Fries, onion rings, a milkshake, the works.'

MaryAnn hugged the detective even tighter until he croaked that he couldn't breathe.

120

'Give me your gun.' Davey stood outside a locked cell door just a short distance from where Zack had rescued Jasmine. The three of them had already looked in the remaining cells and found them empty.

Zack handed over the gun without hesitation.

Davey aimed the small gun at a spot on the wooden doorjamb where it appeared the dead bolt would lie, and pulled the trigger. The ancient wood exploded inward, leaving a hole the size of a man's fist and exposing the iron bolt.

Davey reached in, yanked back the bolt, and threw open the door.

The sickening aroma of burned flesh stopped all three of them in the doorway, and the nightmarish sight in the corner made Davey recoil and Jasmine gasp.

Zack's reaction was different. His gaze was drawn to one of the cell walls covered entirely in repeating images of a teenage girl whose life had been dramatically altered twenty-five years earlier.

One photo, in particular, showed three cheer-leaders. Two bookend blondes and—

Zack entered the cell and looked down at the smouldering corpse. The sight filled him with an incredible, soul-deadening sadness.

'God, I'm so sorry.' He fell to his knees beside the bunk. 'You didn't deserve this.'

Jasmine grasped her husband's shoulder as if to lend him what little strength she had left. 'Did you know her?'

Zack nodded, his eyes filled with pain. 'Her name was Susan Millar. She was an old friend.'

Lucas disappeared through a metal door marked *Maintenance*, which was set into a small alcove just before the station ended. Sam quickly followed, grabbed the door before it closed, and found himself at the entrance to a steep set of metal stairs.

He descended rapidly, taking the stairs two and three at a time. At the bottom, he found himself in a tiny concrete storage room, empty except for dusty bottles of forgotten cleaning supplies and a scattering of rat traps.

Sam spun around, scanned for other exits and found none. He ran back to the stairs, heard someone banging on the door above him, and cursed.

Lucas had vanished.

*   *   *

'We have to move,' Davey said urgently. 'Sam will need us.'

Zack wiped tears from his eyes and rose from the ground with the aid of his wife. Jasmine looked into his eyes with such love and kindness that Zack hated to break the spell.

But he couldn't take another step before she knew the truth.

Panicking from the sounds above, Sam ducked underneath the stairs, his feet colliding with chunks of broken mortar. He spun to face the wall, found where the mortar had fallen from between the bricks and inserted his fingers. When he pulled, a hidden door swung open to reveal a dark crawlspace.

Sam ducked his head and plunged into the darkness.

'Kalli is dead.' Zack's voice cracked.

Jasmine's face aged before him as she tried to shake away his words.

'How can . . . ? How can you . . . ?'

'I was there. Lucas made me watch while the house she was in exploded. I thought you were inside, too, but . . .' Zack's voice drifted.

Jasmine wiped at her eyes and straightened her shoulders, her face set in stone. Zack could tell that although the news stabbed deep, it wasn't something she hadn't already suspected on her own.

'Are you positive?' she asked.

'The police confirmed it.'

Jasmine's lips tightened and her eyes folded into angry slits. She turned to Davey. 'Get us out of here. We're not finished yet.'

121

Sam had only crawled a few feet when the passageway opened into a natural cavern and he was able to stand.

He moved forward blindly when suddenly the cavern blossomed in light from strings of bare bulbs hung haphazardly along the walls. The unexpected illumination caused an angry screech to ignite from the ceiling. As Sam shielded his eyes and looked up, hundreds of bats flapped leathery wings before vanishing into dozens of blunt-mouthed air holes.

When Sam lowered his hand again, Lucas was waiting, a gun aimed directly at his chest.

'Tired of your daughter already?'

'Where's Hannah?'

Lucas laughed without mirth. 'Didn't Zack tell you?'

'Tell me what?' Sam felt the cold worm stir in his belly again.

Lucas's lips curled upwards. 'And you thought

he was a trusted friend. Just goes to show, Sam, you're learning the same lesson I did twenty-five years ago. You can't trust anyone.'

'I know what you made him do, but he never betrayed me. You didn't—'

Lucas pulled the trigger.

Sam spun from the impact, his right shoulder on fire as the bullet cut through muscle before exiting flesh. He fell to the ground and fought the pain to draw his own weapon.

He fired without aiming. The bullet smashed uselessly into the cavern wall.

Lucas laughed and fired a second shot. The bullet tore through Sam's right wrist, breaking bone and making his trigger hand useless.

'You son of a bitch!'

Lucas walked closer and pointed the gun at Sam's face. 'Never knew my mother, Sam. But I am definitely the son of a bastard.'

'A dead bastard, though. Right, Luke?' said an unexpected voice.

Davey appeared from the shadows of another tunnel. He was breathing heavily as though he had been running hard.

'I wondered when you'd show up,' said Lucas. 'I was saving him for you.'

Sam's eyes narrowed, the pieces he hadn't wanted to join finally clicking into place. 'You were both in jail.'

Davey's face lost its mischievous innocence to be replaced by something much, much harder.

'We survived together,' Lucas explained. 'I wanted to die when they locked me away. Do you know what they do to people who look like me, Sam? The freaks? I didn't think I had the will to survive until Davey showed me how to use my strengths to make the other prisoners fear us. And fear they did.'

'Once you got a taste for it you just never knew when to stop though, did you, Luke?' Davey added.

'Why would I want to stop?' Lucas grinned as he turned the gun back on Sam.

The bullet slammed into Lucas like a sledgehammer, dropping him to the ground as a wide spray of blood erupted from his side. He gasped for air, his mouth opening and closing like a dying fish.

The tiny bullet had caused mortal damage and as his chest heaved, his lungs began expelling pints of bright arterial blood at a rapid pace.

'You shouldn't have tried to burn me, Luke. I took that personally.'

'It was a test.' Crimson foam bubbled from his mouth. 'I knew he wouldn't do it.'

The gun fired again and Lucas howled as his left ear vanished in a puff of blood.

'J–Jesus, Davey, we're partners.'

'Partners?' Davey laughed. 'You're living the high life while I make do with fucking hand-outs. I watched your back inside for years and how did you reward me? As soon as you were out you forgot I even existed.'

421

'I–I never forgot,' Lucas croaked.

'Nah, you just never gave a shit. Well, now you know, neither do I.'

Lucas reached out his hands in a plea for help.

Davey shook his head. 'It's not the bullets that kill you, Luke,' he said calmly, 'it's the shock.'

Lucas's eyes grew wider as his breath became more laboured. From there, it only took seconds before a final hiss rattled from his throat and the flow of blood began to ebb.

Davey turned to Sam. A playful smile danced across his lips, but failed to find purchase.

'It was fun being together again. I really missed you, man.'

'Then why, Davey?' Sam groaned as he pushed himself into a sitting position and cradled his broken wrist. 'Why this?'

Davey's eyes turned dark. 'I was angry at you, Sam. I was just the clown, the sidekick, someone to be overlooked. I was the one nobody took seriously – but when we were inside, Lucas listened. He saw what I had to offer and helped make me realize all that I was capable of. Without me, he was weak. But together we were unstoppable.'

'I always knew—'

'Knew what, Sam?' Davey snapped. 'Knew that I was destined for nothing? What did you see when you met me under the bridge? A bum who had wasted his life? Someone you felt sorry for? You never once thought of me back then, did you?

Even when I called from prison, you could never be reached. I was told you would return my calls, but you never did. You were more interested in living *your* dream. But what about mine, Sam?' Davey wiped at his eyes. 'I only wanted you to need me again, like old times, but Luke fucked that up, too. It wasn't supposed to be this way.'

Sam's voice caught in his throat, but another voice spoke the words.

'How was it supposed to be?' Zack walked out of the tunnel, holding hands with a woman of indescribable beauty, despite the cuts and bruises that marked her chocolate-brown skin.

Sam's heart ached when nobody else appeared and the stark realization sunk in.

'I'm sorry, Sam,' Zack said. 'Hannah wasn't there. I prayed we would find her.'

'What about MaryAnn?' asked Jasmine.

'She's safe,' Sam answered. 'Up above.'

'Why don't you join her?' Davey said. 'You've all been in the dark far too long.'

'Just like that?' said Sam. 'You're going to let us walk away?'

Davey shrugged. 'Luke was the one into blood sports. I only wanted some money of my own and a chance to relive old times. I never expected a new life. Besides, I lived better inside jail than I ever did out here.'

'You bastard!'

Davey raised his arms too slowly as Jasmine

launched herself at him, the gun flying free from his grasp.

'Get her off!' Davey cried in panic as Jasmine went for his face.

'Jasmine!' Zack snatched up the loose gun. 'I can end it.'

Jasmine released her grip on Davey as Zack moved forward, aiming the gun.

A gunshot, louder than all the others, made everyone freeze.

'Police, goddamnit!' Detective Hogan entered the cavern from the same short tunnel Sam and Lucas had used. 'Nobody move. You need him alive.'

'Why?' Sam's voice was cold as he stared across at the boyhood friend he had never really known.

'Think about it,' Hogan snapped. 'He has the evidence to clear you. He can show you were coerced to save your daughter.'

Davey and Sam locked eyes, blood dripping from a serious gash along Davey's cheek. In the briefest of instants they shared a hundred memories and a thousand laughs from their youth. But when Davey tried to move, Zack cocked the hammer.

'Don't do it!' Hogan warned. 'If you kill him, it's murder. That's a lot of years behind bars. Your wife doesn't deserve to be without you again. You need to bury your daughter. You need to heal.'

Zack reached his free hand behind his back to be met by Jasmine's. They squeezed tenderly.

424

Switch

'Lower the gun, Zack,' Sam said softly, his own need for violence now quenched. 'It's over.'

Sam turned to look behind him and say, 'He's all yours, Detective,' when his words were lost in the sharp report of a tiny, stainless-steel handgun.

Zack dropped the smoking gun on the ground. 'I'm already going to jail for Ironman,' he said with a shrug. 'Nothing I can do about that.'

He locked eyes with Sam and smiled weakly. 'For Hannah and Kalli, that prick really deserved to die.'

122

Sam found his daughter wearing an oversized cowboy hat and devouring a hamburger within the Victorian-era walls of Wilf's Restaurant connected to the station.

When she saw her father, MaryAnn dropped her hamburger and rushed into his awaiting embrace. Sam dropped to his knees, his broken wrist held tight by his side as his daughter kissed his filthy, unshaven face over and over. Sam closed his eyes and breathed her in, never wanting to let her go.

'Jasmine!' MaryAnn squealed in delight as the rescued woman appeared over her father's shoulder.

Jasmine rushed forward and fell to her knees, too. She patted the girl's face through a veil of tears as MaryAnn wrapped one of her arms around her neck and squeezed tight.

'Jasmine protected me,' MaryAnn told her father breathlessly. 'She was a tiger.'

Switch

'I got my strength from you,' said Jasmine. 'You were so very brave. You remind me of my own daughter.'

More tears sprang to Jasmine's eyes as she moved away from MaryAnn and returned to her husband.

'Where's Mom, Dad? I thought I heard her crying, but . . .' MaryAnn paused at the pain that crossed her father's face. 'She died, too, didn't she?'

Sam nodded, his face wet with tears.

'Why did this happen?' MaryAnn asked.

'No reason.' Sam thought of the two men rotting in the tunnels beneath their feet. 'No good reason at all.'

THE END

Acknowledgements:

My agent, Amy Moore-Benson, for believing; my editor, Selina Walker, for saying 'Yes'; Danielle Weekes for her infectious enthusiasm; Emma Musgrave for her skill and support; and Sally Riley for telling the rest of the world to climb aboard. I would also like to thank the wonderful people at Transworld who embraced the book from the beginning and expressed their continued excitement about it. And to you, the reader, who has taken a chance on a new author. You'll never know how much that means to me.